Gillian Slovo was born in South Africa in 1952 and came to England in 1964. She lives in London with her partner and daughter and writes full time. She is the author of the saga *Ties of Blood* and a political thriller, *The Betrayal*; her most recent novel was the psychological thriller *Façade*. She has written three previous books featuring her detective Kate Baeier: *Morbid Symptoms*, *Death by Analysis* and *Death Comes Staccato*. In 1996 Virago will publish her fifth, *Close Call*.

G000152105

CATNAP

Gillian
Slovo

Published by VIRAGO PRESS Limited 1995
20 Vauxhall Bridge Road, London SW1V 2SA

First published in hardback by Michael Joseph Ltd,
part of The Penguin Group, in 1994.

A CIP catalogue record for this book is available from the British Library

Printed and bound in Great Britain by
Cox & Wyman Ltd, Reading, Berkshire

For Cassie

Chapter
one

My business completed, I was free to go. I celebrated by buying a cheap day return to Dalston.

Dalston, Hackney, that is, one of London's shabbiest boroughs: not your average tourist spot, I know. But then I was hardly your average tourist.

There was nobody at the barrier to take my ticket. Leaving it on the kiosk's ledge, I stepped out into the street.

Momentum had carried me this far – nerves made me stop. I'd been gone five years and in that time I'd been constantly on the move. I'd grown to like it, that feeling of belonging nowhere, of owing nothing to no one. As I stood, quite still, outside the station, I wondered what I was doing back in Dalston.

A queue of ambling buses had compressed the traffic on the two-lane road. I looked beyond them. Ahead, on the other side, was Ridley Road market. To the right, an indoor shopping mall, installed since I'd been away. The building's brickwork was already stained by damp, its glass frontage dingy to match the neighbours. Greyness was the theme, a contrast to slabs of red meat wrapped up in polythene – the local butcher's idea of a beckoning display.

My eyes went down. Dalston, like nature, abhorred a vacuum – every hole and crevice was filled with newspapers, sweet wrappers, and other detritus. A gust of wind disturbed the mixture, and Hackney's version of autumnal leaves swirled round my feet.

I watched an old woman pass by: she was using a beat-up shopping trolley as a walker, her legs, swollen by oedema, held rigid by dark brown surgical stockings. She didn't even look up when a gaunt, wired man in a checked suit too big for him leaped over the pavement railings and ran past her.

It began to pour. I was protected by the station's awning. Scurrying people joined me, emptying the pavement. Only the very stoned, or those with the foresight to carry an umbrella, or children in their plastic pram bubbles kept going, smugly, as if nothing had happened. In the market's mouth, a young man in a Naf Naf jacket struggled to rescue a trolley load of oranges. As they spilled in all directions he was drenched. He didn't seem to mind. His smile, the only one in sight, was radiant.

The rain stopped. Abruptly. The crowd dispersed, me amongst them. I crossed the road, heading for the market. I paused by the first stall. A shaft of light had disturbed the grey, making the droplets on the bruised red plums look almost crystalline. I thought of buying some but water, dripping down my back, moved me on. The market was adrift with soggy trash. I veered away, walking beyond and behind it.

Without the enticement of cheap consumer goods, the atmosphere turned mean. What had been lively, was now enlivened by uneasiness. I watched a toddler yanking at his mother's skirt and saw the sullen set of the young woman's mouth as she slapped the small hand off. Another woman, her shoulders hunched by the double burden of age and poverty, walked by. Her eyes kept shifting to left and right, anticipating bother.

Five years of being a war reporter had given me a nose

for danger, but it wasn't that which made me want to leave. It was something else – some feeling that I was out of place. Go home, I told myself, go home, finish the article and then get the hell out of England.

I should have gone.

I didn't. Something, some kind of mixed-up masochism I suppose, drove me forward. I turned away from company, climbing the set of concrete stairs that lead me round the market. I had no real destination, just a trip down a memory lane which I had, until that moment, shoved into a cul-de-sac.

I kept on going, down a narrow alleyway. Ahead, beyond the ranks of crumbling houses, I saw that they had finished converting the old synagogue. The grey steel of the new mosque's dome glinted in the sunlight. The sight brought memory.

I shook it off, concentrating on the dome, cutting myself quite deliberately loose from that time, that other era, when I had lived close by.

I was programmed to forget but I wasn't blind. And I wasn't stupid either. I saw them coming. I'd been around enough to know that careful swagger for what it was, that way they had of keeping all angles covered without appearing to be looking. There were three of them, working together – three young men in the full perfection of youth, their clothes, costly, American and casual, loose over spare bodies. They kept coming, looping their way towards me. I met one's gaze, his eyes skimming almost lovingly across my face before flitting away. I thought: he's going to mug me.

He passed me by, he and his friends.

They did it from behind. A hand slipped up my shoulder and yanked my bag strap, a foot stretched out in case I turned.

I had nothing in my bag – nothing precious, that is. My

3

passport was safe at home, my purse snug in my pocket. And the bag itself was disposable, an ageing leather pouch without sentimental value.

I was alone, a woman, and outnumbered. I knew the sensible thing to do. I knew I should keep on going.

It wasn't my day for being sensible. I turned and lunged.

So routine was their operation that the men had relaxed their guard. Two were yards away. I faced one, the one who'd met my gaze before. He was holding my bag.

His eyes flared. I saw uncertainty and I saw resolution, and anger that I should dare to challenge him.

I was angrier. My hand grabbed for my bag. His held on. As one of the others shouted in alarm, his arm swung out. Rage made me swift. I ducked, saw his fist punching the air where my face had been. I followed through, yanking my bag at the same time as I kicked out.

It was pure luck that I unbalanced him – that and the fact that what I'd done was so unexpected. I saw him fall. I was on a roll, I could do no wrong. I skipped out of the way so that he wouldn't take me down with him.

I've won, I thought.

But, of course, I hadn't. There were three of them and the other two were upon me. They didn't waste much time. As a shove sent me sprawling, the bag was dragged out of my grip. I didn't worry about it, not any longer. I hit the ground, hard.

And lay there, looking up as the man I'd previously unbalanced sprang to his feet. His face loomed above mine. His lips moved.

My hearing had gone fuzzy. 'Are you crazy?' is what I thought he said. His generous mouth was set into a long, thin line. He was furious. In one sense I didn't really blame him. I had broken the rules. And for what? For nothing.

His movements seemed agonizingly slow. I watched them. I saw his foot swing back and then glide towards me. I had one thought as the moment stretched: if he really beat me badly, I would not be able to leave the country.

I moved instinctively, my arms enclosing my head.

'Stop!' I heard.

The shout came from far, far away. I lay there, clasping tight, ignoring it, waiting for the impact of his boot.

It never came.

Instead the sound of running feet.

I opened my eyes, saw the muggers retreating in the wake of the newcomer's pounding arrival.

Chapter

two

I was on my feet, all in one piece, and ready to leave. But when my good Samaritan insisted that we file a police report, I didn't feel I could refuse.

The visit was the waste of time I'd known it would be. The police were polite but there was nothing they could do. A description of my fight-back earned me a raised eyebrow and a warning that this way I could get in trouble. As if I didn't know. I nodded my head and, having read my statement through, signed where indicated.

I stepped out on to Dalston Lane and didn't stop to think. I began walking. It was only when I reached the corner that I realized what I'd done.

'Shit,' I said. I was going in the wrong direction, towards the flat that I'd long since vacated. I had no desire to go there: coming to Dalston had been a mistake which I did not want to replicate.

I turned abruptly. The street was crowded but I ploughed ahead. There was a man heading towards me along the same channel. I took avoidance action. So did the man – with the result that we remained on collision course. I tried again. As did he. Deadlock.

'I'm sorry,' I heard him saying.

It was as much my fault as his but I couldn't bear the

contact. And, anyway, I wasn't in an apologizing mood. Without looking up, I issued instructions: 'I'll stand still, you walk round me.'

'Kate?'

I looked up.

'It is!' He was smiling through his obvious astonishment. 'Kate Baeier!' He moved closer. He was tall, he had to bend his neck to reach me.

I had no idea who he was, but I did know one thing: he was going to kiss me.

His firm lips glanced against my cheek. I was at a loss since 'Do I know you?' after the kiss, seemed hardly appropriate. People jostled to get past me, their shopping bags cuffing my legs. I ignored them. I narrowed my eyes, locking the man more securely into vision. I saw a long, thin face, overfull, with red lips, dark eyes and thick dark wavy hair, all made more striking by a vivid air of intensity. He was a man who would stick out in a crowd, a man who would not easily be forgotten. Yet I *had* forgotten him.

He knew it too. 'How are you?' he said, slightly mocking me.

I pushed myself into high gear. A name popped out. 'Roger?' That was all I could access, that one name, disconnected from any memory.

It was enough. Roger's face relaxed. 'That's right.'

I smiled, the cogs working harder. Success: a surname. 'Roger Toms,' I said. I was going great guns now – I remembered his profession as well. Of course, Roger Toms, photographer. What I couldn't remember was when I'd last seen him.

'You had us worried,' Roger was saying.

Us? I looked around, wondering which other actors from my past would now materialize.

None: although the pavement was crowded, Roger was by himself.

7

'I thought I'd run into you one day,' he said.

There was something challenging in the way he said it, something that I didn't feel up to answering. I took a step back, pretending to admire his expensive double-breasted light grey suit and matching moccasins while I tried to remember why my distant and fragmented memories of Roger Toms were shot through with wariness.

My silence didn't faze him. 'I'm glad we did meet,' he said, smiling suggestively.

Perhaps that was it, I thought. Perhaps this man had just been too seductive for my puritanical younger self.

His smile deepened. 'So Kate,' he said. 'How are you?'

I shrugged.

He kept going. 'And how long are you staying?'

Another shrug. I was good at them.

'Staying with friends?'

This time I changed tactic. I frowned.

'Or have you rented somewhere?'

I shook my head.

'Kate?'

My silence was heavy, moving into rudeness. I forced myself to speak. 'Someone lent me their house while they're out of town,' I said.

'Round here?'

He was pushing me and we both knew it. I stood there, remembering how determined Roger had always been to get his own way. Perhaps it was because of this that an echo of dislike kept repeating on me.

But what if it was? I was older now and I could be just as determined. 'No,' I said, sharply, closing down on further interrogation.

He got the message. 'Well,' he said, pressing my hand with his. I felt the smoothness of his skin and the toughness that lay behind it. 'Nice to see you again.' He moved on past.

I stood still, feeling the uneasy stirrings of guilt. Five years of mostly solitary travel had diminished my social skills but, even so, I could have tried with Roger. I watched from behind as he prepared to propel himself back into the crowd. I opened my mouth, meaning to call him back.

And snapped it almost immediately shut. My visit to Dalston had already been a disaster. Let him go, I told myself, don't make the same mistake twice.

But I had reckoned without Roger. He had taken only a few steps before he stopped and turned. 'I have a picture of him,' he said.

A shadow fleetingly crossed my retina. 'Him?' As if I didn't know.

'Sam.'

I swallowed.

'Taken a few days before the accident.'

I remembered then where I had last seen Roger – amongst the crowd at Sam's funeral.

'I thought you might like it.' He must have seen the emotion striking at my face: he sounded quite nervous. 'I was going to give it to you at the time but you left so quickly I never had the chance.'

I nodded. 'Yes,' I said quietly, almost to myself. 'I couldn't stay.'

'You should have it.'

I nodded again and at the same time wiped one hand over dry eyes. 'Thanks, I'd like that,' I said, thinking that this was maybe true. 'You still living round here?'

'Sort of.' He didn't say anything more: he was paying me back for my evasiveness.

Oh well, what did I care? 'Could I call you at work and arrange to pick the photo up?'

But no, that wouldn't do either. 'I'm freelance,' he said. 'My office is a mobile phone. I'll post it to you.'

He was so certain, he had his pencil and paper out already, waiting for my address.

I almost refused. I opened my mouth, in fact, to do so. But the knowledge of the photograph's existence defeated me. I couldn't leave it – not with this self-confident, unfeeling Roger. And, anyway, what did it matter if he knew where I was? After all, I wouldn't be there long.

So, instead of saying no, I wrote down my temporary address.

'Good,' he said, and then saying, 'good to meet you, Kate,' walked off.

I watched him go, standing in the centre of the pavement, waiting for the impulse which might make me want to move. I'm sure I looked calm. I was far from calm. I stood there, still, amongst the home-going bustle, my thoughts chaotic. I was angry, really angry – with myself.

This trip to London hadn't been my idea. I'd come under protest and for only one reason – to sign a document, one in a series connected with my mother's estate.

Before she'd gone on her last, fatal drinking spree, my mother had taken uncharacteristically subtle revenge against the husband she hated. She had left him all her money but then tied it up so he could only withdraw a yearly, and specified, sum. Worse still for a man whose life was driven by egotism, he had to have my consent before he did so.

My father's way of overcoming this obstacle was predictable – he referred it to his minions. He was rich and ruthless enough to buy their absolute devotion: if ever I refused to sign, they just kept on tracking me. So this time I'd said yes right away – as long as they made it easy.

They'd given me the choice of going either to a London solicitor or to a firm in Lisbon. Lisbon was the city of my birth and the site of my father's main home. I chose London.

But London also had its sting. In choosing it I'd promised myself something: that I'd concentrate exclusively on the business in hand. A visit to Dalston had not been part of that bargain. And I should never have made it. If I had learned anything in my years' absence it was that I'd managed to bury the past. Stirring it up would only cause me pain.

'Excuse me.' A woman with one shopping bag too many was trying to manoeuvre round me.

As I got out of her way, I also pushed off regret. There was no point in it. What I had done was over, it would not be repeated. And, anyway, it hadn't turned out so badly. After all, Sam had been mentioned and I had not collapsed.

Chapter
three

I was still half asleep when the phone began to ring. Instinctively my hand stretched out. But no: I dropped it. I wasn't ready for the world.

The phone kept on going. It was getting on my nerves. I threw the covers off and climbed out of bed. I missed the cat which, intent on pinning a mutual dislike on me, had planted itself in my way. I'm not normally vindictive but I couldn't resist shooting a triumphant smile its way. 'Fooled you,' I said.

Its answer was an outraged glare, a disdainful flick of its tail, and a walking away. Not too far though: at the door, it stopped, turned, opened its mouth and yowled. It was hungry.

'So when aren't you hungry?' I said. I was rewarded by a narrowing of its yellow eyes. 'Oh all right.' I moved towards it. The ringing, thank God, had stopped. I padded over thick pile, following the cat. Down the elegant, curving stairway we went and into the basement kitchen.

I fed the cat and me – in that order – and then I went out and bought a paper. I almost read it as well, over my second cup of coffee, but the thought of my unfinished article drew me reluctantly from the kitchen. Taking the coffee, I began to climb the stairs. On the ground floor, I stopped. I was frowning, trying to pick up the thread of the argument that I had abandoned yesterday.

The article – an in-depth comment on the culture of violence – should have been easy. Violence was my subject: I'd followed it around the world, earning my living by being in its midst and by writing about it. But this piece was proving much trickier than anything I'd anticipated. As soon as I focused my thoughts on the writing, they became constipated. Yesterday I had tied myself into such a verbal knot that I'd had to stop.

Well, I was leaving soon – it had to be finished. I took a step forward. I was standing by the drawing-room door. I let my eyes range round. What I saw was Pam and Greg Willis's idea of perfection: a huge, elegant room; high ceilings, low, soft furniture, muted colours; the vast walls painted an unfamiliar shade of dusty pink which had been matched exactly by the material covering a triumvirate of couches and by a double set of full, silken curtains. It was lovely, but it wasn't me. Too solid, too safe, too darned respectable.

And it, I thought, it and the rooms that surrounded it, were probably to blame for my writing block. After all, how could I talk about violence and the things that violence makes people do, so secure in this Chelsea haven?

But maybe, I thought, understanding this, I could mobilize myself. I walked up the stairs and into Greg's study, which I had colonized. My typewriter, the draft in it, were waiting. I sat myself down behind Greg's polished mahogany desk, ripped the paper from its slot, replaced it with another, virgin, piece and began to type.

The words were flowing smoothly when the phone rang. I ignored it, typing my way through the sound of Greg's stiff voice giving tedious instructions on how to leave a message. When the bleep sounded I went on typing.

'Kate,' I heard. My fingers froze. 'Are you there?'

I knew that voice. It was Bev, an acquaintance who'd

always assumed a greater intimacy than we had ever actually had.

'You must be there,' she continued. 'Pam said you were using the house while she and Greg were away.'

I gritted my teeth, cursing Pam.

'Anyway, long time no see and other clichés,' Bev said. 'Give us a ring, hey, stranger?' A silence so extended that I began to think she'd guessed that I was listening. But no, she was only waiting to see if inspiration would strike again. When it apparently did not, she said, 'Call me. It's Bev.' And hung up.

My fingers had dropped on to the keyboard, locking a trio of hammers. As the impact of the call sank in, I lifted my hand off. I didn't bother untangling the typewriter. I was concentrating on only one thing; the fact that my cover was blown. If Bev knew where I was staying then so would the rest of my old circle. Which meant that I was about to be inundated. I stamped my foot down. Damn Pam, I thought, for persuading me to stay here.

At that moment the phone began to ring. I knew who it must be: another one-time friend stretching out the hand of reconciliation. I didn't want what they had to offer – the cushion of their soft embrace or their affectionate sympathy. I'd already rejected all that. I had never wanted sanctuary. What I had wanted was out.

A wave of anxiety swelled, clogging my throat. It brought with it a single impulse – an urge to run. Shoving the typewriter away, I got up. But I had already hesitated too long – the phone's recording mechanism had been activated. 'This is a message for Kate Baeier,' I heard a mellow voice announce.

I didn't wait to hear the rest. I left the room and ran downstairs. At the ground floor, I stopped again. I didn't know what I was going to do. All I knew was that it had been mad to come and, now that my whereabouts were known, even madder to stay. I should leave – right now.

And why not? The idea took hold. I had an open ticket. I could do it, could just get up and go.

I turned. This time, I hit the cat. My foot crunched down on to its tail. It gave an outraged yelp, a mixture of triumph and of pain, and skittered away. It didn't go far. Once safely out of range it stopped and, turning, scowled.

The cat! I couldn't leave. Not yet. That had been what Pam had asked, that I stay as long as her 'daily' was away. I scowled at the beast.

It looked smugly back at me, its thick, white fluff expanding and then, disconcertingly, it began to purr. I shook my head. 'You're unbelievable,' I told it as I began to move closer. But stopped. It looked so satisfied and so well fed. Too well fed. In my travels I'd seen babies who weighed less than it. The germ of the idea expanded. I nodded: a few days alone would do it good.

It stopped purring and, for the first time since we'd been introduced, it looked uncertain. A good move: seeing it deflating, I felt my resolution wane. I remembered Pam speaking of the cat. I remembered how her voice had softened, her normal brisk, businesslike tone almost mushy. There was no avoiding it: Pam loved the cat.

And she had entrusted it to me. I couldn't let her down. Even though I knew the cat would be all right, I couldn't take the risk. I frowned. 'You're a bloody liability,' I told it. It looked at me and I could have sworn that its expression had changed and that it was smiling.

'Come on,' I said, moving towards it. The drawing-room phone began to ring. 'Come on,' I snapped, and, using my foot to nudge the cat into an approximation of speed, walked briskly away.

Memory of the previous day's stupidity soon slowed me

down. And that wasn't all. Old terrors, fears that I thought long discarded, were returning. I stopped, realizing anew what I had always known – that Britain was bad for me. It seemed so domestic compared to other places and then it whacked it to me, shoving its underbelly right into my face, making me drop my guard. Which I couldn't afford to do. Not now. Not ever.

I had to get out – anywhere – I had to or else I might go mad. Grabbing an umbrella and throwing the cat a cursory farewell, I ran to the front door, punched a code into the burglar alarm's side panel, and then, pulling the door securely behind me, left.

I stepped out into uninterrupted grey. It was relentless, a designer gloom, a moist sky weighing down grey pavements, drops of dirty water clinging to grey guttering. I shivered. Years of travelling in the southern hemisphere had diminished my tolerance of this dank cold which was a British speciality.

I rounded the corner and walked to the Embankment. Ahead was the Thames. I crossed the road and stood on the pavement, staring into the murky water. Sam and I, I thought, had used to come here. I stood there, remembering how we had walked, arm in arm along the river's edge.

What had been a faint smile became a stony grimace. I must not think of Sam, not here in London. Sam was gone. He had been killed five years ago, run over one dark night by a stranger who hadn't bothered stopping to check out the damage.

I'd left the country soon afterwards and spent a long, long time learning to accept that he would never come back. Five years later things had changed. I'd negotiated a couple of dramatic if ultimately unsatisfying love affairs and was even able to laugh again. I had regarded myself cured – until, that is, I'd wakened up one day in the grip of a new delusion. It went like this: it's over, you can safely visit London.

Safely, indeed. After only three days, the notion was exposed in all its absurdity. I wasn't safe. I was on the brink all the time, fearful of so many things: that I would meet somebody I knew, or go to a place containing too many memories, or that I would feel – I don't know what – something nameless that I did not want to feel. I had thought myself completely self-sufficient and self-directed. And yet I had come here, disastrously, thinking that it was preferable to Lisbon, only to find myself face to face with the remnants of a past I no longer understood, trapped by a disagreeable ball of off-white fur. Except ... I had it suddenly. I didn't have to choose between staying or catricide. All I had to do was find a stand-in.

I was smiling. I mean, how hard could it be to find someone willing to live in luxury, feed the cat, spritz the plants and, finally, leave without even having to clear up after themselves? I didn't need to go to the old crowd – I knew others in London, people I'd met more recently. Amongst them, I was certain, would be an eager volunteer.

      That decided, I relaxed. I expanded the boundaries of my walk and ended up strolling through one of London's most exclusive shopping streets. Although the media was full of stories about the way eighties' ostentation was no longer fashionable, nobody had bothered to tell my fellow streetwalkers. They stepped from glistening BMWs and Mercedes, their faces glowing with the natural vibrancy that is a result of ownership of unnatural quantities of cash. In and out of shops they swayed, Gucci around their bronzed arms and waspish waists while their nails, long and shiny red, fondled bow-topped packages.

I stood watching as, gift-wrapped in wealth, they fluttered into coffee shops, indulged in mutual cheek-pecking, arranged themselves in plush chairs and ordered bottled water. I was entranced, unable to disengage. I stood wondering how it must feel to have so much of everything. Pretty good, I thought.

But no – I shook my head – that wasn't right. These women didn't have everything. For here, amongst the pastel and the hush, life had gone walkabout, crowded out by too much cushioning. The women were smiling but their faces were like masks. There was no oomph about them, none of the urgency that I'd seen in Dalston.

Except I couldn't believe my own naïveté. Who cared

about 'life' any more? Five, ten years ago it might have mattered. These days it was different.

'Table for one?'

I had loitered too long. The maître d' was pretending to believe that I might be a potential customer. I shook my head. 'Sorry,' I said and, seeing his top lip curling up into a disdainful sneer, I added: 'Your flies are undone.'

He blanched and looked down. Great, I congratulated myself. I had flustered a flunky. With that hollow victory settling on my stomach, I left.

I walked straight back to the house. The more I thought about it, the simpler it seemed. I knew plenty of reliable but nomadic Latin Americans, who would be only too pleased to protect and serve the Willis mansion in exchange for a short stay there in the sun. By the time I got back, I had completed my mental shortlist. I pulled the door shut and then turned to the alarm, which needed immobilizing. I stood by its control panel and tapped in the code. That done, I continued standing, concentrating now on remembering where I'd left my address book.

A faint, familiar cry distracted me. I knew that sound: it was the cat. I smiled. I wasn't going to worry about the cat – I'd solved its problem. I ignored the cry.

It came again then, from the living room. Oh no. I started down the hallway. I must have locked it in. I speeded up, praying I'd reached it before the destruction proved terminal. I was at the living room. I opened the door and took one step inside.

I had just enough time to glimpse the havoc that someone had wrought, black paint sprayed across Pam's immaculate walls, when all hell broke loose. I don't know which struck me first, the sight or the sound, but it was the sound, an ear-piercing, mind-blowing squeal, which endured. It was the alarm, bombarding me from all sides.

At that moment the cat took a running leap off the sofa

and landed on my back. I felt its claws digging in and I shouted at it, trying to bat it off, but as the cat clung harder, drawing blood, the siren drowned out my protests. The alarm was my first priority. Cat in situ, I began to move – but stopped abruptly. I saw the alarm's panel, flashing red, and beside it the gaping of an open front door.

My stomach lurched. I had closed the door, hadn't I? Out of the corner of my eye I saw motion.

The cat had more sense than I. It took off. I was too slow. I was slammed against the wall, my arm twisted until the back of my hand almost touched the base of my neck. I yelped. 'Don't bother struggling,' a voice snarled and then, raising his tobacco-ingrained tone, shouted to his companions: 'It's OK, she's mine. You get the others.'

There were no others, only me, but it took some time to convince the police (for that is who they were, responding to the alarm) of that. They checked me out, rifling through reams of documentation as well as Pam's last-minute in-structions, before reluctantly conceding my rights of resi-dence. But they got their revenge. Having accompanied me around the house and confirmed that apart from the destruction in the living room nothing else was out of place, they told me, with some relish, that the break-in had been my fault. Their reasoning went this way: there was only one possible inlet into the house – the front door – and that should have been guarded by the alarm. Since it wasn't, I must have fucked up. When I said that I definitely remembered switching the alarm off, if not on, the one who'd pinned me against the wall, almost crowed. 'You didn't turn it on when you left,' he said, 'so what you did on your return was to activate it.'

'And then,' added his colleague, 'you crossed the elec-tronic beam in the living room.' He waved his hand, ushering his troop out. He was the soft cop. He threw me a hard-boiled, but simultaneously sympathetic, sideways nod. 'Tough break,' he said. He'd obviously been watching too much *Miami Vice*. 'Got any enemies?'

I shook my head. 'Not that I know of.'

Nice cop shrugged. 'It's a terrible thing, he did, defiling the living room. They're the worst, the ones who add destruction to theft. Although this one didn't get anything . . . did he?' His voice, which had descended into doubt, was revived. 'We'll do our best to catch him.' He shook his head sorrowfully, implying that their best would probably not be enough. 'In the meantime,' he said, 'we'll give your name to the local victim support group.'

I didn't say anything. I stood on the doorstep, watching them getting into their panda and driving off. And longer than that as well, delaying the moment when I had to go back inside the house and face again the results of my own incompetence. But I couldn't delay for ever. Having seen the men in blue depart, neighbours emerged and began throwing suspicious looks my way. I used a smile I didn't feel to shut them out and then, walking inside, I shut the door.

I moved fast after that. I strode along the hall and, reaching the living-room door, flung it open.

It was the wall opposite that had been defiled, with large scrawled black words which made no sense. I stood in the doorway, facing the smeared message, wondering what kind of twisted mind had produced it. It was four lines laid out like a poem. I read the four together:

> I saw your face yesterday,
> Oh yeah, oh yeah.
> Getting closer,
> Yum yum.

I shut my eyes. Nothing – or at least nothing that made

sense. It had a feel of muddled Beatles songs, but no more than that. I looked again.

I saw your face yesterday. Not the muggers, surely?

No. Of course not. They were not going to take the risk, not after they'd got away. And besides, how could they have found me?

Roger Toms then. How about him?

The idea brought a smile to my face. Since meeting Roger, memory had trickled back. I'd realized why I'd associated him with unpleasantness. It wasn't to do with me, it was to do with Sam. Roger had worked occasionally for Sam's father and that had made Sam jealous. With reason, I suppose, since Sam and his father hardly ever talked.

But even though I could just about imagine Roger in the role of interloper, I didn't think his taste ran to weird warnings. He had been a yes man – that's what had driven Sam so crazy – hardly the type to involve himself in an unprovoked kamikaze mission.

I pulled the door shut. Not the muggers then, nor Roger. Which meant that the explanation the police had come up with – that the message was either the random scrawlings of a junkie so far off base that he forgot to steal anything, or else it was directed not at me, but at Pam or Greg – was probably right. Which had, I realized, an added bonus: it let me off the hook. I smiled.

Not for long. I had to face the truth. I wasn't in the clear because no matter what the target, I had been the message's conduit. By my own carelessness, I had brought it into the house. Which meant that I must make it better.

I went to the kitchen and brewed fresh coffee. By the time it had filtered through, one thing was clear. My plans were nullified. I couldn't leave. The Willises were my friends; they had trusted me. I couldn't let them down. I could have used their emergency fax number, I suppose, and canvassed their opinion, but I didn't have the heart. They'd been so generous. I didn't want to spoil their holiday.

I would have to act. I picked up my coffee and going to Greg's study began searching through his desk. It didn't take long to find his address book or the number of his insurer. A simple question soon confirmed what I had previously suspected: that because the alarm had not been functioning, the insurance company would not cough up. Which left me with only one option: I would have to organize and pay for the repainting job myself.

The money was no problem. Travel was my main expense; for the rest I lived cheap and always managed to keep an emergency stash in my London bank. Since, in my view, collaborating in the desecration of the house you're meant to be protecting counts as an emergency, that disposed of the finances.

Finding the exact same shade of living-room pink proved more difficult. There was nothing in Greg's book to suggest a paint shop – decorating was, I guess, Pam's province. Plumping for active research, I cut off a bit of identical grey-pink from the curtain hem, and took it round the shops.

I learned a lot about pink but nothing about the one I was trying to find except that we were talking neither Dulux matchmaker, nor any other conceivable and well-publicised brand name. Five hours later I returned, exhausted and empty-handed.

I did then what I should have done first. I opened the Yellow Pages and began working methodically down a list of interior design firms. After a while my list expanded. From one I was handed on to another, in an entirely different location, and on again in quick succession. My story – that I was a Willis cousin intent on surprising them on their anniversary with a matching set of brushed silk cushions (the real story being too unlikely) – began to feel increasingly ludicrous but it seemed to pass muster. I kept on going, jabbering out my request, met by a constant line of nos. It was so tiring I ended up hoping that the next lot would ignore the bloody phone.

That was when I hit pay dirt. 'Willis?' a fruity voice asked and, before I had time to launch into the full patter, it added. 'Are you perhaps related to Pamela Willis?'

I cut the snow job and moved directly to the point, asking whether I could be told the name of the Willis drawing-room pink. 'Pink?' said the voice and there was the sound of rustling paper. 'Ah yes. Friedrich Pink.' A pause and then, into my silence, an explanation: 'After Caspar David Friedrich. He was a friend of Goethe's, you know.'

'Oh yes. Of course he was,' I said. 'Can I buy some?'

That was no problem, said my saviour.

'Fast?'

That didn't faze him either. He would mix a batch up overnight, he said. I could fetch it in the morning.

I thanked him more than once and said goodbye. Restraint fled. I jumped up, punching my fist into the air, yelling with delight.

'OK,' I told the disapproving cat, 'so it's an over-the-top reaction to Caspar David Friedrich Pink but why should you care? You'll get some Sheba out of it. In fact' – I was feeling so relieved that I even forgave it the claw marks on my shoulder – 'you can have as much as you can possibly eat.'

Chapter
five

The next morning found me at the kitchen table, mesmerized by small print. The book was a dishevelled *A–Z* which I'd been using to plan out a route to the paint shop. But my vision had veered off course, my eyes focusing on one street, a tiny cul-de-sac with a familiar name: Lambton Place.

I shook my head. It's not possible, I told myself. Of course, of course it wasn't possible. I mean, we were talking of one brief mention, and under the least auspicious of conditions. Move on, I told my eyes, move on.

I didn't move on. No matter how vehemently I tried to deny it, I knew that there was no room for doubt. Despite the fact that I'd spent years pretending that I'd forgotten Anna and Daniel's new address, preferring, in the beginning, to send occasional postcards to their defunct US home, I had not forgotten.

I hadn't forgotten anything of that week, neither the look on their faces as they had stood on my doorstep, nor the glance away as they told me that Sam was dead, nor their silence as they waited out my reaction. I remembered each instant that had followed that one: the lonely, sleepless nights; the days jammed with unwelcome well-wishers; the funeral itself; and the weeping. My recall was total and it included Anna's staccato burst of information.

Even now, after all this time, if I closed my eyes and

concentrated I could hear her voice. 'We're moving back to London,' is what she'd said. 'We've found an apartment in Notting Hill.' She had paused then before adding what I had considered, in the circumstances, to be irrelevant '14, Lambton Place.' That done, she'd responded to my unspoken command, moving off, leaving me to myself. Expecting me, of course, to contact her when I was ready. 'I'll always be available,' she'd said.

I snorted. Always indeed! It was the kind of word one *always* used at funerals, positing a living infinity, I suppose, in the face of death's finality. But funerals were one thing and reality another. I was pretty sure that, in reality, 'always' would not have stretched beyond the five-year limit. Not that it mattered. There was no going back for me.

I slammed the *A–Z* shut. The cat had gone and done the unthinkable, jumping up to settle itself purring in my lap. 'I'm not going to see them,' I told it. It was unconcerned. 'There's no way that they'll still be there,' I said. 'Their wanderlust would have moved them on.'

The cat dropped its head and lay there, innocent, its eyes half closed, the underfelt of its soft white neck rumbling gently. I stroked my hand along its velvety back, amazed that it tolerated the attention. 'And all for a change of diet,' I told it. 'Now that's what I call fickle.'

I was on the tube eavesdropping. I nearly missed my stop. Two young women, certain in the way that only late adolescents can be, were standing talking in cheerful voices about the best method of deterring a rapist.

'Kick him in the balls,' one said loudly. 'Or better still, grab hold and twist.'

'Nah.' Her friend was having none of that. 'You gotta go for their eyes. Jab at 'em with your finger. That'll bring 'em up short.'

26

I looked up and saw the tube doors about to close. I made a run for it and only just got through. I pushed all thought of the conversation aside. I had a busy day ahead.

My plan was simple. I would pick up the paint, take it back to Chelsea, dust-proof the living room and be in good time to welcome in my friends, the painters I had booked. The sooner they started, the sooner they would finish, and when that was done I could leave with a clear conscience. The prospect was tantalizing; I increased my pace.

I needn't have bothered. I found the shop easily enough, nestling in an exclusive row adjacent to Notting Hill Gate tube, but it was guarded, windows and doors alike, by snugly fitting wrought-iron shutters. Peering through the lattice-work, I saw a faint notice on the door. The shop, it informed me, would open at eleven. I sighed, mentally kicking myself. I should have checked, especially after he had answered the phone so late the previous evening.

Oh well. I only had an hour and a half to kill. No problem. I would get a coffee and a paper and if I was still too early after that, I'd treat myself to some unhurried window shopping.

That's what I told myself I would do. What I did was different. I walked straight to number 14, Lambton Place. I didn't even pause to admire the row of trees, their leaves a dazzling autumnal fusion of golds and reds and browns. I climbed the broad stone steps.

I kept telling myself that what I was doing was a waste of time: Anna and Daniel would surely have moved on. And even if they hadn't, they would both surely be out at work.

I rang a bell, any bell, the first to hand.

As soon as I heard the distant ringing, I began my retreat. They're not going to be there, I told myself, turning. I heard footsteps. It won't be them, I thought,

27

and was down the first step. Behind me I heard a door opening.

I turned. I had to. I turned and there she was standing above me, looking down. She seemed completely unsurprised. Of course – she was bound to have been top of Bev's list. She knew I was in town.

She stood there, quietly.

It was so different from the past. Then, she had been my soul mate. I had known her almost as intimately as I had known Sam; I was able often to predict what she was going to say. Now I wasn't even in the ball park. The possibilities – from a puzzled 'What are you doing here?' to an outraged 'Off my steps' – seemed boundless.

Her face had changed. Like mine, her jaw line had been breached. And also like mine, her skin was no longer as firm, and there were lines there, etched deeply in the shadows beneath her eyes.

Her eyes were fixed on me, waiting. I cleared my throat.

She spoke before I could. 'So. Our lady of the postcards.'

'You got them?' I smiled. Or tried to.

She nodded. 'Years ago. Redirected from the States. We assumed you'd forgotten our new address.'

'I thought I had.'

She frowned and lines which had been only faintly etched on her forehead five years previously dug deeper. 'The cards stopped coming some time ago.'

'I suppose I ran out of steam.'

Her face darkened. I bit my tongue. I shouldn't have said that, especially since it wasn't true. 'I'm sorry,' I said.

A pause and then: 'Well,' Anna said, and for one dreadful moment I thought she was going to turn away. She didn't. Of course she wouldn't. Flight had never been part of *her* repertoire. 'I'm glad you finally made it,' she said.

That sentence changed everything. I could have left

before. The sight of her, middle-aged like me, would have been enough to drive me out. But hearing her speak and hearing as well this first hint of acceptance, I felt my resolution dissolve.

I swallowed, trying to swallow down a lump. 'Can I come in?' I asked. Tearfully.

'Oh, Kate.' Her voice had softened. 'Of course you can.'

She reached out, pulling me to her, hugging me tight, and the years of separation were revoked. It was so wonderful, that embrace. And alien as well. I'd forgotten what real friendship could feel like. During my travels I had made many friends, amongst them some I considered to be good friends, but the parameters were entirely other. For when I was with people post-Sam, there had always been words, waiting to protect me. With Anna, it was different. With Anna, silence would do as well as explanation.

She spoke into my withdrawal: 'It's not easy, is it?' and in her voice I heard disapproval.

I nodded, my thoughts confirmed. What I had done was irrevocable.

Her voice intruded. 'Come in,' she said and, without waiting for my reply, walked briskly up the stairs.

I was thankful that they had moved. The familiarity of their Islington house, the place where our foursome, Anna and Daniel, Sam and I, had once hung out, would have been intolerable. Not that this large second-floor flat was entirely unfamiliar. For even though there had been changes, Anna's style remained sovereign. I didn't recognize the turquoise vase, standing there in the corner on a low long table against the brick-red wall, and yet, in a blind trial, I would have guessed that Anna's was the guiding hand behind the combination.

But wait. I stood in the centre of the open-plan living

area, looking round. There was something different. Something missing. I frowned.

Anna was silent, watchful. Searching for clues, I looked beyond and past her, looking for the notice-board she would surely have. I found it, hanging strategically on the wall between the living area and the kitchen. One glance, even from a distance, was enough. I got it then: what was different.

My first impression had been wrong. Something was not missing, something – someone – had been added. Her photos dominated the notice-board collage, including one which, stuck in the centre, was larger than all the others. I looked at her: she, Anna's spitting image, looked back. She had the same sparkling blue eyes and the same cheeky smile. I blinked and I saw her differently; this time, I saw Daniel's face looking back, his mop of curly brown hair, his hint of gravity about her forehead. I blinked again and the separate parts were recombined: she was her own person and, at the same time, her parents' child.

Of course. I couldn't believe my own stupidity. Of course the room was different. The splendid, luscious, perfect sheen that is the luxury of childless couples had been disrupted. I turned to Anna. 'How old is she?'

'Almost five.'

Five? Anna had been pregnant when Sam had died!

But hadn't told me. Well, of course she couldn't. I bit my lip.

'Is she at school?'

A nod. 'She started this term.' A pause. 'We named her Kate.'

Kate, I thought. A name chosen in good old Jewish fashion after somebody who had departed from this earth.

'Hey.' Anna's voice punctured my mental blurring. 'Hey, Kate.'

'It's all right,' I said. 'It was just a shock.'

Anna laughed. 'For you and me both,' she said. 'I mean, I was hardly prime motherhood material, was I?'

Looking up, I saw how her smile softened her face and I saw as well that, despite the fact that she was more lined, she was also much less jagged. It was almost, I thought, as if she had ripened rather than aged. 'It suits you,' I said.

She nodded. She was beaming.

'And Daniel?' I asked, meaning did it suit him too?

Her smile evaporated. 'He d –' she began.

I couldn't bear it. I half rose. 'He died?'

She laughed. 'No. Not died. Another D.' As I fell back into my chair, her laughter got a bitter edge. 'Don't panic,' she said. 'D as in he divorced me.' A pause. She was no longer even smiling. 'I suppose that's unfair,' she said. 'What I should say is that we divorced each other.'

'Oh, Anna.' That's all I could say. Anna and Daniel had always been an item. I couldn't imagine them apart.

Which she did not appreciate. 'It didn't work out,' she said in a steely voice, willing me to take this in my stride. 'Having Kate had a lot to do with it, I suppose. We waited too long, couldn't find a way of slotting it all – careers, baby, and our relationship – together.' She shrugged. 'I could just about balance childcare with life in the cutting room. Anything else felt like too much.'

She spoke bravely but I thought I heard an undercurrent of misery threading through. 'Tell me,' I said.

She told me then, all about her parting from Daniel. I found myself listening hard, not only because I needed to know what had happened but also for another reason. If Anna and Daniel had separated, I thought, then nobody was safe. Perhaps . . . as I shivered, my thoughts came rushing out: perhaps if Sam had not died then he and I would also have eventually gone our separate ways.

Anna had always been able to read my mind. 'You

31

romanticized our relationship,' she said. 'Things were not that good.'

I couldn't let her get away with that. 'Things *were* good,' I insisted. 'I remember how they were.'

She smiled. 'It's your fault, then. You shouldn't have left.'

'Come on,' I said softly.

She shrugged and her voice was no longer teasing. 'Time changes everything,' she said, shrugging again. 'We're only human, all of us.'

'I suppose so,' I said, thinking, however, that it wasn't true. Death can make people more than human. It was ridiculous, I know, but I sat there feeling almost envious of Anna. She at least had been given the opportunity to face up to who Daniel really was, whereas I . . . I had only memories of Sam, and in those memories he was young, energetic, full of hope.

'Kate. Where've you gone now?' I heard her asking.

I couldn't speak. It was over, over. I had got over it. I didn't want to have to think of it, none of it, not Sam, not life without Sam, nor the changing world, nor anything. 'I'm not the same,' I said.

'Hey,' she said, softly. 'Relax. It's over.'

'Perhaps,' I said, but remembering some of the places I had been and some of the things that I had witnessed, I couldn't stop myself. 'But sometimes,' I said, 'sometimes it feels as if things are never over.'

Chapter
six

We steered away from homespun philosophy and concentrated instead on filling each other in on the times we'd missed. It was all quite superficial, but since superficial had, in our relationship, always played a role, it was also reassuring. For hours we talked, pausing once so that Anna could make lunch and once again when I remembered to put the painters on temporary hold.

At three o'clock, Anna checked the time. She looked vaguely guilty. 'I'm in between cutting films,' she said. 'I promised Kate I'd fetch her.'

Kate. It was odd to hear Anna use my name on somebody else, especially somebody so precious. I smiled and stood up.

'You sure you won't come?'

I shook my head. 'It's enough for one day,' I said.

She didn't argue. She also stood and, linking her arm to mine, began walking me out.

At the ground floor I felt Anna's arm tensing. I knew immediately what the general arena of her next comment would be.

'It's been great,' I said quickly.

She flashed me an uncertain smile. 'Um,' she murmured and then, letting go of my arm, she turned away and clicked on the hall light. The action appeared to give her courage: as she twisted back, she also spoke. 'I saw

Matthew the other day,' she said, the apprehension in her voice belying her composure.

Matthew – there, it was out in the open, that name which had lain between us since the first moment of our reunion.

'I see him occasionally,' I heard Anna saying. 'He's a good kid.' I looked at her: she dropped her gaze. She was as uneasy as I.

'He's no kid now.' I was attempting my own version of nonchalance.

'He's fifteen.'

Fifteen. Of course I knew that. I smiled. 'I bet he's spotty.'

'No.' She shook her head. 'Actually he looks a lot like Sam.'

Like Sam. Of course he would. He always had done, had Sam's only child. I felt something stabbing at me, a pain the like of which I had assumed had been for ever stilled. I could not speak.

Neither it seemed could Anna. We stood, in silence, for so long that the hall light clicked off. I was grateful to it. Closing my eyes, I turned away.

There was another click. 'Will you visit him?' I heard Anna asking.

I shook my head and, since my eyes were still mercifully dry, turned back. 'No.' I was quite positive.

She frowned. 'Why not?'

I shrugged. Nothing, not even Anna's disapproval, was going to change my mind.

'Why not?' She was belligerent.

My eyes met hers. 'Because I did enough damage, leaving so soon after Sam's death,' I said. 'He won't want to see me.'

'You mean you don't want to risk it.'

When I said nothing we faced each other, our masquerade stripped bare. Our time together had been a few hours of absurd make-believe, grown women pretending that the missing years could be ignored.

Anna was like a yapping terrier. 'That is what you mean, isn't it?' she snarled. And then abruptly her voice softened. 'But is it really what you want?'

What I wanted was out. I felt it physically, the urge to flee.

Her will was at least as strong as mine. 'You should go and see him,' she repeated, adding: 'You owe him that.'

I looked up, staring, my mouth shut tight. What the hell did she know? Divorce or not, her life was one continuum: her home was here, her choices clear. Not mine. My life was different.

'You owe him.'

I narrowed my eyes. If this was the way that Anna was going to play it, then I would show her. I would show her that she did not have the monopoly on anger. 'I don't owe anybody, anything,' I said slowly, leaving a space between each separate word.

As the full force of my hostility hit her, her expression changed. Her face went pale, her jaw tightened. I knew that words were forming behind this barrier, and I knew also that once these were packaged, there would be no going back.

I waited, hopelessly, for her to say it, the thing that would end everything.

'I'm sorry,' she said. 'I always was an interfering cow.'

I didn't trust myself to speak.

'It was great to see you.' She stepped closer and before I realized what was happening she had embraced me. I almost pulled away. I managed to stop myself. I felt her determination and the contrasting softness of her body against mine, and I felt myself involuntarily relax.

'I missed you,' she said.

35

'Me too,' I said, or tried to. It came out all blurred.

She let go of me, leaning across and opening the front door. 'You better go,' she said. 'Before I cry.'

'Drive me out then,' I hectored. We exchanged a smile.

'See you.'

I nodded and walked out.

I was halfway down the front steps when: 'Kate?'

I felt adrenalin resurge, pumping toxins through my veins. I was furious. Why couldn't she let it alone? I turned.

But I was wrong. 'Are you sure you're not going to do another midnight flit?'

Relief must have made me look quite gormless. 'I promise I'll phone,' I said.

She nodded and then, blowing a kiss my way, she shut the door on me.

I was still so hyped up when I arrived at the paint shop that I pushed the glass door too forcefully. It swung backwards, banging loudly, drowning out the tinkling of a bell. As a result, 'I'm sorry,' was my opening phrase.

It was downhill from then on. There was a man standing in front of the counter, his dark green trousers firmly pressed into place, his open-necked shirt gleaming white against a ruby cravat. As I came nearer he threw me a look which left me in no doubt that I had relinquished all chance of a customer popularity prize. Not that he glared, far from it. He merely raised one disapproving eyebrow. 'May I help you?' His cultured voice was icy.

'I'm Kate B –' No, that was wrong. I changed tack. 'Kate B. Willis,' I said.

'Yes?'

I smiled ingratiatingly. 'Pam Willis's cousin.'

'Ah yes.' A pause. 'The Friedrich.'

Another pause, so prolonged that I eventually realized he was waiting for me to speak. I spoke. 'Is it ready?'

He nodded. 'Naturally.'

'Well . . .' I tried an uneasy smile.

'You did say that it was urgent.'

Oh. The penny dropped. I was in trouble because I was late. 'I'm sorry,' I said again, 'I got held up.' And then, when he did not speak, found myself saying, 'I'm sorry,' for a third time.

'That's quite all right,' he said, turning away.

While he was gone, I passed time rooting through vast books of wallpaper samples. Brocade, ornate and glitzy, was, I saw, all the rage, as were some rather lurid swirling patterns. I turned to one page where the mix was particularly ghastly, sallow yellows and sickly greens interwoven into a complex design. It was so ugly it was engrossing. I stared, disbelieving, at it.

The man had made a silent reappearance. He was standing by my shoulder. 'That,' he said, pointing, 'is one of our most popular lines.'

'Oh.' What else could I say? I had spent much of the last five years with people who considered themselves lucky if they had a wall: I was hardly in any position to pass judgement on wallpaper fashion. I smiled ingratiatingly. 'Have you got it?'

No dice. 'It?'

I sighed, wondering why this was proving so hard. 'The Friedrich,' I said.

'It's on the counter.'

And so it was, an array of tins swathed in string to make them easier to transport, along with a computerised bill. I glanced at the latter, whistled through my teeth and paid.

'Thanks,' I said, balancing tins on either side.

'A pleasure,' he said, although his half-scowl made it clear that it was no pleasure. What was his problem? I wondered. I moved away.

As I was opening the door, clumsily trying to hold on to the paint as well, he spoke. 'You can tell Mrs Willis that her drawing-room maroon will be ready as requested,' he said.

I nodded. I had not the faintest idea what drawing-room maroon was, but I certainly was not going to ask. I pushed the door with my foot – too hard. It banged again.

'Sorry,' I said, and left.

Chapter
seven

It was dark when I got home. I hadn't eaten much at Anna's and, as I slipped my key into the lock, I realized I was starving. So, it seemed, was the cat. It started meowing when I opened the door, raised the level when I de-coded the alarm and was at fever pitch as I picked up the post. 'OK, I'm coming,' I said, glancing idly at the batch of letters.

I froze. I had flipped through quickly but there was no denying it. I had seen my name, not once, but twice. I started rooting through the post, looking unseeing at the names in front, until I had the whole bunch fanned out in my hands – like Tarot cards. The thought was so ridiculous, it brought me to my senses. I concertinaed up the pile. I didn't have to face this: Not now.

The cat's yowling had moved beyond frenzied. 'OK, OK,' I shouted. I went downstairs. The cat did not let up. I threw the post on to a counter and found myself bending down, stroking it. When that only increased its protests, I set to work with the tin opener. I whirled the electric monster around some Sainsbury's Supreme. The cat was quite frenetic, weaving itself maniacally in and out of my legs. When it didn't even occur to me to kick it away, I realized, with a sinking heart, that I was actually growing to like it.

It was growling. I set its bowl upon the floor. 'What's

there to like?' I asked it. It was too busy stuffing its mouth to spare me a second glance. Pam had told me that she was afraid to put it in a sanctuary while she was away because it had been acting ill. Some illness, I thought, as I watched, disgusted. I knew that it would soon start spraying most of what it was pretending to consume all over my spotless floor. 'Relax,' I told it. 'I mean, it's not as if your food supply ever dries up, is it?'

The cat looked up – once only – before launching its head back into the centre of the bowl, jamming a wodge of food into its mouth and then sneaking off. I knew from past experience that to try and get it back would only cause further devastation. I let it go. 'Don't worry about me,' I told it's retreating back. 'I'm going to eat too.'

Straightening up, I wondered what should come first: food or shower. I was hungry but also feeling grimy. Shower, I decided. I turned.

The post was there, lying on the counter, too powerful to ignore. Its pull was such that I couldn't go upstairs. But I also wasn't ready to open it. 'I'll eat first,' I said out loud, ignoring the other thought.

I put a pot of water on the stove and, while it was heating up, I concentrated on making a marinara. I skinned garlic, threw it into hot olive oil, and followed through with some roughly chopped tomatoes, a pinch of dried basil, some salt and fresh ground black pepper, before turning down the heat. The water was not yet boiling. I decided on antipasti. I took the raw ingredients – salami, an assortment of cheeses, olives and some greens – from the fridge and laid them on the counter. The plan was to arrange them beautifully on one of Pam's bone china plates. I even started doing this, managing in the process to hum a few bars of a song I thought I'd long forgotten.

But stopped abruptly. All this activity, just to avoid

what I would eventually have to face. Laying down my knife, I turned off the sauce.

The post consisted of a bundle of business letters for Greg, a catalogue, an air mail letter, two postcards for Pam, and the two envelopes for me. I walked to the counter and got hold of them. I had one in each hand. The one in my left, a large manila with a reinforced back was easily explained; the other, now in my right hand, white and official looking, was less comprehensible.

I tried to work out which would be the least upsetting. In the end, I chose the white. When I saw what it contained, I smiled. Of course – I should have guessed. It was a diplomatically worded invitation from the local victim support group to contact them. I wasn't sure for which crime they were offering counsel – the mugging or the break in – but I don't suppose it mattered. I set the letter aside, knowing I'd never use it.

That left the other. I thought about leaving it, there on the kitchen counter. But that wouldn't make it go away, not unless I stopped eating altogether. I came up with another option: I could stow it at the bottom of my suitcase. But that, of course, was sillier than the first, for I would soon be packing up to go. The only other possibility, that I throw it away unopened, was unthinkable.

I was trapped. I stood there, flailing against the knowledge, until something in me rebelled. I refuse to be trapped, I told myself. I'll choose option number one, I'll never open it. I nodded decisively and, with that decided, walked away. I threw tagliatelli into the water, now boiling, and reheated the sauce. After that I turned, walked three paces forward, picked up the envelope and, using a kitchen knife, slit it open.

There was no accompanying note: just the photo. Black and white, it was, a portrait of Sam taken as dusk fell. Sam smiling at the camera, his face grainy against the blurred background of a spreading tree. I couldn't tear my eyes away. Whatever else one could say about Roger Toms, he sure knew how to get a likeness. He had captured Sam exactly, as Sam had been: so handsome, so energetic, so vital, so . . . so bloody alive.

The kitchen timer went off. I put the photo down and drained the pasta. Having put it into a bowl, I added olive oil, a helping of the sauce and some grated Parmesan cheese. I sat down to eat.

All the time I was busy, Sam smiled at me – just as he used to when I cooked this dish for him. The scent of the sauce I'd made came wafting up.

'Smells delicious,' I told his photo.

He carried on smiling. I got up, grabbed a bottle of Greg's French vin de pays from the wine rack and poured myself a glass. Sitting down again I raised the glass. 'To us,' I said, sipping wine. I put the glass down. I was hungry. I picked up my fork. Sam and I had used to make pasta together. I dug my fork in, twisting it, and as I did so I saw an image from the past – the two of us, in the kitchen, working together, sensing what each other needed, criss-crossing and making contact without getting in each other's way. No, I thought: I won't remember. I lifted the fork and ate what was on it. I couldn't stop myself. Chewing, I remembered standing by a vast pot and tasting a single strand and no longer being alone, feeling Sam's hands around my waist, his body hugging close to mine.

I put the fork down. I watched my tears splashing on to my plate. I swallowed but they kept on coming, streaming down my cheeks and dropping from my chin. There was nothing I could do to stop them, they had a life all of their own. It was a quiet crying, a welling of something that was too old to be simply labelled grief, and I sat there enduring it. When finally it abated, I got up and washed my face in cold water. I dried it with a bit of kitchen towel and, going back to the table, sat down again.

Sam was smiling.

I felt tears welling again. I used words to forestall them. I pointed my fork at Sam. 'Why did you go out?'

He kept on smiling.

I managed to return his smile but, unlike his which was fixed in grey, mine went sticky. I shook my head. I was quite determined: I wasn't going to cry again. And didn't need to either. The tears had worked. I sat there, staring at Sam, and realizing that they had not been tears of grief as I had hitherto experienced them. My grief had brought anger, denial, pain and eventually a kind of inner deadness. Now I felt myself warm – alive. For the first time in five years, I felt how much I missed what I had lost.

Five years ago I'd left the country because I couldn't bear facing Sam's death. Now I was back and some of what I had cut off by leaving was returning to me.

Is that why, I suddenly thought, I had allowed Pam to persuade me to stay here for a few days, rather than doing what I had originally planned – a quick hotel trip? Because, by staying in London, I could acknowledge what I had once had and, in facing that, could make myself whole?

Whole – that was a bit portentous, wasn't it? I shook my head and finished up my pasta. I did not, however, immediately get up. My shower could wait. I had something else to do, something important. I pulled the phone to me and punched in Anna's number.

She answered on the second ring. 'Hello,' she said, sounding breathless and simultaneously irritated.

'Bad timing?' I asked, above the sound of high-pitched screaming.

'Kate,' Anna said. Just that – 'Kate' – and the anguished squeals came nearer.

I felt like duplicating those noises. But I wouldn't. 'I could ring back,' I said, mock cheerfully.

'Don't.' Her voice was loud. 'Hold on a mo'. I'll move phones.' All sounds were abruptly cut off. I waited, the phone pressed uncomfortably moist against my ear. 'Sorry.' Anna was there, backed by silence. 'It's mayhem here,' she said. 'Typical, isn't it? On the one day that I have time to fetch her from school, she throws a mega fit. Enough to make a person guilty.'

'Guilty?' I asked, thinking that guilt and Anna had not previously been companions.

'Comes with the territory,' she said. 'Cross a workaholic with a single mother and what you get are sacks under the eyes and bagfuls of portable guilt.' Not that it seemed to bother her – there was laughter in her voice. Until that is, she softened it. 'I'm glad you phoned.'

'Me too,' I said, an uncomfortable lump swelling in my throat.

Silence until: 'Oh no,' from Anna. An unearthly wail engulfed the airwaves. 'Discovered,' Anna said. 'I'd better go. Look, come to dinner, why don't you? Soon?'

I said I would and, after I agreed that she could invite other guests as well, we fixed the day. The wail got louder. 'I'll give you a ring,' Anna said, her closing gambit.

I took a deep breath in and, before she could hang up, shouted: 'Stop.' I followed that with a garbled sentence. 'Can you give me Matthew's number?' is how I think I phrased it.

A pause and then, thank goodness, Anna skipped a comment. 'Sure,' is all she said, 'hold on.' A bumping sound and an impatiently yelled, 'Wait, can't you?' which was, I assume, directed at her angry child, and Anna was back. 'He's living in Kingston. In John's new house,' and, moving quickly over the disparaging remark she knew I was tempted to make, she gave me the number.

'How is he?' I asked as soon as she had finished.

'Matthew? He's fine.'

'No. Not Matthew.' I would never ask her that – not over the phone. I had thought about him too much, had hugged my guilt at leaving him too long around me. 'I meant John.'

A sigh. 'John. Well, what can I say? He's John.'

'Yeah,' I said, knowing exactly what she meant. 'He always was.' In the background I could hear a child's voice, sounding pathetic. 'You'd better go. Speak to you soon.'

'Yeah. And Kate? . . . Thanks for ringing.'

'Sure.' I put the phone down.

And found myself alone. The cat had disappeared, gone to eat in secret, I supposed, in case I decided suddenly to take its food away. I sat there, quite still, thinking vaguely that it must be nice to be Anna, who, having hung up, would have a crying child to comfort.

The thought amazed me. I wasn't the type to envy motherhood. I got up. 'You're just feeling sorry for yourself,' I said out loud and then, shaking off self-pity, I went upstairs to shower and then to finish up my article.

Chapter

eight

I slept, soundly, without dreaming and for a very long time. I slept so soundly, in fact, that I slept through my alarm and, if my painters had been ordinary, I might have also slept through them. They, however, were not ordinary and they had survived greater challenges than me. When the bell proved useless, they began to knock and, when that was also unsuccessful, went into overdrive.

I was awakened to a tremendous battering on the door, accompanied by a bellow. 'Katherine,' I heard Jurek yelling, except it being Jurek, it sounded more like Kazerino. 'Katherine.'

I hauled myself out of bed. 'Coming!' I called. I needn't have bothered: sated by sleep my voice wasn't even strong enough to breach the bedroom door, never mind travel downstairs.

'Katherine!' and, immediately afterwards, a series of explosions. I pushed my sluggish body into action, fumbling for my dressing gown which I wrapped around me as, against the background of accelerated hammering, I stumbled my way downstairs.

'Katherine.' It was really loud now.

The repetition was driving me wild. Wrenching the door open, I opened my mouth and yelled: 'How many times do I have to tell you that my name is Kate?'

'Katherine.' Jurek's arms wrapped right round me. 'How are you?'

'Umph,' was all I had the strength to say.

It was enough. Jurek let go and, leaning down, grappled with paint trays, brushes, dust covers and the like, all of which he soon contained within his angular arms. That done he surged on past. He was a fast mover: by the time Maria and I had exchanged greetings and a kiss, Jurek's equipment was on the floor and he was halfway up the stairs. 'I cannot work without first having a feel of the house,' he announced before bounding out of sight.

My head was aching. 'He's impossible,' I said to Maria. 'How do you control him?'

She, all five foot nothing of her, shrugged. 'I have my ways.'

Jurek was back. 'Nice,' he commented. 'Very nice. But, Katherine.' His smile had faded. He was deadly serious. 'You must make your bed. Every morning. It is good for the mentality.'

Oh Christ, I thought, remembering how bad for the mentality Jurek could be.

'The kitchen is downstairs?' he asked.

I nodded and as Jurek dashed off down the hallway I stood rooted to the spot, wondering what I had done. What yesterday had felt sensible – the hiring of Jurek and Maria – now seemed preposterous. After all, to preside over the disarming and destruction of someone else's house was in bad taste but to trust its restoration to a madman and his sidekick! . . . This surely was vile. And besides . . .

'Hey,' I called. 'It's not the kitchen. It's the living . . .'

'Don't worry, my Katherine,' Jurek said. 'Maria and Jurek will take care of everything. You go now, brush your teeth. It will make you feel much better,' and with that he disappeared.

*

I hate to admit that Jurek is ever right but, by the time I got downstairs, I was feeling much better. Not for long though. As I walked into the kitchen, I was assailed by an incredible, and at the same time horrifyingly familiar, stench. Jurek was by the gas hob, his lanky frame bent almost double as, simultaneously muttering to himself in Polish, he stirred a saucepan. My heart sank.

Jurek had heard me. 'Good timing, Katherine,' he said, looking up, 'the coffee is almost prepared.'

I had tasted Jurek's foul concoction only once before just after I'd first met him and Maria in some Godforsaken town in Albania. That had been once too often.

'With sugar or not?' Jurek was smiling proudly.

I grimaced. No amount of sugar would ever make it palatable.

'You're quite right,' he said. 'Without sugar is much healthier.'

Healthier! I almost laughed but, seeing Jurek so pleased with himself, I remembered how easily he could be upset. I swallowed, thinking that if the worst came to the worst, I would also swallow down his coffee.

But I had reckoned without Maria. 'Kate will be having tea,' she announced.

I nodded vigorously.

'You.' Jurek pointed an accusing finger at Maria. 'You, I have given up trying to civilize. But Katherine is different. She is not a useless Greek. She is Portuguese. She appreciates the good things in life. She is a coffee person.'

'Kate will be having tea,' Maria said. And that, I was relieved to discover, was that.

We sat down together, drinking our separate beverages and eating toast. As the minutes ticked by, I felt myself relax. My initial reaction had been wrong: I hadn't made a mistake. Jurek might be an over-optimistic Polish emigré with a personality as flamboyant as his long hair, but he

48

could also be surprisingly on the ball. He listened carefully to my requirements for the paint job and then he detailed exactly how he would achieve the desired effect. 'As in our relationship,' he said, 'I supply the speed and Maria the finesse. Your friends' sitting room is safe with us.' He flashed me a dazzler of a smile. 'And you,' he said. 'How do you plan to spend the day?'

I didn't stop to think. 'I'm going to Kingston.' I frowned. That's where John Layton, Sam's father, lived. Why on earth should I be going there?

'Ah, Kingston,' Jurek was off. 'I know it. Battersea, Wandsworth, Roehampton, Robin Hood's Gate and then the jewel, Kingston Hill.' He frowned. 'The route is relatively simple. The potential trouble spots are . . .'

I cut him off. 'I was thinking more of Sloane Square, Waterloo, Kingston, taxi,' I said, although what I was really thinking was that I would not go to Kingston.

'What? You have no car?' Jurek slapped a broad palm against his forehead. 'But of course,' he roared: 'you will take our van.'

I shook my head. I had spent sufficient time with Jurek to know that any van of his meant trouble. And anyway, what I had said had been all wrong: I wasn't going to Kingston.

Jurek was unstoppable. 'You must take the van,' he said. 'I insist. You will solve our parking problem while we will save you from travel on the filthy underground. You come back any time. We go to the movies, this evening after painting. We will pick the van up after eleven.' When I did not reply, he frowned. 'Come, Katherine,' he urged. 'You are pale. This London is not good for you. Take off: take the van. Make a day of it.'

I nodded, thinking that he was right. London wasn't good for me. It threw me out of kilter, making me say all kinds of preposterous things. Like: *I'm going to Kingston*, something that I was certainly not going to do.

'Here,' Jurek said, misinterpreting my nod and handing me his keys. 'The van is outside. I will walk you to the door and there you can show me how to operate the capitalist's alarm.' He was on his feet, grinning, 'Hurry,' he said. 'We must start work.'

He was too energetic for me. I got up and walked with him upstairs. I shoved my completed article into an envelope, addressed it, and then showed Jurek how to operate the alarm. I gave him and Maria their own special code. And then, with Jurek watching, I got into their disreputable-looking van and drove off.

I went to Kingston. Jurek's detailed route plan, delivered on the door step, made it easy. As I drove slowly (slow and stop being the van's only two modes) through dreary urban blight into zones of middle-class comfort and back again, my mind was vacant. Over the wastes of Putney Heath I went, past sedate Richmond Park and finally left as instructed, at Robin Hood's Gate, on to Kingston Hill.

I was inching into the presence of great wealth. Nature smoothed my way: as the van struggled up the hill, the quantity and variety of green was correspondingly upped. And not only that: everything else was different. I gazed around, counting the changes. We were no longer in either terraced or even semi-detached territory: in their place were high walls and long driveways. There were, of course, gardens, but in versions so large they were almost estates. I couldn't comment on the houses for what money bought in this department was invisibility. I didn't see a single dwelling, only lines of trees winding gracefully towards them.

I ignored the numbers on the gates and kept on driving. I topped the hill and went over it and the tranquillity brought on by affluence began to diminish. Life got more crowded, the green less bright, the houses closer to the road, and there, nestled in the distance, I saw a council estate and a Barnado's home. I slowed down almost to a halt. There was no doubt about it: I had passed my destination.

I didn't turn. I moved the van slowly down the hill as one question kept repeating on me. One question – What am I doing here? – which had one answer. It was mad, that was the answer, to drop in unannounced on John Layton. We had never liked each other, and since Sam died the only thing we had had in common was Matthew – who was sure to be at school.

I put my foot down on the accelerator, drove straight ahead, away from Kingston Hill. I would find my way back eventually but my return route would give this place a miss. I'll ring instead, I told myself, and arrange to meet Matthew (if of course he agreed to meet) at some neutral venue. Yes, I nodded, and with this decided, felt almost happy.

I had reckoned without Jurek's van. It was unimpressed by happiness. As it gathered speed, it also began to knock. Or something did, something on the undercarriage. Glancing at the dashboard, I slowed right down. I saw another symptom – the heating dial moving into the forbidden upper zone.

There was a lay-by to my left. I pulled in and waited for a moment, watching the dial return to zero. I sighed and, getting out, opened up the bonnet and stuck my head under it. I was at the limits of my mechanical expertise, but I knew enough to remove the radiator cap carefully. After the first rush of steam had cleared, I took a closer look. I should have guessed: the radiator was empty.

'Shit,' I said and kicked the hub cap. That got me nothing but a sore foot. 'Shit,' I said again and, getting back into the van, I started it up, turned it in the road and slowly, slowly drove back up Kingston Hill.

Chapter
nine

I had no trouble finding John Layton's new house. It was on the crest of the hill, its entry point a set of imposing, and open, wrought-iron gates. I drove through them.

The engine noise was deafening. It had its uses: worrying that the van might blow up disposed of other fears. I manoeuvred slowly forward, edging along the elegant avenue, past sentinel intermixed plane and chestnut trees, the tyres rolling over fallen conkers. Behind the trees were rolling lawns, so substantial that the wide herbaceous borders that lined them made little impact. There was wildlife as well. I heard a gang of dogs barking and what I thought was the clip-clopping of hooves, and I could almost swear that the item standing on the edge of the furthest lawn, by the high wall that separated John Layton's land from Richmond Park, must be a deer. I never got the chance to check: hearing the van backfire, the beast took off.

I turned, a corner and there, at last, it was – the house. No bigger than the majestic boulevard had led me to expect, but no smaller either. A mansion, fake Tudor, with leaded windows dotting the pattern of wooden beams arranged against rough white plaster walls.

I braked and the engine banged and died. I got out and crunched my way across a gravel forecourt, past immaculately coiffed shrubs and an old and cranky-looking stone lion. I paused, patted it gently on the head. 'You're a bit out of period, aren't you?' I asked it, and then, walking on, found myself thinking idly that I seemed to be developing a thing for cats.

I was almost at the door. My doubts resurfaced. It was crazy, I told myself, what I was doing, just pitching up like this. I stopped a moment, on the threshold, playing with the idea of turning back. But no. If I turned away I knew what would happen. I would lose the courage to contact Matthew. This was a test which, for some mysterious reason, I had set myself and, because of this, it had become a test I could not afford to fail. Lifting my hand, I pressed the bell.

I wasn't surprised at the speed with which the door was opened – after all the van had telegraphed my presence. What I hadn't expected was that it would be answered by the man himself. The man – Sam's father – John Layton.

'Kate,' John said, exhibiting, after five years' separation, not the slightest surprise. I don't know why that disconcerted me – I suppose I was still kidding myself that I was incognito in England. Whatever the reason, I stood there feeling vaguely stupid, wondering who, amongst my circle, had forewarned him.

But then I frowned. A distant voice – Sam's voice – sounded from the past. *My father is never surprised by anything*, Sam had said. *After all, God only invented poker so that John Layton could win at it.*

'Come in.' The door was pushed open wide.

I caught a taste of what lay inside – an entrance hall far more spacious than Tudor in its native form could offer. Seeing the sheer power of John's wealth, I wondered again what I was doing there.

'Kate?'

My eyes met his. I froze. Not because of anything he did, but because of the way he looked.

How he looked made me ache with longing. He was standing in partial shadow, which must have helped annihilate the lines, and so what I saw wasn't the man but the man as a version of his son. I saw Sam. They were a generation and a half apart – Sam had been thirty when he died while John must now be in his mid sixties – and yet it was as if time had stopped. The same blue eyes stared out at me, the same broad forehead, the same full and sensuous lips. Is this, I thought, is this why I have come?

'Kate?'

I couldn't keep on standing there. I pushed myself into motion. I walked across an elaborately inlaid oak floor into a vast gallery. Once inside I stopped. I almost whistled. All around were polished mahogany banisters leading to a high balcony, and from the dark wood ceiling hung a glittering chandelier. And that wasn't all: the walls, oak panelled to waist height and lined, after that, with the kind of brocade that I'd seen in the Notting Hill Gate paint shop, were dotted with wood-framed paintings – English country scenes, a horse, a dog, the kind of stuff that reeks of Stubbs.

Another transformation, I thought, thinking that five years ago in John Layton's previous house the interior designers had gone for minimalist modernity. All that was over, now everything was solemn, solid, organized to impress. It worked. I couldn't help myself – I was impressed. I stood there, dumbfounded, digesting the totality of John's transition from nouveau riche into wealthy Edwardian. Whatever it was that had happened to the British economy in the last few years, it certainly hadn't happened to John.

He was watching me, expecting praise. I couldn't give it to him. I was too assailed by memory. It came back to me, so clearly, that time I had suppressed: the time that followed Sam's death. I remembered John looking at me as we stood opposite each other, separated by Sam's coffin. I remembered the pain written on his face, pain that had made me want to reach across to him. And I remembered something else as well: I remembered how, seeing my eyes on him, his face had closed against me, shutting me out.

As I remembered this, the hallway seemed to darken. All that wood was no longer impressive: it was sinister. I tried to domesticate it by saying the first thing that came into my head. 'The falling pound's going to blow a hole in all of this,' I said.

'Not if you're also into Deutschmarks,' was his instantaneous reply.

Of course, I thought: of course John would be into Deutschmarks, just like he was into property before the crash, and futures before the fiasco of the London futures market, and uranium before nuclear power got iffy – and out of all three when the time was right.

He had moved to the wall. 'But tell me,' I heard him saying. His hand hit out. 'Why are you here?'

The chandelier caught sudden flame, flooding the hall with brightness. John was looking straight at me, one feathery eyebrow raised. What I had thought before was wrong. John did not look like Sam – he was far too aged for that, his forehead covered by a myriad fine lines.

'What do you want?'

I cleared my throat. 'Actually,' I said. 'I want to see Matthew.'

He raised a second sceptical eyebrow.

While I stood there thinking that he was right: this really did seem ludicrous. 'He's at school,' I said.

A faint nod.

'Yup.' Of course he was. 'What school?'

'Dulwich.'

Dulwich? Oh sure: Dulwich College, Raymond Chandler's old alma mater, an establishment on the grand old scale, all spires and playing fields – a far cry from the state primary where Matthew had begun his school life. I should have expected that. One glimpse of John Layton's entrance hall was enough to show how dramatically Matthew's material life had been transformed.

I wondered if contact with all this ostentatious wealth had done him any good. I wondered if he was happy. 'Is he a boarder?'

Another nod. 'Weekly.'

Which meant that Matthew came back every weekend. I waited expectantly but my waiting was rewarded by a silence which told me that John wasn't planning to invite me back. 'I guess I could arrange to see him during the week,' I said.

John hesitated and in that moment it returned to me, more of what he'd done, that time, five years ago. I remembered a raised voice, mine not his, and tears, again mine, the only tears that I had shed. And then I remembered John stooping and, having hugged Matthew, removing him.

Something started burning inside me then, burning with ferocity. I breathed in, trying to hold it back.

John had sensed the change. He too was transformed. His eyes hardened, glittering with malice. I could no longer believe that I'd seen in them my gentle Sam's eyes. Here, behind a suave exterior, lurked a bully happy to use brute force if that way he could win.

Well, I would not let him win, not this time. My anger was a match for his. 'Don't try and stop me.'

John smiled, his lips tightening into a long thin line, wiping out the last vestige of Sam. 'I don't need to stop you,' he said. 'Because Matthew will.' And then, before I could butt in, added: 'Have you ever considered the possibility that my grandson' – *my grandson*, spoken with an air of possession and of pride such as one might say my Rolls or my country mansion – 'might not want to see you?'

56

Of course I had considered it. For five long years.

'After all,' I heard John saying, 'you deserted him.'

Deserted him. I remembered how as soon as Sam had died everything – access on the telephone, the doors to his house, the post – had all been closed to me.

'Fortunately Matthew has put all this behind him,' John was saying. 'He never speaks of you.' His voice oozed satisfaction.

I knew precisely what he was saying. He had got what he had always wanted – his grandson. He had won. Why should he need more?

'Why did you want to keep me from him?' I asked, as I should have asked before.

His only reply, a dismissive shrug, was answer enough. I stood there thinking that Sam had been right: it was a mistake to think of John as human. And that what I had assumed at Sam's funeral – that John's antipathy was caused by his terrible upset – was bullshit. 'You never did like me, did you?' I said.

'I did not particularly dislike you.' His tone was almost uninterested, his voice disengaged. 'You were a bad influence on my son. You turned him against me.'

My son, he said, claiming Sam. Sam who had spoken of his father only with bile.

'You wanted Sam to be another Roger Toms,' I said. 'Responsive to your every whim.'

'Roger?' John's smile was barely amused. 'He's a functionary. Sam was different. He could have been much more. But you encouraged him to inhabit a fantasy world, refusing to grow up.'

'Refusing to play by your rules, you mean.'

'Not by my rules, by the rules of the world,' John replied. 'Just look at you.' His pointing finger located my shirt and the smear of grease that the van had deposited there. 'You have nothing. Nothing. You were a competent journalist but no, you decided to run a detective agency. A detective agency!' His snort was explosive. 'And after that didn't work out, what have you been doing? Playing at journalism again?'

What I'd been doing didn't seem the point. 'Sam was a mathematician,' I said.

'At a university,' he said. 'Struggling to get a permanent contract, complaining about his lifeless students. Compare what he had with all this . . .' His hand swept up in a high arc, encompassing the high space, the solidity of his possessions. 'I came from poverty, worked my guts out to protect my family from similar insecurity. What can you give Matthew when compared to this?' He was goading me now, almost gloating. 'Come on,' he said. 'Tell me what.'

I stood my ground, looking calmly at him, and the words I spoke came easily. 'Some people work all their lives to save a little money,' is what I said. 'And then it is taken away.' I said it quite deliberately, to see what he would do.

His reaction was extraordinary. Pink, red, puce – each in turn flashed across his skin. 'Get out.' He was spitting with rage. 'Get out of my house.'

As he advanced on me, I knew I had gone too far. He'd remembered them, just like I had, those words that Sam had yelled into the phone, using them as a bludgeon with which to batter at his father.

That phone call, I remembered it so clearly. It had happened on Sam's last day alive, the last time, therefore, that he had spoken to his father.

John grabbed me by the elbow, propelled me to the doorway, shoved me out. 'Leave Matthew alone,' he said. 'I am all he has. Don't try and come between us.' The door was swung back. The knuckles that gripped the frame were white. 'Keep away, Kate Baeier,' John Layton said. 'Or I will break you.' The door slammed shut.

Chapter
ten

I was outside and moving mechanically. The way behind was barred so I went forward. I moved slowly and jerkily and without thinking until, eventually, the sound of my feet hitting the gravel brought me to my senses.

I stopped and stood still, frowning. Now that John was no longer towering over me, what he'd done seemed like a drastic over-reaction. OK – so I had spoken out of turn, throwing in his face his son's last paroxysm of wrath, but John Layton, especially this strong, rich, remade John Layton, must surely be the equal of that? And besides, I realized that potential conflict had been flaring well before I spoke. John had been almost rude, neither offering me a drink, nor suggesting that we move out of the vast hall to somewhere more comfortable – hardly a case of the prodigal almost-daughter-in-law returns. And since John was always in control, his lack of hospitality could only mean one thing: that, right from the start, he had been planning to evict me.

I saw it plainly now, what had happened. It wasn't, as I had first assumed, a matter of like or dislike, it went deeper than that. John Layton had answered the door ready to repel me, because, whether he had expected me that day or not, the last five years had been preparation for the moment when he would stake his final claim on Matthew.

Another echo from the past, Sam on the subject of his father: *'John doesn't know how to love'* – Sam's voice stiffened by bitterness – *'all he knows about is ownership.'* Sam's voice which had been so long silent, coming back clearly on his father's forecourt.

The voice persisted, echoing that single word: *ownership*. I kept on hearing it. *Ownership*. I stood there, trapped by remembrance and as I continued to stand there, I felt myself boiling. It began as a simmering resentment somewhere far back which caught fire. It was a physical sensation almost, a burning in my veins, a surge of . . . of what could only be fury. I was enraged. Not at the man, but at his son, at stupid bloody Sam who, knowing what his father was, had died intestate.

There was nothing, nothing I could have done. When Sam died, John had a phalanx of lawyers and a budding empire behind him. All I had was my grief, my failing detective business, and my unofficial bond to Matthew. No court on earth would have chosen me in preference to John. If I had tried to persuade them to, I would have been pulverized.

I was so angry, thinking of it, that I lashed out, kicking gravel. Too hard, my swinging foot made contact with the stone lion's flank. Pain, shooting through my toe and upwards engulfed me, forcing out words. 'You stupid idiot,' I shouted at myself. 'You idiot.'

I bit my lips, felt tears stinging at my eyes. But as I stood there, waiting for the pain to lessen, I knew that the tears had nothing to do with physical sensation and everything to do with guilt. Guilt that I hadn't tried harder; that I had abandoned Matthew. Gripped by my own grief, I had not had the strength to help him in his. I'd let John make the running, had gone away, had told myself that it would be better if the break were absolute.

Now I stood, wondering how it might have ended if, instead of fleeing, I had stayed to fight.

A sound, distant, clamorous barking, cut through my speculation. I pushed it off. 'I couldn't have done any different,' I said, directing my words at the sad stone lion. It stood, impassive against my denial. I looked more closely; saw a rivulet of brownish-yellow rust staining its yawning mouth. 'I couldn't have changed it,' I told it. It was true: and I repeated it to myself: I couldn't have done any differently.

But then, I thought, neither could Sam. His failure to make provision for his son could be judged only by a hindsight which paid no heed to the reality of the times. And the reality was that we were, all of us, young, children of the sixties who, although we considered ourselves grown up, had not yet come to terms with death. Sam, I, our whole circle, we thought ourselves immortal.

I wasn't angry any longer, I was melancholy. 'If we'd known then . . .' I told the lion. I didn't bother finishing the sentence. Instead I patted its tawdry mane and walked on.

I reached the van. Not thinking properly I got in, inserted the key, and turned it. To be met, of course, by a roaring, a clattering and a stoppage of the engine. My head fell forward, on to the steering wheel. The horn blared.

I lifted my head up, but not for long. I let it go again and this time it went backwards, falling against the seat. I closed my eyes. I was exhausted. I had no idea what next to do. Only one thing was certain – under no circumstances would I go back and ring John Layton's bell.

Time passed as I sat, in my own constructed darkness, blankly waiting for I don't know what. For night, perhaps, or the strength to get out and start walking down the drive.

'Can I help you?'

My eyes flicked open.

'Mr Layton,' the voice continued, 'asked me to enquire whether you needed help.'

I tilted to the right, looking out, and saw the person whom I had expected to answer John Layton's door – a maid dressed in conventional black and white, a Filipina with a sweet, sweet smile.

A smile which was growing a trifle strained around its edges.

Thinking that I must look as ghastly as I felt, I straightened up and returned the smile. Or tried to. My facial muscles were so stiff that what emerged was more a smirk and, by the look on the maid's face as she took one involuntary step backwards, an ugly smirk at that.

She didn't, however, go into full retreat. Of course she wouldn't. After all, she worked for John Layton: she must be tough.

She was. Her voice, although soft, pressed insistently at me. 'Is there anything you need?'

A tow truck, I nearly said, but, knowing how long that might take, I went instead for half-measures. 'I think the radiator's dry,' I said. 'Some water would be great.'

She nodded and was off, walking quickly towards the rear of the house, her steps as silent as they must have been when she had come my way.

As I sat, waiting out her return, I felt my heart softening. John, I thought, could have easily left me in the driveway, stewing in my own humiliation. And yet he hadn't. Seeing my predicament he'd quickly sent help out. Perhaps, I thought, perhaps I'd been too harsh on him. After all, John had also suffered. He had experienced a similar loss to mine and his reaction might well have been dramatic. Little wonder then that he, having lost his son, should be terrified of losing his grandson too.

But before I could go too far down that road, a sceptical voice, Sam's voice, took over. *Never underestimate my father*, I heard Sam warning. Remembering how vitriolic Sam had been in his refusal to see John, I nodded. John had lost his son long before death, had lost him because, as his son said, John Layton was a streetfighter, his first impulse was to hit out and only afterwards ask questions. *He's most dangerous*, Sam had said, *when you think he's being nice.*

This time as well, I thought. I could not afford to feel grateful to John. All he'd probably done was tell the maid to get rid of me – he always was a delegator, was John. How the maid chose to do it was her own affair.

How she chose to do it was with grace and skill. When she came back she had with her two jugs of water and some plastic gum. She handed me the first of the jugs and, after lying on the gravel and poking her head under the van's front, she ordered me to pour. When the water began to leak out, she took the gum and stuck it on a spot, stemming the flow. Out from under the car she came, her uniform still immaculate, and, having poured the contents of the second jug into the radiator, firmly did up its cap. 'It will hold until you reach a garage,' she said, and then proceeded to tell me how to reach not the nearest, but the most reliable, one.

'Tell them Lilia sent you,' was her parting shot. She stood and watched as I got into the van and drove it off.

Just before I rounded the corner I looked in my rear-view mirror. The maid was standing there, on the gravel, her arms akimbo. Behind her was a ground-floor window, framing something, a blur, a face, John Layton's face, I suppose. Whoever's face it was, I didn't want to know. I pressed my foot down on the accelerator and the van rounded the corner.

The name Lilia worked miracles on the Kingston mechanic. Within seconds his face had changed from glum to optimistic. The Mercedes he'd been working on was rapidly evicted, its place taken by Jurek's van. I was even, wonder of wonders, offered tea, which I gratefully accepted.

I stood there, sipping at the sweetened brew, listening vaguely to the mechanic's stream of consciousness. Lilia's influence did not, apparently, extend to compliments about the van. 'Look at this, look at this,' a voice from underneath was continually muttering. At one point he poked his head out: 'This thing's a fucking death trap,' he said. 'How you got an MOT is beyond me.'

Since the only honest answer was that Jurek, whose stay in successive countries was always brief, had a respect for national laws that was even briefer, I kept quiet.

'OK.' The mechanic had finished. 'I've patched it up,' he said, sliding himself out. He got up and began wiping his hands on a cloth. 'It won't last long,' he said. A pause and a sardonic smile: 'But then neither will the van.'

The rate at which he charged me was so low it was almost third world – another consequence, I assumed, of his admiration of Lilia. 'Tell her she's welcome here any time,' were his parting words before he turned and began reinstating the Mercedes on the ramp.

Chapter
eleven

    With one eye on the van's temperature gauge, I drove round Kingston. The choice of eating places, I soon discovered, was between a greasy spoon which smelled of stale fat and a bijou coffee house which stunk of chicory. I plumped for bijou, partly because, since the only other customers were a couple locked in silent combat, I thought I might get served fast. Big mistake. I spent some time with my hand in the air, waving it uselessly about in an attempt to attract the attention of a waitress who had raised neglect of service to high art. When finally my persistence, and my shouting, paid off and when my sandwich (salmon – tinned with a shred of cucumber as decoration) and my beverage (chicory with coffee flavouring), pitched up, I knew why she had been so reluctant to start up the whole process.

    Oh well, I'd been waiting so long, this would have to do. I wolfed it down and then, feeling almost emptier than when I had arrived, ordered a Danish. That did the trick. Sweet and sticky it sank, overtaking fragmenting bread crumbs and flakes of salmon essence, to deposit itself in my stomach's basement. There – that was done: if I wasn't satisfied, I was certainly full.

    And cleansed as well, it seemed, of my encounter with John Layton. Now that I had moved out of his orbit the man had lost his bullying power. I was now thinking of him not with anger, nor pity either, but with vague interest. It must be quite a strain, I thought, always to hit out first. I smiled.

'What do you mean you don't trust me?' I heard. I looked along the row of pink spotted tablecloths. The couple had moved from silent resentment into open battle. She had her lips pursed in disapproval while he was leaning forward, berating her. 'I could teach you a thing or two about trust, my girl,' he hissed.

My girl, I realized then that my tolerance of John Layton's behaviour was utterly misguided. This was the way he had always treated me: as some obnoxious girl. My smile faded. I sat there, thinking that John Layton was not only bullying, he was vindictive, and not only vindictive but also unrelenting. It came to me clearly what his next step would be. He'd phone Dulwich College, that's what, and put me on the 'wanted' list. If I was to see Matthew, I thought, I must hurry. I shoved my chair aside and got up. The waitress had vanished. I tossed some money on the table and left.

Dulwich College was surrounded by green, a slab of England's pleasant land, complete with avenues of chestnut and lime, and all of this smack in the middle of suburban London. I drove into the grounds, parked the van and got out. In front of me was a cluster of magnificent buildings, red brick and brownish terracotta and some spires to top the lot. I walked along, heading for a central double-layered item which had covered cloisters on left and right leading in turn to yet more of the same. I couldn't help myself this time. I whistled: if John Layton's mock Tudor had been designed to exhibit wealth, this was something else. This was history – three hundred tangible years of it.

It was also extremely alert. 'Can I help you?' a polished voice inquired.

I turned, expecting an adult. What I got instead was an adolescent bean pole. He was well over six foot and lanky with it, his pock-marked face topped by a thatch of brown hair which flopped down over one eye. But his face was not the main attraction: it was the badge on his blue striped blazer that fascinated. An ornate thing in orange and grey, with Latin on its base, it had a surprising top: a hand emerging from a flamed vase, and in the hand an orange heart. Above all this, some words in English: God's Gift.

Its owner certainly had an air of absolute self- confidence. 'Can I help you?' he asked again.

The badge had slowed me down. 'I'm looking for a boy,' I said. Stupid, I thought.

'Oh, we have a lot of those.'

We tittered together before I elaborated: 'Matthew Layton,' I said.

'Ah yes, Layton. He's in the fifth, I believe. A weekly boarder?' I nodded. 'An Ivyholme chap then.'

He'd lost me there but I didn't think it mattered. I nodded again.

'They'll be on the playing fields,' he said, his hand fluttering, gesturing beyond the courtyard to one of the many stretches of green. 'If you go to the office' – his hand now pointing straight ahead – 'I'm sure somebody will be available to escort you . . .'

I shook my head. Escorts meant questions, and questions meant that, if John had not already called, the call would soon be placed with him. I smiled. 'It's OK,' I said, 'I can find my own way,' and turning, walked off.

He was too well bred to hold me back. I heard his voice, more vulnerable now, pursuing me. 'You should have an escort . . .' I heard him calling. I didn't stop to hear the rest. Instead, holding up my hand in what I hoped was a confident dismissal, I quickened my pace.

*

The playing fields were, at least by the roundabout route I took, a brisk walk away. I was breathing heavily when I arrived. Not as heavily, however, as the boys. My guide had been right: the College had a lot of them and most appeared to be dressed in long socks, filthy shorts and stripy shirts, grunting ferociously as they threw themselves into a rugby scrum.

As I stood on the side lines, watching, hearing shouts of encouragement mixed with disparagement, I began to feel quite dumb. I don't know why I hadn't thought of this before: that the boys, even when they had emerged from the midst of their mutual grappling, would look, to my eyes, so much the same. Surely not, I told myself, and kept on looking. But as I stood there, despair took embarrassment's place. I watched the boys butting at each other, and I saw the lot collapse. As they got up, laughing, I felt as if the wind had been knocked out of me. There was no point, no point at all, in my standing there. It had been so long since I'd last seen either Matthew or a photograph of him, that I didn't even know whether, if confronted head on by him, I would recognize him. What chance, then, did I have of identifying him amongst this mob of churning manhood?

'Buck up,' I heard, shouted across the field. Of course, I thought, I would buck up. I would not despair.

What I needed was help. What I would do was go and find it. I turned.

And crashed into a man who had been hurrying towards me. He was extremely chivalrous: even though the collision had been my fault, he apologized. Having got that over, he added: 'Can I be of any assistance?' He was smiling at me, and he delivered the words casually but by the way he looked at me, calculating my nuisance potential, I knew that I had been found out.

He was waiting politely for me to explain myself.

Rapidly I invented a story, opening my mouth to deliver it. But: 'I'm looking for Matthew Layton,' is what I said. There was no point in lying. After all, this man worked in a boys' school. He was bound to be used to more creative liars than I. And besides, I was pretty sure he already knew what I was doing there.

He nodded. 'And you are?'

'Kate Baeier.'

He nodded again. So he knew that too. My paranoia had been well founded. John Layton must have picked up the phone as soon as my van chugged out of sight. 'Is Matthew here?' I asked.

The man's smile was generous, but tinged, at the same time, with apologetic regret. 'Ms Baeier,' he said gently. 'Matthew's grandfather feels that it would be better if you were to meet his grandson in a more natural setting. At home perhaps. If you would like to phone Mr Layton . . .?' He had placed a gentle hand on my shoulder and was turning me. I did not resist. I didn't tell him that, ten to one, if I phoned Matthew at home John Layton's staff would hang up on me. I didn't tell him either that Mr Layton was a bastard. I was too experienced for that: I'd been bounced from too many settings. Admittedly, never so courteously, but nevertheless I knew a bouncer when I saw one, especially when one of his sure hands was on my shoulder.

I allowed myself to be led, unprotesting, to Jurek's van. Climbing into it and seeing, when my companion gently closed the door, how rickety it looked, I was glad I hadn't tried to fight. The van, me, my quest – they were all at odds with this peaceful, sure place.

'Safe journey,' my escort called as I pulled out. I smiled and waved, thinking that he was probably a nice man.

I drove on, out of the College grounds, remembering Sam talking with anguish about own exclusive education.

And if Sam had had trouble, how much worse it must have been for Matthew – Matthew who at age six, had, as his ultimate ambition, a desire to cross light sabres with Darth Vadar.

Poor kid, his mother dumped him when he was two. His Dad died when he was he was ten, then I left him . . . And now this school. I pushed the thought away, told myself that things had surely changed: in a modern world such schools could no longer be places where brutality and Latin walked hand in hand. I nodded to myself: I was sure I was right. Or – my nod grew much less certain – at least I hoped I was.

I headed straight for Chelsea. I had no trouble with the route. Even the van behaved itself, manoeuvring round corners as if the amateur dramatics that I'd previously endured were all counterfeit. That didn't feel like cause for celebration. As I drove closer to Chelsea some of what I'd felt on the playing fields came back to me. I saw them, in my mind's eye again, that frisky, throbbing bunch of young men, and I remembered Matthew as he'd once been: a child, a compact body full of energy, a puppy unformed yet by the stringent demands of gender. All that must now have changed. All those years while I'd been gone he'd been growing up, not under my watchful eyes, or his father's, but moulded instead by John Layton into someone, presumably, of whom John Layton would approve.

The more I thought these thoughts the more I knew I could not go home. I wasn't ready to face Jurek and Maria. Not them, especially, but any friends. I glanced in the mirror and my fears were confirmed. No friend of mine would be able to look at me without immediately asking what the matter was. And I couldn't risk that. I was managing to hold myself together, but only just. One tiny scrap of sympathy and I would collapse.

70

In the end I turned away from Chelsea. To my old stamping grounds of north London, I went, heading straight for Hampstead. There I got out and began to stride across the Heath.

Chapter
twelve

I arrived home at around nine to find the house in darkness. There was a note lying on the hall table telling me what I already knew: that Maria and Jurek had gone to the movies and would be back after eleven. 'If you want to go to bed,' Maria had written as a postscript, 'leave the van's keys here.'

Bed, that sounded tempting. I yawned. But it was far too early for bed. I put the note down and yawned again. Don't be fetishistic about time, I told myself, my own Jewish mama – you're tired, so go to bed. I'd treat myself to a long, hot bath, that's what I'd do, and after that to bed. Putting the keys down, I headed deeper into the house.

I was halfway up the first flight of stairs when I heard it, a faint and angry cry. I stopped. I knew that cry – it was the cat – and I knew where it was coming from – the living room. Bloody cat, I thought, knowing already that even though Maria and Jurek had locked it in, I was going to get the blame.

I turned and went downstairs and, going to the living room, opened the door. The cat was waiting and my forecast was proved right. Hostilities had broken out again. It stalked straight past me, its face averted, its tail rigid. I nearly started berating it but I couldn't: my heart wasn't in the conflict. I stood there, watching its dignified retreat, thinking that I must face facts, the most embarrassing being that I had definitely grown to like the cat. 'It's not my fault,' I said. It merely carried on, walking huffily away. Oh well, knowing now that the shortest route to its heart was through its stomach, I also knew that, if I splashed out on a fresh consignment of Sheba, it would probably forgive me. 'You will, won't you?' I said.

The cat was gone. Feeling faintly ridiculous I turned and looked into the room. What I saw – the walls stripped of the offending slogans and already relined – disposed of earlier doubts. Aside from the fact that the room was still in transition – the walls an interesting fusion of Friedrich Pink and lining paper grot – the Willises might never have guessed that I'd had the burglars in. The place was immaculate; they'd even taken the trouble to hoover carpet and dust sheets alike.

I yawned and turned again, meaning to leave. But didn't. Something stopped me – my foot buffing against something small. Glancing idly down, I saw a white envelope lying beside my right foot. Must be Maria's or Jurek's, I thought and, thinking that I would leave it with their keys, I picked it up.

It was not their envelope: it was mine. My name was neatly typed on the up side. Apart from that, the envelope was blank: it must have been hand delivered.

I stood there looking at it, wondering how it had ended up on the living-room floor. The answer, or at least a choice of answers, soon came to me. Of course: having picked it up from the hallway floor, Maria or Jurek, intending to leave the envelope in some central place, had accidentally dropped it.

I suppose I knew then, before I opened it, that something about the envelope was wrong. I must have known. Why else was I standing trying to explain its presence on the living-room carpet? I told myself to get on with it but was strangely hesitant. I ran my hands across its edges, feeling out the contents.

What I felt was more rigid than paper but more flexible than card. A photograph, I thought.

So that was it: another portrait of Sam. I felt myself relax. It's just like Roger Toms, I thought, to turn a simple gift into a complicated double-sided manoeuvre. I tore the envelope open.

It was a photograph, all right, but not of Sam. It was of no one that I knew. Or at least I hoped I didn't know her. For the woman in the picture was naked, stretched out, her arms tied up above her head, her mouth open, her legs, also tied, pulled to each side. It was an ugly, porno-graphic image of a woman helpless. I didn't want to look at it. I turned it over.

There was a message on the photo's flip side, a simple message. *Still thinking of you.*

I frowned and reread it. *Still thinking of you.* What the hell was that supposed to mean?

I flipped the card back and saw again that sight, a woman splayed out like a piece of dead meat. My hand went slack: the paper fluttered down. I stood quite blankly, watching it. But then, as it hit the carpet, I remembered where I had found it. I knew then that my previous assumptions, that Jurek or Maria had dropped the enve-lope there, were wrong. I frowned, my mind still moving lethargically, trying to remember what had brought me to this room.

The cat, of course, that was it: the calling of the cat.

The cat! It came back to me how, the time before when they'd written on the wall, how the cat had also been the trigger that had led me to this room. And yet . . . At that time the police had convinced me that the burglary had been my fault, that I had gone out without first priming the alarm.

This time it had not been like that – or had it? I frowned and half closing my eyes, mentally retraced my steps. I saw myself, standing in darkness by the Willis front door, pushing my key into the lock. I saw my hand twisting and the door opening. And then I saw what had happened afterwards: the alarm blinking and myself disarming it.

No. It couldn't be. It wasn't possible.

I continued to stand in the doorway, shrouded by a haze which distanced me from panic. My thoughts were coming, orderly and strangely remote. I must check it out, I thought. I turned and walked slowly, slowly to the front door. Opening it, I went outside, closing it behind me. Then I reopened the door and, at the same time, glanced quickly at my watch. After that, I speeded up. I walked forward, closed the door, punched numbers into the alarm, marched down the hallway, pretended I heard the cat, opened the living-room door, took one step inside and checked my watch.

Twelve seconds. I blinked. Twelve, not ten.

Well, perhaps I'd remembered it wrong, perhaps the lapse time had been twelve? But no: I stood there hearing Greg Willis's genial voice clearly teaching me how to operate the alarm. *Be careful he'd said: If you don't immobilize the alarm within ten seconds, it will go off.*

Ten; not twelve. Which meant only one thing: that the alarm had been set off, that first time, not by my mistakes but by something other. Something other. There was only one possible explanation. I had not been alone. I had come in, defused the alarm and walked to the living room, and then, while my back was turned, someone must have crept behind me, switched on and triggered the alarm, before opening the door and leaving.

And leaving. I stood there, thinking that was what I should do. But didn't. I stood motionless as the two words repeated on me, muffling thought.

It was then I heard it. A sound. Of movement. Some-where in the house. I was still partially befogged. It's the cat, I told myself.

I was suddenly alert: what if it wasn't the cat? An image flashed on to my retina, the woman splayed out for con-sumption. What if the man (for man it surely must be) who had left the picture was still in the house? I saw her mouth open in a silent scream. What if . . .

That did it. I had two choices: to leave the house or go upstairs. I didn't stop to think. I went upstairs, almost sideways, my back so close to the wall that as I went up I could hear the sound of my coat scuffing the wall. Just that – no other sound. The higher I got the more sure I became: there was no one but me in the house.

I kept on going anyway, hitting each switch as I passed it, flooding the place with light. I was driven by instinct, climbing to the top and into one of two rooms on the highest floor that I'd only ever briefly glanced at. This time I entered it. I don't know why. I entered, my thoughts a constant string of reassurance. I was alone in the house. I was.

The room, a bedroom complete with en suite bathroom, was modelled on the one below it, although furnished on less grand a scale. I walked across the beige carpet, feeling the familiarity of the room's proportions. I was no longer scared: I was convinced I was alone. It was odd, I thought, that Pam had insisted I sleep in their bedroom – this one would have done equally as well. I went to the bathroom, checking it out. It was perfect, its white tiles sparkling, its luxurious white towels hanging neatly over gleaming chrome rails. The towels looked soft and homely. I went over to them and buried my head in one.

It was then that it happened. Darkness. My neck went rigid. I lifted my head. Darkness: sudden and complete. Someone had switched off the light. I whirled round. 'Who's there?' My voice eerie in the black.

I heard breathing, soft and methodical in contrast to my anxious rasping which all but drowned it out.

'Who's there?' My voice was cracking.

A soft footfall and a click.

I stood, silent, the towel rail digging into my back. That way I was facing the door and the bedroom beyond. My eyes were growing accustomed to the dark: I could see the outlines of the room, the bed-post, the side table next to it. It was all variations in grey and black – no yellowing streetlight. Whoever had come into the room must have drawn the curtains.

Whoever had come into the bedroom. I thought of the picture of the woman, stretched out, and those words *yum, yum* at the end of the message on the wall. I thought how stupid I had been to trap myself in there, alone with a madman who was playing games. I thought how even in this small bathroom there were many places that he could snare me, banging my head against the hard tile surfaces, my blood smearing the pristine white. And as I thought of all this, I knew I must move.

I grabbed what I could: a tooth mug, which I brought down hard against the basin. It shattered. I left the pieces where they fell, taking only the fragment that remained in my hand. The temptation was to hold it out in front of me, a warning to any assailant, but I knew how easily my wrist could be turned. I forced my hand down.

Slowly, slowly, I advanced. As quietly as I could, holding my breath, listening out for his. I could hear nothing but traffic flowing past on a distant road.

I stepped into the bedroom and, lifting my other hand up, switched on the light. The wrong light: behind me the bathroom was illuminated. Up went my hand again and this time when I flicked the switch the bedroom's overhead went on. I could see clearly. The room was empty. The door was closed. The click I'd heard had been the man leaving.

Leaving: but how far? Could he be waiting outside for me? My eyes swept the room. It was as I had remembered – all mod cons save for a telephone. I stood, quite still, thinking that I had to move. I had to; or else become the victim that the man expected me to be. I took a step forward.

I thought I heard another sound. I stopped. The sound was gone. Me moving, perhaps? I had no way of knowing. All I knew was that I must keep going.

I was over by the door. I stretched across and put one hand on the knob while the other, still grasping the glass fragment, I held behind my back. I breathed in. I pushed the handle down.

The door opened inwards. I pulled it to me. What faced me was more darkness. Whoever was in the house must have followed me upstairs, switching off what I had just switched on. I took one step forward, my hand went up: the hall was illuminated.

I didn't stop after that. I went as fast as I was able down the steps. A phone, I thought, I need a phone, but I couldn't risk going into any of the rooms. Down the stairs I ran, telling myself to keep an even pace, my senses wired so hard that with every movement I imagined something else.

I was almost on the ground floor. Walking straight, I thought: I will walk straight out. I went down the last step.

I heard a sound. A key turning in the lock. I saw a shadow beyond: I was not imagining it. I glanced at my watch. Nine-thirty: too early for Jurek and Maria. I was trapped.

I heard a voice, gabbling. My own voice, I dimly thought.

'Kate?' Maria and Jurek were in the hallway, their faces looming as if distorted by a wide-angled lens. 'Kate?'

I didn't answer. I pitched forward. The last thing I saw was a hand grabbing out. The last thing I remembered was the smell of Jurek's skin, turpentine against a background of something much more fragrant.

I was lying flat out on the floor.

'Kate?' I heard. Opening my eyes, I saw Jurek's face framed in mist. 'Kate?'

Oh God, I thought, Jurek is calling me Kate. I knew what had happened: I'd died and gone to heaven. I lifted my head.

'Kate?'

I frowned. What kind of heaven would let Jurek in? My head was aching. I closed my eyes, slumping down.

'Here,' I heard a voice, Maria's voice, gently saying. Forcing my eyes ajar, I saw her hand, and in it a glass. I licked my cracked lips and nodded. The glass came closer and, while Maria supported my head, I took a few grateful sips.

'How are you feeling?' Maria said as she withdrew the glass. I began to push myself up. It was quite an effort. 'Humiliated,' I croaked. 'I mean, this isn't me. I never faint. Ever.'

'Sure you don't.' Jurek's hand was there, waiting. I took it, and felt myself lifted to my feet.

As soon as I was upright, Maria's arm linked mine. 'Come on, Superwoman,' she said. 'Let's go downstairs.'

We sat at the kitchen table, drinking brandy. In silence. They were waiting for me to speak but I had no words to give them. Until, that is, the brandy hit target. 'What happened to your movie?' I asked as I downed the last sip.

I saw a look – exasperation – exchanged. Maria shrugged. 'Too much angst, not enough action,' she said. 'We walked out.' She stretched across and poured me another stiff one. 'And you?' she prompted. 'What happened to you?'

I was beginning to feel quite drunk. 'What happened when?' I asked stupidly. 'You mean before Jurek caught me?'

Another look, even more perplexed. Jurek leaned forward, about to butt in.

But thinking suddenly that I might as well get it over with, I beat him to it. I took a deep breath in and started from the top, from the moment I had begun to climb the stairs.

They listened intently, without interrupting. Only when I finished, and when he was sure I really had, did Jurek get up. I heard him, climbing stairs, walking down the hall. Then he was back. 'The house is empty,' he said. He had the photo held gingerly between thumb and index finger. 'What kind of ugly mind would do this?'

The kind that wants to get me, I thought. I kept my mouth shut, watching as Jurek slowly eased the porn back into its containing envelope. That done, he looked straight at me. 'Shall we phone the police?'

I shook my head. I was too tired for the questions that would inevitably ensue. The questions like how did they get in? and who are your enemies? and where were you when someone waltzed into your house? and how come they keep managing to do this to you? I was too tired.

'I'm going to bed,' I said. Picking my brandy up, I began to walk towards the door.

'We're staying the night,' I heard Maria telling me from behind.

I nodded but did not turn. I was too tired; too tired to thank them even. Wearily I hauled myself upstairs.

Chapter
thirteen

I fell into bed thinking that nothing on earth could stop me sleeping. I was wrong. When I hit the pillow, something did. My head – it hurt. I ran my hand across the back of my skull and found a small bump. Strange, I thought and then, telling myself that this must, of course, be the result of my ridiculous fainting jag, I closed my eyes.

In sleep's place came a question. If Jurek caught me, then how come I had a bump?

I didn't want to deal with that. I kept my eyes shut tight, summoning up sleep. No luck. Flashing images – myself in the hallway falling backwards, a hand held out – jolted me awake. A cut to another vision. Two hands juxtaposed together, two different hands.

My eyes snapped open. Of course! I remembered now. My bag which had been stolen. It all slotted into place. The police had been right – it *was* my fault. I'd thought there was nothing valuable in the bag, but I'd been wrong. There had been a piece of paper with some numbers written on – the alarm's combination. I'd made it easy for them. My address must have been written down there too, along with the alarm's code. It was all my fault. My fault . . .

I was awakened by the phone's insistent ringing. My

cover was already blown, there was no point in lying low. I grabbed the receiver. 'Hello,' I croaked, my voice thickened by sleep.

I heard a bleep, some distant crackling, and someone doubtfully pronouncing my name: 'Kate?'

'Pam?' I didn't wait for confirmation. 'Are you all right?'

'Sure.' Her voice, stronger now. Of course she was all right. Why should she not be? After all, she was in the Bahamas. It was me who was here, and me who was not all right.

'Just checking that everything's in order.'

Everything? I thought, wondering why she sounded so uneasy. I squinted at my watch. It was just gone six.

'Is it?'

I thought of the graffiti on the walls downstairs and decided I wasn't going to tell her – not after I'd gone to all this trouble to repair the damage. 'Everything's fine,' I said.

'Oh.' A pause and then: 'Good.' Another silence, this one so protracted that I thought we'd been cut off. But no: her next sentence came out, suddenly, in a rush. 'Are you planning to stay long?'

I reacted without thought. 'Why?'

'Because I was . . . I mean . . .' Her voice died out.

I waited, for quite a while, and then said 'Pam?'

I could hear her breathing at the other end. This was really odd – not at all like the cool, confident Pam I knew. I wondered what on earth was bugging her.

But before I had time to ask, she had pulled herself together. 'I was thinking,' she said, 'that we've been unfair. I know you like to keep your plans flexible. If you want to go or anything, don't worry about the cat . . .'

Don't worry about the cat? I frowned.

'I mean, you know I didn't want to send it to a sanctuary,' she continued. 'But it's just occurred to me. Our friend, Mona Hanson, will look after it.'

I sat up.

'Mona's number is in Greg's address book,' Pam said. 'Which is in his study. It shouldn't be difficult to find.'

It isn't, I thought, remembering how I had already used Greg's book to contact the insurance brokers.

'So – feel free if you . . .' She left the sentence hanging, almost making it a question.

I was more confused than ever. I turned my wrist, looking at my watch again in case I'd read it wrong. But no, I hadn't – it was just gone six.

'Kate?' Pam's words *had* been a question.

I gave the only answer that I could think of. 'Thanks,' I said. 'It's useful to have an out.'

'I know,' she said. 'The cat can be a pain.'

This phone call was getting stranger by the second. *A pain* – coming from a woman who had previously been gushing with cat love?

'I'm actually growing to like it,' I said.

'Oh.' Pam sounded surprised. 'Good. Anyway . . . thought I'd phone and tell you. Just in case.'

In case of what? I thought. 'Are you all right?' I asked again.

'Yes.' Her voice was loud and strongly definite. 'Of course I am.'

I heard what sounded like a siren. 'That's the boat,' Pam said. A pause, another long one and then: 'I'll have to go but remember you're not under any obligation. Don't stay on our account.' A blip and the satellite hung up on me.

I was wide awake, staring at the receiver. I put it down and continued staring. The phone call had confused me. It wasn't like Pam – she was usually so clear, so sure of what she wanted and yet, just then, her voice had seemed

83

diffused and unfocused, as if some delicate agenda were concealed behind the words she used. A wish that I would leave, perhaps?

No, how could that be? I mean, it wasn't as if I'd pushed myself on her. It was she who'd offered me her place, who'd insisted that I'd be doing her and Greg a favour. So why the change?

I thought about it but no answer came. I yawned. It was too early for puzzles. I got up, picked the debris of my previous day's wear off the floor, went to the bathroom, threw clothes into the laundry basket and turned the taps full on.

That's when the meaning rather than the context of Pam's words sank in. I could go. Maria and Jurek didn't need me and neither, apparently, did the cat. I could pack up and go.

I licked my lips: I was parched. I went to the kitchen and as I stood there, squeezing oranges, I thought how fruit in England was never quite authentic. It never tasted the way it did, picked fresh, in other countries. I twisted an orange and thought longingly of blue skies, bright light, un-English vitality. I felt my spirits rising. This place is getting me down, I thought. I'd better leave. I nodded. I would go. I poured the juice into a glass and carried it upstairs.

The cat followed me up. As I lowered myself into the water, it installed itself on the porcelain's edge. It sat there, looking particularly fluffy, the gleaming white of its neck which had previously looked sleek now seeming vulnerable. I held my glass up in the air. 'Here's to us,' I said, taking a swig, thinking it would soon forget me.

It fixed its mournful eyes on me.

'I never meant to stay here anyway,' I said defensively.

Which was true. A chance encounter on a Rumanian border post had led me here. I had just completed an

84

assignment for *The Guardian* and was on my way out, while Pam, going to ministrate to orphans, was trying to get in. We knew each other vaguely. When I had still been living in Britain, we had occasionally landed round the same dinner table, a connection made only slightly more firm by the fact that the Willises and Sam went further back than that. We were friendly but had little in common.

Out there, however, stuck in no man's land, it felt good to speak English. At first, thinking we would soon part, we kept the conversation on the surface. But then we discovered that both our clearances – mine to exit, hers to enter – had got lost. We were trapped.

We spent three long nights together, stretched out on concrete benches, trying to get to sleep. During the daytime, when we weren't either arguing with hard-nosed officials or using the phone to pull rank, we kept each other company.

It was a strange, uneasy time and I found myself gabbling out all manner of half-formed thoughts. Like it was five years since I'd left England and that I was scared of my prospective return. Pam had listened in a kind of queasy silence and that had, for some strange reason, made me talk more. I ended up telling her things I never would have before, like how odd it would be to find a hotel in the city that had once been my home.

At first Pam seemed disapproving. But after one of her long calls to Greg, she changed her tune. She hit me with a proposition: that I stay in their house. She and Greg were off on a long jaunt, she said, and they didn't like to leave the place empty. She was quite insistent: when I refused, saying I would be in London only briefly, she lapsed into petulant silence. I thought she had given up but, two hours and one more phone call later, she upped the stakes. She replayed in enormous detail Greg's account of the recent strange behaviour of her much-loved cat. 'I'm worried,' she kept on saying. 'I can't put it in a sanctuary. It hasn't been itself.'

I'm no cat lover. I kept on saying no. But as she pleaded with me, using ever-spiralling superlatives to describe how much the cat meant to her, I felt the strength of my refusal waning. I'd been travelling continuously and it would be nice to stop. The more Pam talked, the more was I tempted. It's safe and comfortable and quiet, she'd said and, after scrutinizing my unwashed face, added: 'restful as well.'

So I'd said yes, if only for a short time. I'd known it was the right answer when I'd seen relief coursing round her face.

And now? Now it seemed that Pam might want me gone.

'She always was an odd woman,' I said. Out loud.

The cat stared, unblinking. I winked. Its eyes stayed frozen, punishing me because I was planning to leave.

Well, it could damn well stop. 'No need to act like that,' I said. 'Pam or no Pam, I'm not going anywhere.'

The cat jumped down and walked haughtily away.

I lay still, thinking that Pam hadn't actually asked me to leave. And without that, a direct request, I wouldn't go – not after what had happened. I couldn't let those bumbling punks scare me off. And I couldn't, after last night's little offering, let them alone either. Nobody sends porn and stalks me and gets away with it. Nobody.

I dressed and, going straight to Greg's study, scanned his filing system. The alarm's manual was easily located and the briefest flick through told me what I needed to know – that changing the alarm's code was a simple enough procedure. I took the book down with me and did just that, altering both mine and the painters' programmes. There, that was done. If my muggers thought of returning they would find themselves stymied.

With impeccable timing, Maria and Jurek appeared. I was full of energy. I cooked us all a massive breakfast – porridge, toast, omelettes – only half of which was eaten and, over it, I told them about the changes I had made to the house's security and of my decision to stay and face my tormenters down. They didn't, either of them, comment. Neither did they mention the police. I realized then what I should have known the night before, that their papers were probably in dubious order and that they would not welcome an invasion of the boys in blue.

'Kate.' Jurek's voice, sounding curiously uneasy, distracted me. I looked up. 'How will you go about locating these men?'

It was the obvious question and I had already, somewhere in the back of my mind, worked out my answer to it. Now I forced myself to say it: 'Carmen.'

Carmen who had been my detective agency partner. It was a long shot but it was the obvious way to go. Except . . . I shivered. If Anna, my best friend, had been hard to face, then how much worse would Carmen be?

My tension must have been palpable. 'Do you need help?' Jurek asked.

It was tempting – I felt myself aching to accept. But, 'No,' I said, knowing that to pitch up with a bodyguard would be disastrous. 'No,' I said again, shaking my head for emphasis.

'Take the van,' Maria tossed the keys my way.

'Thanks.' I caught them. 'I better get off.' I sat quite still.

They looked at each other and then at me. 'Good luck, Kate,' Jurek said. I was dismissed.

I was dismissed: I had to go. I got up and left the room, realizing as I went that it was the proper use of my name which had made Jurek sound so odd. I better get him back to Katherine, I vaguely thought, as I went upstairs to fetch my coat.

Chapter
fourteen

As I walked down the hallway, the phone began to ring. I didn't hesitate. I picked up the receiver and gave a bright and sparky hello.

'Kate. I'm glad I caught you.'

I froze.

What came next was even more extraordinary. 'Come to tea tomorrow,' John Layton said.

'To tea?' My voice rose.

'Yes. Matthew will be there.'

Matthew!

'You will come?' John sounded almost anxious. Interesting, I thought: first the Godfatherly 'I-will-break-you' routine and now the grandfatherly invitation to tea. With biscuits, probably.

'That's quite a turnabout.'

His answer was a non sequitur. 'The College can be rather over-protective,' connected to, 'I apologize on their behalf.'

'Oh yes?' I made no attempt to conceal my intensifying incredulity.

John Layton, the chameleon that he was, was oozing charm. 'My major concern,' he said, 'was that a sudden encounter at school might be a shock for Matthew. I think it better that you meet at home, don't you? At least the first time.'

The first time, I heard, and, as I stood there, hope wrestled with disbelief. Perhaps John's not so bad, I thought and I opened my mouth, planning to throw some conciliatory tidbit of my own into the encounter.

But before the words were out, it repeated on me, how he had driven me from his house. My mouth slammed shut.

John spoke into the void. 'Matthew, um . . .' There was a cough. 'Matthew heard about your visit.'

Ah.

'He . . . he has asked to see you . . .' John let the sentence, the closest I'd ever heard him come to pleading, hang. That was it – as far as he would go. The rest was up to me.

My decision wasn't difficult. I knew how proud John was and I knew that, if I took too long accepting the invitation, he was bound, Matthew or no Matthew, to launch us into a fresh round of vindictiveness.

'Thanks,' I said. 'I'd like that. Tea?'

'Yes.'

'At four?'

'Precisely,' he said and, having got precisely what he wanted, he hung up.

Leaving me standing in the hall, frowning. Which is how Maria found me. 'Trouble?' she asked as she rounded the stairs.

'No.' I shook my head. 'In fact the opposite,' and, letting those foolish words dangle, I left the house.

It was a lovely autumnal day, bright light glinting against softly changing leaves. To make things more perfect, the van went from Chelsea along the embankment and towards Camden Town without a single irregular dial movement.

I headed north. This London seemed to be almost entirely up for grabs – wherever I looked I was met by an interminable display of 'for sale' signs. I kept on driving, thinking that it was probably a good time to buy – my money would go a long way in this moment of Britain's decline.

But then I turned into the Holloway Road, without a doubt one of the world's least attractive thoroughfares. The idea of buying here was so preposterous, I burst out laughing. I was still laughing as, dodging the flow and fumes of articulated lorries heading for the M1, I turned again, into the back streets of Finsbury Park.

My laughter was abruptly stanched. I couldn't set aside my nervousness, not any longer.

What if she's moved? I wondered, and immediately replaced that with a complementary and equally disturbing thought: What if she hasn't moved?

She hadn't. I put my finger on her bell and was immediately buzzed in. I climbed up the dimly lit stairway to the second floor. The closer I got, the slower I went. I kept remembering what Carmen had once been to me; my employee, my partner, my friend. We'd been a team, in sync together, had worked as one and played together as well: the three of us – Sam, Carmen and I – relaxed in each other's company. And yet, even while this was going on, there'd always been a part of Carmen I couldn't touch. Gender and political outlook united us; race ensured we could never entirely relax. And not only race, I thought, as I slowly, slowly went up the remaining stairs, but Carmen herself. Carmen who could be a loyal friend and equally a terrifying enemy.

I was there, by her flat. I knocked.

'It's open,' I heard her calling. I turned the knob and the door swung open. I found myself standing in her tiny cubicle of a hallway.

I couldn't see her. 'Go straight on in,' I heard her shouting. 'The money's on the table.'

I took one involuntary step forward and then abruptly stopped. 'Carmen.'

'On the table.'

'Carmen.' Louder this time.

There was a muffled and once familiar, sound – Carmen swearing – and a footstep. I twisted my head to the left. I saw her standing in her bedroom's doorway. I was in darkness, she framed against the flaring of sunlight. Her hair was unbraided and the light made about her head a burnished halo. I stood there, staring, thinking that she hadn't changed. But as the silence between us was stretched taut, I looked at her tall figure and her smooth brown skin, and I knew this wasn't true. What had in fact happened was that age had improved her. While any other woman would have looked unkempt in that faded brown candlewick dressing gown, she managed to look spectacular.

'It's you,' she said. Her voice was deadpan.

I nodded. I didn't know what else to do.

'Go on in,' she said, pointing straight ahead. She withdrew, closing the door behind her.

I did as instructed. I walked forward, and, entering the sitting room, stood at its centre, gazing round. The room was bright and bare – little changed, in fact, except that it was exclusively adult now: in place of the childish drawings which used to line the walls were the occasional photograph of an elegant young woman.

I heard the sound of footsteps. I turned.

'Here.' She was carrying a huge stack of files. She had changed her clothes – exclusively to black – but left her dour expression on. 'Here.' She shoved the armload at me.

The pile teetered. I moved closer. Too late – the whole lot overbalanced, tumbling down on to the patterned carpet. When Carmen made no move to rescue them, neither did I. I raised an eyebrow. 'Nice to see you too,' I said.

She clicked her tongue impatiently. 'What you doing here, girl?'

I shrugged. 'Revisiting old haunts?'

She stood, glaring.

'I came to see you,' I said quietly.

'And?'

So this is how it's going to be, I thought. No quarter given. I felt my own gaze harden. 'And' – I stressed the word just as she had – 'to ask for your help.'

Carmen nodded as if she had expected this. At that moment, the buzzer sounded.

It took me by surprise. I jumped. Not so Carmen – she calmly left the room and I heard her press the release button. Then she returned and, standing opposite, looked at me.

That's how the milkman found us – locked in voiceless discord. He bounded into the room, saying: 'It's only –' and, seeing us, he stopped. His eyes flicked, first in my direction and then in Carmen's. Watching, I saw him ask of her a silent question and saw that her answer was the briefest of head shakes. I swallowed, thinking enviously that communication between Carmen and me had once been as easily conducted as this.

'On the table?' the milkman said. Carmen nodded. Walking forward, he swept coins into his apron's large front pocket, said a quick, 'Catch you later,' and left.

Leaving us alone.

'You want some tea?' Carmen said.

For a moment I thought that the offer might signal the easing of hostility. But looking at her, half meaning to accept, I saw her face as stern as ever, her dark brown eyes as belligerent. I shook my head. If this was how it was going to be I did not want tea. What I wanted was to get it over with.

'Sit then.'

I sat. But couldn't help myself. My eyes were drawn to the photograph opposite. 'She's beautiful,' I said.

I thought I saw Carmen's face softening. Her words, however, remained accusatory. 'She missed you when you left.'

I was getting sick of this. '*She* missed me,' I drily commented. 'Not you.'

I shouldn't have bothered. I should have known that once Carmen had decided on a course of action, nothing could deter her. She sat, waiting.

Oh well. In as neutral a tone as I could muster I told her all about it: about muggers I'd inadvertently challenged, and how, after it was over, someone had come after me. I told the story flatly, without inflection.

'The muggers were black,' Carmen said. It was a statement, not a question. I nodded. She followed through with a second statement: 'That's why you came to me.'

I couldn't let her get away with that. 'I would have come anyway. You were my partner.'

'I was your assistant,' Carmen said. 'Once. A long time ago. And now you come waltzing back, expecting me to surrender some of the brothers to you.'

Some of the brothers. In the old days Carmen would have been more careful about using this category. But then, I thought, what Carmen's behaviour proved was that the old days were long gone.

Well, I could match her indifference. I restricted my reply to a mild: 'I'm not going to set the police on them.'

'Aren't you?'

I felt my composure slipping. 'Come on, Carmen,' I said. 'You know me better than that.'

'Do I?'

I bit back my anger. I would not give her the satisfaction of rising to her bait. 'I just want to bang their heads together and get them to leave me alone,' I said. 'Will you help?'

'Will you pay?'

So it had come to this! I flushed. 'If needs be.'

'I'll see what I can do.' Our interview was over. She rose. 'You're at the Willises'?'

So she knows that, I thought, wondering who could have told her. I sat tight.

'Are you?' She was looking down on me, demanding a reply. I couldn't bring myself to speak. I nodded.

'I'll put the word out,' she said. 'And ring if anything comes back.'

'Fair enough.' My voice was businesslike.

So was hers. 'I'll send the bill to Chelsea,' she said. 'You won't leave without telling me, will you?'

That did it. I stood up, matching her height with mine. 'What the hell's the matter with you?' I hissed. When she didn't react, I raised my voice. 'OK,' I said, 'so I left without telling you. We were friends and I deserted you. It was wrong. I know that now. But there were reasons for what I did, and you know them as well as I.' I looked across the space that separated us and, seeing her stand, unmoving and unmoved, felt even angrier. 'Can't you' – I was spluttering with rage – can't you, even after five years, let it go?'

Carmen waited until I had finished before she spoke – calmly, quietly and without compassion. 'No, I can't let it go,' she said. 'Not until you acknowledge what you did.'

She sounded like a pompous schoolteacher. I sniffed.

'There is no forgiveness,' she continued. 'Not without remorse.'

Remorse – another word she'd never have used before. I was drained of anger. 'I'm sorry,' I said. 'I shouldn't have gone. Not like that. I should have come and talked to you first.'

She shook her head, slowly, from side to side. 'It's not me you let down,' she said. She raised her hand and pointed it at the floor, to where the files lay scattered. 'It's those people, those faceless names in there. You said you'd help them, but when the going got tough you packed up and left.'

The going got tough. I suppose that was one way of talking about Sam's death.

She hadn't finished. Not yet. 'And then you come back and expect everything to be the same. But it's not the same, is it? You're in Chelsea now.'

The word *Chelsea* was spat out as if it was the embodiment of evil. Could this be it? I thought: Could this really be what was riling her?

Having got into her stride, Carmen was relentless. '. . . and those people' – her hand was almost shaking as it pointed at the floor – 'they're where they always were. But you don't worry about them. You think only of yourself and your precious pain. You've crossed the line, girl, you've joined the other side.'

'The line? The other side? You never used to talk like this.'

'You've been gone too long, Kate,' she said quietly.

I registered this first use of my name. I blinked.

But it was purely incidental. She was warming to her theme. 'Nothing's the same, not any longer,' she said. 'All those slogans we used to whoop: sisterhood, all that posturing – it's gone. This country has been split apart. You spent a lifetime straddling different cultures, moving between them and us. You can't, not any longer. You have to choose. Between the Willises and the Wilsons. Between –'

She was in mid sentence when I turned my back on her. Deliberately. There was no other course open to me, no other way of stopping her. The last thing I was going to do was submit myself to a two nations lecture with myself as target. I turned my back and, kneeling on the carpet, began to gather up the files.

She made no move to help me.

Oh well. Bundling the files roughly together, I stood up. She wouldn't look at me. Her eyes were focused on my feet. I shrugged. 'I'll be off,' I said to nobody in particular and I walked past her, through the doorway, into the hall, out the second door, and down the stairs. That's it, I thought. The end.

But no matter how she had changed, she was still Carmen and, being Carmen, could not resist a parting shot. I heard her voice calling to me from the stair well. 'Watch out, Kate Baeier. You should choose your friends more carefully.'

Too right I should, I thought as, opening the door and stepping out, I remembered how I had once counted Carmen amongst my closest friends.

Chapter
fifteen

I drove off. Time passed, I kept on driving. I didn't think of Carmen. I didn't think of anything – not, that is, until I saw the petrol indicator blinking, and then my only thought was that I was lost. I drove some more. When I came across a petrol station, I pulled in and filled the tank.

The pimpled cashier wasn't into originality. 'Cheer up, love,' he said as I reached his glass enclosure. 'It may never happen.'

I scowled and asked him where I was. Barnet, he said, proudly, as if Barnet was the only place to be.

Barnet is almost as far as you can go without quitting the London directory. Too far. I began driving back the way I had come, concentrating on heading towards familiar territory. Until, that is, I saw nestling snugly on the corner of a suburban roadside a small squat building. I took my foot off the accelerator. A sign confirmed my guess: it was a library.

I stopped and parked and, with Carmen's files under my arm, walked in.

There was not a soul in sight. I didn't mind: I didn't need anyone. Pushing the wooden barrier aside, I followed signs to the reading room. I found it easily, a cramped, overheated, book filled-space about the size of a large store cupboard and containing only two tables – both empty. I chose the furthest one and, sitting myself down at its scratched surface, began sorting through Carmen's files.

Correction: my files. The compleat collection: the records, from day one, of my detective business. I sat for a moment, staring at them, wondering why Carmen hadn't thrown them out. I wished she had. They stank of a past which was gone and which was better gone. Well, I wasn't going to keep them. I tore my eyes from them and, scanning the room, spotted a metallic waste bin. I began gathering them up.

Yet the memory of Carmen's accusations proved too powerful. My hand went slack. I couldn't junk the files – not without first knowing what had so enraged her. I would have to read them.

Gingerly, I scanned their covers. They were, I saw, neatly kept; catalogued, each one, by name and date. The fall in Carmen's apartment had mixed them up – I reordered them. When that was done, I sat for a moment hesitating, responding to an inner voice which told me that the files were better left unread. I almost listened to it, but in the end the pull of what I didn't know was too strong. I grabbed the topmost file, opened it and began to read.

I was flung back into the distant past, to my first case. It wasn't as bad as I expected; in fact it wasn't bad at all. I read my notes, the sting removed from what had once been a potentially explosive investigation of a group of colleagues. I found that I was smiling, my amusement directed inwardly at that foolish, optimistic, gawky younger self who had seen, in the detective business, an alternative to the monotony of freelance journalism.

It seemed, in hindsight, a zany idea, except that it had worked. I had managed to make a living from the agency. Never a great deal, but enough to pay for me, an office and, eventually, an assistant as well.

An assistant – Carmen – my one-time friend.

No, I would not dwell on that. Putting one file on the discard pile, I fetched another. I skimmed quickly through the series until I reached the point where Carmen had joined me and then, began to read slower, trying to get a handle on her fury. It was an eerie process, this ransacking of my past, made more bizarre by a memory loss which, as I got closer to the time when I had abandoned the agency, kept enlarging.

And now . . . I pulled the last folder forward. There was a date at its head: the September 15, 1988. September 15: one week before Sam's death. I looked at the file's nameplate and I saw a simple heading: Agnes Wilson.

Wilson was the name Carmen had mentioned. I turned the page. I was looking at a kiosk photo, this one more mediocre than the usual. Agnes Wilson's skin had gone a waxen yellow and a good half of her face was hidden because the stool was too low. As I stared at her, only one of her rheumy eyes stared back. But that one said it all. Memory filtered through the intervening years.

She'd arrived without an appointment, apparently on impulse. I closed my eyes and summoned her back, seeing her come limping into the office. Carmen had been there as well but Agnes had made straight for me. She had tossed a photo – this photo – on to my desk. 'The bleeding pyrotechnics caught me on the hop,' was what she said, followed by an assertive: 'It will just have to do: I'm not going back.'

I had shrugged. I didn't need a photo anyway. Thinking already that she was unlikely to be a payer (Carmen and I had just decided we could only afford to work for money), I'd asked her what she wanted.

Sitting in the library, I reopened my eyes. I pushed the file away. I had no need for it. The curtain had been lifted and I remembered clearly what had happened next.

'I want what's mine,' she'd said, in her frail old woman's voice, and in the silence that followed her pale blue eyes peered out from under heavy lids.

She seemed fragile; I was gentle. 'What's yours?'

She was old but she wasn't fragile. She shot a disdainful look my way before launching into a concise account of her working life in a small clothing company which had recently gone bankrupt. 'Nearly fifty years I worked there,' she said: 'I was due for retirement when it closed.' She pursed her lips and the puckering made her look older than she had before. She did not speak; she was eying me, as if it was my turn.

But I was confused. 'What do you want from me?' is all I could dredge up.

She didn't hesitate. 'I want my pension,' she said.

My pension? I felt an eyebrow rising.

'Or at least I want to know where it went,' she said.

My pension. Of all the odd requests articulated in my office, this surely was the oddest. But then I shrugged. I'd done missing dogs and missing husbands, why not missing pensions? 'Yes?'

She launched into the second part of her tale. It was an account of how a complicated sequence of company take-overs, involving her employers, had ended in bankruptcy and the discovery that, somewhere along the line, the pension fund had been consumed. As she guided me through the minutiae of her story, I listened politely. I was interested but uninvolved: although I felt sorry for her, I knew that there was no way I could help.

She read my thoughts. 'I don't want your pity,' she said. I must have jumped. She smiled. 'What I need is your skill.'

Her eyes, wet but not weak, seemed to have been cemented to mine. She was so determined, so convinced that I could help her. I couldn't drop my gaze, nor find a way to tell her the truth – that in this area I had no particular skills. I asked her more, writing down, for form's sake – and to break the strength of her gaze – the names of the companies that had sunk together. That done, my courage had risen. I told her that she needed an accountant.

'Accountants,' she snorted – she had a great line in explosive snorts – 'should be banned. They don't give a stuff, not after the money's already gone.' Having thus disposed of all accountants, she directed her energy at me. 'You can help me,' she said. 'you know that. You know it's not right what they did.'

With hindsight, I can see that this was how Agnes hooked me in, with that sentiment: 'It's not right.' Combined with the ferocity of her determination, that phrase landed me.

Even so, I flailed, momentarily, against the inevitable. I started speaking, reasonably enough, telling her why I could not take on her job. But she was indomitable. No matter how hard I tried, I couldn't faze her. The more obstacles I produced, the quicker she disposed of them until, at last, against my recent decision that we must no longer take charity cases, I found myself agreeing to investigate. 'I can't promise anything,' was my only rather feeble rider.

'I know that, love.' She'd pushed herself out of the chair. 'But I also know you'll do your best.' And, with her arthritic hands grasping her knotted cane, she hobbled out.

Leaving me to face Carmen. 'I see our management, after long and well-considered discussion, has opted for a change of tactics,' she remarked.

I'd tried to brazen it out. 'It might lead to something bigger.'

'Of course it might.' Carmen's snort was almost as professional as Agnes's. 'Which is why you didn't ask for a down payment. You were worried she'd move her custom elsewhere.'

Elsewhere ... Sitting in the library, trying to shut out Carmen's words, I closed my eyes. Without success: vision joined sound. What I saw was us – me and Carmen – in our office. The mental snapshot made me ache with longing. I saw us, looking at each other, smiling as she teased me. Smiling because we had been friends, because my new-broom attempt at sound economics had lasted less than half a morning, because we both knew that, in my shoes, Carmen would have done the same thing.

When the wells of her mockery had finally run dry, Carmen got down to business. 'So who's to do it? Me or you?'

I frowned, both in the then and in the now, thinking about the decision. Of course, now I realized why I had forgotten Agnes. I had got Carmen to do the first leg of the investigation. She was to check the pedigrees of the interconnected companies, to try and sort out how it was that they had gone down together, and to present her findings for discussion, at our next weekly meeting.

Which never came. Before the meeting could be held, everything had changed. A car ran over Sam. Sam who ...

'What are you doing in here?'

My eyes snapped open.

I was where I had been before memory engulfed me, in the library's tawdry room, but I was no longer alone. The sentence: 'What are you doing here?' was repeated, this time more stridently. I saw a woman standing in the doorway. I was in trouble: her feet were astride, her hands planted on her hips. 'What ...'

I'd got the message. 'Reading,' I said and when she continued to stare accusingly at me, added: 'This is the reading room, isn't it?'

The woman visibly relaxed. 'This is the store cupboard,' she said and, enunciating each separate word very clearly as one does for crazies, added helpfully: 'The reading room is next door.'

'Oh.' I scrambled to my feet and, slipping Agnes's photo back into its folder, wondered how I could ever have called myself a detective.

'To the right,' the woman directed as, folders in hand, I turned to the left. 'The right,' I heard. I took no notice. I kept on walking.

Chapter
sixteen

According to the file, Agnes Wilson lived on an estate near Kings Cross station. I found it easily enough. I parked the van in a metered spot and walked through a set of rusting iron gates and under a concrete archway.

I was in the centre of a group of tenement blocks which, although they were comparatively young, had already passed their sell-by date. I walked across a courtyard which was surrounded on all sides by buildings whose most prominent features were stairways, iron and concrete, and the stink of decay. Following signs to Agnes's block, I went under a second arch, past piles of rotting garbage. On my left was a narrow alleyway: I glanced down it and saw a brightly coloured child's trike abandoned amongst screwed-up scraps of burned aluminium foil. I put my sense of smell on hold as I headed up a concrete stairway, keeping to the centre to avoid the stains of urine which ran down each side. I kept my emotions on hold as well. I couldn't imagine how Agnes Wilson could tolerate living here. I couldn't imagine how anybody could.

'Psst.' I turned. Nothing. I went on climbing. 'Pssst,' followed this time by echoing laughter. Another turn, another blank. I walked faster, thinking that Agnes who, five years ago, had walked with a heavy limp, must find this last stretch torture.

On the second floor I stopped and checked the numbers.

I turned right. I walked along the narrow balcony, looking across at another whose glass sides were covered by putrid graffiti. *Send them home*, and scrawled underneath that another: *Or better still, kill them all.*

My heels clacked against the concrete. I kept imagining an after-sound as well but every time I turned, the space behind me was empty. Telling myself that my fear was just the after-effect of the intruder in the house, I increased my speed, aiming for the balcony's far end.

I reached it soon enough. Because there was neither bell nor knocker, I rapped against the door's scratched green wood. I sensed something, a presence behind it, but nobody answered. I flicked the metal letter box up and down, and, when that got me no results, did it again. I was sure that there was someone there.

There was. 'Who is it?' An anxious voice, too young and un-English to be Agnes Wilson.

My name would mean nothing. 'I'm looking for Agnes Wilson,' I said. I heard vague fumbling noises – someone manipulating the door's spy hole. I took a step back to provide a longer view. 'Is she in?'

I heard a soft click – the peep-hole cover dropping down – and then a sentence spoken with finality. 'Agnes Wilson does not live here.'

'Do you know where she's gone?' I got no reply. I tried again, louder this time. 'Can you tell me where Agnes Wilson is?' No answer. I dropped down to my knees, lifted the letter box's flap and peered through. The box had been entirely lined: all I saw was more tarnished metal. By the accent of the woman within and the vindictive slogans opposite, I thought I knew why.

I didn't want to scare her further but I needed to know where Agnes was. I rattled the letter box.

She must have been standing very close. 'Go away.' Her voice was breathy.

I stayed right where I was. 'Look,' I said. 'I don't want to hurt you. My name is Kate Baeier and I'm a friend of Agnes Wilson. Tell me where she went, or even when she went, and I promise you, I will go away.' Silence. 'I'm getting up now,' I said. I got up. 'I'm going to step away from the door.' I stepped away, moving backwards until I was jammed tight against the balcony's low wall. I heard more fumbling – the woman taking another look. I tried to smile, but not too widely – I knew what deformations those fish-eyed lenses could make of human features. I stood, patiently, waiting for her to see that I was harmless.

It worked. There was a sound of a bolt jerking along its casters. I stepped forward – but not close. Another bolt, this one coming out with more of a rattle and then a third after that. I stood still, trying to keep my expression neutral. A last clanking sound and the door shivered and then was slowly opened. Not fully, of course – one solid steel chain was still firmly linked.

The dark eyes of a woman – in her mid thirties I guessed – peered through the door's chink. 'You say that you are a friend of Agnes Wilson?'

I nodded.

Her eyes were boring into mine. 'A true friend would know where she had gone.'

'I've been away. For more than five years.'

Her face closed down; she dropped her gaze. I stood, waiting. When she looked at me again, I knew what she was going to say. 'I am sorry that a stranger should be the one to tell you,' she said. 'But your friend is dead.'

Which is what I had expected. Agnes Wilson, who had stayed in the same job all her life, would never have moved from home.

'She died three years ago,' the woman continued. 'We moved in after that.'

'Was she sick?' There was a slight tremor in my voice.

The woman heard it. 'I do not know.' Her voice was gentle. 'She was old.'

Yes, I thought, remembering the sight of Agnes's veined hand resting heavily on my desk. I forced myself to speak. 'Do you know anybody who might know more?'

She didn't answer – not immediately. Her face was a battleground of conflicting emotions – dismay, refusal, sympathy – all clashing with each other. In the end, sympathy won out. 'Agnes Wilson had someone who calls himself a relation on the estate,' she said slowly, as if the words came at great cost. 'You could speak with him.'

I nodded. I should go. I had told this woman that if she pointed me in Agnes's direction, I would.

'He lives over there.' One finger pointed through the crack at a building beyond. 'Number 135, Makepeace House.'

'Thanks,' I said and, having apologized for disturbing her, began to walk away.

Her voice tracked me. 'Lady,' I heard her calling.

I stopped.

'You must be . . .'

I looked back but that didn't help. She was shaking her head. 'Nothing,' she said quickly. 'It is nothing.' She closed the door.

I listened to the sound of bolts sliding into place. I didn't bother calling out. I had seen her face closing down on me: she wasn't going to help me further. And so, after the last of the bolts had skidded home, I left.

Her anxiety pursued me. As I walked away from her flat the feeling that I'd had before, that somebody was following me, intensified. I told myself that I was being paranoid. I made myself slow down. But I was in the wrong environment for relaxation. I walked out of the building and over, through an uncared for open space, to the adjacent one, and all I saw was more degradation. Noises – a child's shrill protests, some teenagers laughing spitefully, glass shattering – bounced off the grubby walls, while the occasional person, head held well down, scuttled across my path.

Makepeace House was one of the biggest in the estate, its blackened brick smothering the skyline. I had worked out the rules by now: number 135 would be on the ground floor. I moved along the concrete walkway, looking at the numbers.

I needn't have bothered: number 135 was unmissable. In this place where security was paramount, its occupants had gone overboard. Instead of dingy wood, its door was made of shining sheet metal; where others might have two locks, this door had four; and over the small windows which stood to either side were thick metal bars.

Wondering what kind of relative of Agnes this could be, I put my finger on the bell. I had been expecting a loud buzz; what I got instead was a melodic and eerily familiar tune. Except I couldn't place it. I listened to its dying out and then, getting no answer, I pressed again and heard the whole routine repeated. No joy – either in identifying the music or in bringing someone to the door. I turned.

It happened again then, that feeling that something was watching me, something malevolent. I turned again, going full circle, looking at the door and the windows, but there was nothing there – or at least nothing that I could see. Telling myself I was imagining things, I turned again and walked, quickly out.

Apart from paranoia something else was bothering me. When I reached the van I checked it out. I opened Agnes's file and turned the pages to the very end, confirming that, apart from my brief notes on our initial interview, the rest was blank. When I closed the file, I was frowning. I distinctly remembered that Carmen had agreed to start the investigation. But she hadn't – or at least there was nothing in the file to show that she had. I thought fleetingly of ringing her and asking why but decided that it wasn't worth risking another harangue. I shrugged. But knew that if I let it go Carmen's inexplicable tantrum would continue to bug me. It was easy enough for me to finish where she had patently failed. I fed more coins into the meter and walked briskly to the tube.

Companies House was where it had always been – a short walk from Old Street Station. From the outside it looked unchanged, although I suspected that the rectangles of stucco under each regularly spaced window might be cleaner than they used to be. It was hard to tell: the building had about as much charm as the headquarters of the South African security police in Johannesburg.

The inside was just as uninteresting, except it had been changed. It had gone modern. In the low-ceilinged central room, computers had replaced the once unending ranks of card cabinets. Static had edged dust out. The tone, compared to what had been, was muted: soft voices of officials instructing punters on how to access the new technology having replaced the frantic barking of agents making and unmaking companies.

I opened my bag for inspection and then, passing through the barrier, found a free computer. It was friendly: I had no need for the explanatory leaflet, nor for the woman who was giving explanations as she trod amongst my fellow searchers. I followed the instructions: typed *Permog*, Agnes's employers' name, and there on the screen, came its official number along with a D for dissolved. Any more information required, the computer told me, and I would have to pay.

I paid. Above the going rate. I didn't want to wait two hours so I got the process speeded up by handing twenty quid to the uniformed woman whose hatchet face was just visible behind her high desk. It wasn't graft exactly but a levy on impatience.

In the twenty minutes I had to spare, I walked back to the tube and bought myself a sandwich: plastic cheese and floppy tomato on French bread, which was marginally more palatable than the coffee the Companies House machine produced. I threw it and the plastic container into the bin and fetched my microfiche.

The tape whirled through the machine. It wasn't long. What it told me was Permog's birth (incorporation documents and liquidation date), a list of shareholders and its last three years' returns where dwindling reserves ended eventually in bankruptcy. Nothing on pensions.

I hate microfiche. I took the canister over to the photocopying attachment and, feeding in ten pence pieces, made copies of those pages of the accounts which listed the directors. I also, just for the hell of it, took a shot of the shareholders list. Once the details were on paper, I let my eyes run down the names. Still no joy: none of them meant anything to me.

The sandwich, instead of energizing me, had made me tired. Or maybe it was my lack of progress. I wondered whether Carmen's failure to act had been because she'd met this same deadend. Wondering that made me more determined. I went back to an introductory computer, clicked it on, and typed, where it asked for company names, *Perm*. That got me on to a different folio: a list of companies whose names started with the PERM. I ran my eyes down the string of names. Permog was in the middle, and to either side of it, two other dissolved companies: Permole and Permore. There were others similar but economic considerations prevented me from selecting them. I took down the numbers of the nearest and handed them, with forty pounds, to the axe murderer.

Which left me with another twenty minutes spare. I sat in a Dralon chair and flicked through a discarded financial magazine. It seemed to be having the same problem with the British economy as the current Chancellor of the Exchequer was, but used less words to tell me slightly more. By the time my waiting was over there was one thing I knew: that I was glad I wasn't the Chancellor.

The new microfiches delivered results. My hunch had paid off. Whoever had founded Permog had been uninventive: he had chosen sister companies with practically the same names. Each company had directors in common. But it was even more incestuous than that – when it came to money it was a case of what's mine can also easily become yours. As I flicked through the accounts of one company I noted down the large transactions. Then I took the second company's accounts and stuck it on the microfiche. Sure enough, there were corresponding sums entering or exiting the accounts at a frenetic rate. When the third was on the microfiche I matched other amounts. It wasn't entirely a closed circuit – there were obviously other companies involved – but what I was tracing was a rapid downward spiral. Money was passing from one to the other as unsecured loans, spent on high directors' salaries and perks. It was so organized it was obviously deliberate: whoever had controlled those companies had bled them dry. The end product – bankruptcy for each in turn – was inevitable.

So I knew now why Agnes's company had gone down the tubes. Not bad management, but a hit and run merchant who was interested only in extracting the maximum short-term gains. What I didn't know, however, was what had happened to Agnes's pension scheme. It should have been protected by its trustees, but none of their names nor any other details were in the accounts. I was pretty sure I knew what had happened – that the pension fund itself had been loaned to another company which, going bank-

rupt, took the pension with it – but there was no way I
could prove that from what I had here.

I took a few more photocopies and went over to the
coffee area. Every conceivable British telephone directory
was available there. On my third guess, Newcastle, I
found a registrar of pension schemes listed. I dialled the
number, got first a machine and then a very helpful
individual who promised to send me three forms by
return.

That was it. As much as I could do. I slipped my
microfiches into my pocket, my sheets of photocopies into
my bag and left.

I got back to Chelsea to find the first coat of paint on the
walls and the second about to go up. Maria and Jurek
would soon be gone and, with them, their van. I knew that
if I was being drawn back into the detective business, I
would need a car of my own. I spent some time organizing
my finances and then phoned a local leasing agency. I
toyed with the idea of arranging for another place to live
but didn't. It wasn't necessary – whoever it was that had
got into the house before would now be tripped up by the
alarm.

Maria and Jurek finished at five. I paid them and,
taking up their offer of a lift, went to pick up my car. It
was bottom of the line, a red Renault 5. I drove it for a
while, picking up some food, dropping off some dry clean-
ing, and then went home.

Home. That's not what it felt like when I entered. It
felt hostile. I turned the keys in their respective locks and
pushed the door open. My heart was pounding. I dropped
my shopping and, looking straight ahead, switched off the
alarm. And then tentatively I began to walk along the
hallway.

The house was quite empty, except that is for the cat

which, as soon as it appeared, began to make nice-nice with my shopping. I couldn't resist – I allowed it to lead me downstairs. When it had slunk off with food in its jaws, I sat at the kitchen counter.

The ringing of the phone punctuated my action. I picked it up. 'Hello?'

Carmen wasted no time. 'Be at Ridley Road at midnight.'

'Tonight?'

'Tonight. Stand halfway down. Somebody will come get you.'

'Roger,' I said.

Her finale was as abrupt as her opening. She hung up.

'And out,' I muttered and, slamming the phone down, I left the kitchen.

Chapter
seventeen

I was due at Anna's for supper. I went upstairs to change. Faced with the impending polarization – a dinner party followed by a midnight rendezvous in Hackney – none of my clothes seemed quite right. In the end I settled on a pair of brown silk trousers and black silk shirt which might, in the darkness, pass as cotton.

Anna had told me to come early and meet her daughter. I had thought before that I wouldn't; now I changed my mind. I got into my hire car, which after the slackness of the van's controls seemed unnecessarily frenetic, and drove to west London.

While Anna cooked, I spent a couple of hours with my diminutive namesake. To my surprise I found that, instead of resenting the child, I actively enjoyed her. We played, she and I, quite shamelessly with make-up: when the time came for her to go to bed, both her face and mine were a riot of clashing colour. We scrubbed up together.

She wormed her way in front so that the mirror framed both our faces. 'You must come again, Kate two,' she said.

I looked ahead and seeing her shining, chubby cheeks remembered other cheeks like them.

Her high voice slicked through memory. 'You will, won't you?'

'Yes.' I nodded. 'I will come again.' The bathroom door was opened and Anna appeared. I spoke into the mirror. 'I'm seeing Matthew tomorrow.'

She nodded. 'John phoned to get your number. He's being very civilized.'

I shrugged. Carmen and Agnes Wilson, I realized, had done me some good: they'd stopped me worrying about John Layton's motives.

'Mummmeeee.' Kate had wriggled out from under me and was launching herself at Anna. 'I'm not going to bed, I'm not, I'm not . . .' Her voice grew gradually more distant as Anna carried her off.

As far as I was concerned, dinner was less successful than its warm-up. Anna had decided to side-step our shared pasts and so I knew few of my fellow guests. They were a nice bunch and happy to include me – the trouble was, I didn't co-operate. I looked along the varnished table at the elegant, self-assured company and compared this with the image of the woman behind her bolted door. I remembered what Carmen had said and thought that she was right: there was a visible line in the country that had not been there before

Except . . . I shook my head. What did it have to do with me?

'You disagree, Kate?' someone said.

I tried to concentrate better after that but it was a losing battle. By ten-thirty, I surrendered. My silent presence was having a dampening effect on the rest of the company anyway; I muttered platitudes about fatigue and stood.

No one tried to stop me going. 'I'll walk you to the door,' Anna said.

We went down in silence. 'Still talking to me?' I asked as I was about to step out.

She smiled, briefly. 'Still talking to yourself?'

I had no reply to that. I kissed her on both cheeks, promised to keep in touch and left.

*

It was still too early for Ridley Road but too late for an interim return to Chelsea. I drove in the general direction of Hackney, thinking that the sensible thing to do would be to stop somewhere for a caffeine jolt. I did not, however, do the sensible thing. What I did was drive to Kings Cross.

I parked almost in the exact same spot as before. It felt different: night had given its daytime dilapidation a sinister edge. Stepping out of the car, I pulled my coat closer. It was a dark, cloud-covered night. What lighting there was was dim. It was cold and the streets were empty save for a few lone men, one of them heading straight for me. As he passed under a yellowing streetlight, the dome of a shiny bald path set amidst greasy hair caught my attention. With my eyes focused on that, it was not until he was almost upon me that I saw that he was wearing trousers but no shirt. The hair on his chest was fibrous. As he came closer he launched himself at me. He was only half trying and the smell of spirits explained why. I moved out of his way.

I kept on moving, through the gate that I hadn't realized earlier squeaked when it was touched, under the archway which in the darkness seemed much lower, and into the courtyard. Makepeace House was a huge smudge on the horizon. I went towards it. My footsteps sounded unnaturally loud. I wished I'd taken off my jewellery. I walked under the second arch and heard sounds – breathing. Not mine. I stopped and it came more clearly: an emphatic, panting sound. I took a step forward. I was by the alleyway; the panting was louder, issued with pained exertion. It was a familiar sound: someone had been hurt and needed help. Peering into the blackness I took one more tentative step forwards. At the alley's end, I could just make out a dark, contorted shape.

'Are you all right?'

Movement: a head, a woman's head, turning to look at me. My eyes were more accustomed to the dark by now: I saw that what I had assumed to be one body was in fact two. The man, his back to me, continued pumping. His breath was rasping, ugly.

'I'm sorry.'

The woman looked blankly unconcerned. I turned and left.

As I walked across the courtyard the image of that loveless coupling kept invading my mind's eye. I dismissed it. I didn't know why it even affected me – in my travels I'd seen hundreds of such sights. I slowed myself and my own breathing down and tried to concentrate on the job in hand.

It wasn't easy. The feeling that I'd had earlier, that someone was following me, had returned. My heels clicked loud against the ground. The dark invaded. I didn't stop – I knew that if I turned there would be nobody there.

Number 135 was in darkness but I'd come so far I had at least to give it a try. I rang the bell, listening to its soft refrain. In the daylight it had sounded vaguely familiar: by night it just seemed eerie. I rang it again, to prove I wasn't scared.

All I heard was a squeak: the estate's gates opening. I turned and peered through the gloom.

'What the fuck do you want?'

I whirled round and for a moment thought I was going mad. The door to number 135 had been opened, I could see a dingy hallway, but there was nobody there. Except – I lowered my eyes. There was someone. A man. 'Who the hell are you?' His face was broad, chipped granite set in straight, long, brown hair. His upper body, powerful muscles running along its sinews, leaned forwards. The rest I could not see – it was covered by a dirty tartan blanket tucked into his wheelchair. 'You gonna answer then?'

I tried to smile. 'My name's Kate Baeier.'

'So?'

'I was looking for Agnes Wilson.'

When the man grinned, he exposed a row of uneven, yellowing teeth. 'Agnes,' he said. The grin was stretched. 'You do know you're a bit fucking late, don't you?'

'I know she's dead.'

'You found that out then?' The grin had gone. 'Brilliant. You must be a fucking detective.'

A detective? A warning flashed though my mind. This man already knew who I was: he'd been expecting me. I kept my face neutral.

'I was told that you were related to her,' I said.

The grin – except it wasn't a grin, it was a leer – had returned.

'Who told you? Miss Prissy upstairs?' It was too dark to be sure but I thought I saw spittle running down one side of his mouth. 'I bet you two got on like a house on fire.' It was spit. The back of one calloused hand swiped it off.

I hid my aversion behind persistence. 'Were you related?'

'Yeah. In a manner of speaking. Old Aggie called herself my stepmother. What she really was was an old tart who spread her legs for my father when he wasn't too pissed to perform. But' – he rolled his wheelchair nearer – 'since most of the slags on this estate did likewise, I've got a big family.' He was almost upon me.

I knew he was going to do something. I didn't move. I was much more mobile than he: I don't know why I didn't get away. All I can say, in hindsight, was that his eyes, glinting in the darkness, exerted such a pull on me that it was as if I and not he who was paralysed.

He was fast. His arm shot out and grabbed mine. He pushed my coat sleeve up. His fingers were digging into skin. He yanked me, pulling me down so that his face and mine were almost touching. I glanced down, saw his right hand gripping my arm, saw a circular ridged Sikh silver bracelet around his wrist. It seemed so out of character: I wondered what it was doing there.

His talking stopped me wondering further. His voice was soft, gentle even. 'You've got something on your conscience, Kate Baeier,' he said, 'so you're sniffing round here.' I looked up. More spit bubbled from the side of his mouth. He didn't bother with it. 'I'll tell you this for free,' he said. 'You stick your long nose into my affairs and you risk getting it . . .' His mouth opened. I got a whiff of something putrid. I wrenched my face away. He still had me by the arm. 'Bitten off,' he said and plunged his mouth into my flesh. His bite went deep: pain stabbed my forearm. I yelped and pulled away.

He let go, suddenly, so that the force of my own momentum threw me backwards. I landed, hard, on the ground with my legs sprawled out. I saw the wheels of the chair moving slowly. 'Go on,' I heard. 'Run.' I couldn't help myself: I shuffled backwards like an upturned crab. As the wheelchair moved again I heard another sound. Savage and unrelenting. The man was laughing. And then he was gone.

I got into the car and made sure all the doors were locked. I clicked on the light. My arm still hurt. I rolled my sleeve up and took a look. The bite had been ferocious – I saw a ring of purplish indentations and in two places, spots of blood welling. I sat and kept on looking, feeling thankful that my shots were all up to date. Then I remembered the thing I hadn't been inoculated against, the thing for which there was no inoculation – AIDS.

I needed a drink. I looked at my watch. It was almost eleven. Cursing Britain for its licensing laws I drove the car down the road, parked outside a pub and rushed in with my order. Three quick whiskies later, I was more worried about being breathalysed than AIDS. I left the pub and, grown brave with drink, walked around the block a few times. It was time then to get going for my rendezvous. I got back into the car and drove slowly and carefully to Dalston.

While Kings Cross had been sinister, Ridley Road was sensational. Or at least the part that housed the twenty-four-hour bagel shop was. By day it had melted into the surrounding dilapidation; by night it strutted its stuff. Huge gold lights which I'd not even noticed before were bolted high up on the wall, their beams, burning what seemed like thousands of watts, directed at the shop's entrance. Which was buzzing: young men, mostly, hanging out in groups, the smell of strong grass wafting from their midst. And then their was the music, turned up loud, on the edge of distortion, pulsing as I walked on in.

The action was all outside; the interior was calm. Not that I cared. The anaesthetic effects of the whisky had worn off. My arm was stinging. I asked for disinfectant and a plaster. I guess it was a routine request: within seconds, both were produced. I pulled my sleeve back and put a few drops of Dettol into the tiny cavities, wincing.

Behind the counter a woman watched curiously. 'Met a vampire, did you?'

'Something like that.' I stuck a plaster on, bought a bagel and left.

Leaving the shop's glare behind, I began walking into darkness. I wasn't hungry but I ate my bagel. I can't say it was nerves – as I began walking, I wasn't feeling nervous. I wasn't feeling anything.

Carmen had told me to stand halfway down – somewhere in the dark, uninhabited section of the street then. I walked until I reckoned I was in its middle. I stopped and stood, waiting. In the distance the music's beat continued to pound, making where I was standing seem even quieter.

Midnight went and kept on going. I'd learned the art of waiting on my travels, but this kind of waiting, in the cold, was different. I wondered whether this was a charade dreamed up by Carmen to punish me for unnamed transgressions. I thought of appropriate reprisals but, when they got too vengeful, I pushed them away. I tapped my feet against the paving stones, trying to keep the circulation going. Eventually I invented a new game of guess and go and played it. Without counting, I had to guess each five minutes as it passed and if I was less than three seconds out, then I could go.

On the fourth round, I won. That's it, I thought.

Great timing. At that moment I heard a cracking sound – stone hitting glass. The night darkened. I frowned and blinked. How could it have got darker? I was outside. And yet . . . it felt as if someone had switched out the lights.

Someone *had* switched out the lights. The bulbs in the two streetlamps closest to me had been simultaneously broken. I turned my head; I saw a dark figure moving closer. When I turned my head the other way, I saw its mirror image – another figure, closer than the first. I was impressed. And scared. I took a step backwards.

It was a perfectly choreographed move – straight into the arms of a third man. He'd crept up, I don't know where from, and he'd been expecting me. One arm gripped my chest, restraining both my arms, the other went higher – a blade, an old-fashioned razor, against my throat.

I could just about speak. 'I'm impressed,' I managed.

'What do you want?' a voice hissed.

His razor hand tightened, making me gag. Even in the darkness the jagged steel blade glittered. I knew I should keep quiet but knew also that if he got any more excited I wouldn't be able to talk. Ever. I choked out an 'Ease off.'

His reply was threefold: a grunt, a slackening of the pressure on my neck and a repetition: 'What do you want with us?'

'I want you to leave me alone.'

'*You* want *us* to leave you alone? Very funny.' He didn't sound the slightest bit amused. 'We didn't ask for this meeting.'

I heard soft footsteps: his companions coming closer. I raised my voice. 'I had to see you because of what you've been doing. I want you to stop. I don't know who you are. I don't care who you are. Just leave me alone.'

A chuckle from somewhere close by. 'We ain't been doing nothing, lady.' It was a different man speaking in a voice I hadn't heard before. 'Apart from minding our own business. Which is what we'd advise you to do.'

'You haven't come to my house?'

Silence.

'Or sent me a photograph?'

'We're not into pictures.' The second speaker again. 'Unless they have a silver thread running through them.'

The hand around my neck was tightened. 'We don't care about you. Not if *you* leave *us* alone. Alone. You get it?' And then the pressure was off. 'Look down,' the first voice said. A hand pushed the back of my head. I looked down. 'Count to twenty,' his voice again. 'Slowly. And when that's over, go. And don't come back.' There was a soft thud, some softer footfalls and then . . . nothing.

I counted to twenty. Very slowly. And then, when that was over, I raised my head. They should have specialized in urban insurrection rather than mugging: they had gone, completely, and I had no idea where. I turned.

My foot hit something soft. My bag. Bending down, I hooked it up and left.

Chapter
eighteen

I drove to Chelsea with everything – thoughts, feelings, questions – on hold. By the time I got back it was two a.m.; the house was in darkness. I let myself in, demobilized the alarm and stood in the hallway, leaning against a wall. The cat joined me. It seemed pleased to see me: it began weaving itself, purring, through my feet. The welcome brought me back to life. I knelt and stroked it, feeling its warmth against my cold until I was ready to move again. I went upstairs.

My bedroom was home to the alarm's second master switch. 'You're going to have to spend the night with me,' I told the cat as I closed the door and primed the alarm. That done, I went into the bathroom and ran myself a full, hot bath. Getting in, I went under, head and all. I was sealed off from the world, insulated from sound, the heat warming my bones and stinging my face. I lay there for as long as I could manage – and then shot up, gasping. The cat, which had been sitting at the end of the bath, hissed and left. I lay back. Resting my head on the bath's curve, I closed my eyes.

My thoughts began from then. I thought about the man in the wheelchair, his jaw closing on my flesh, and I thought about the careful choreography of the three at Ridley Road. Both meetings had been very different in style but at both I had been given the same piece of advice: Get out.

Out? I frowned. Of what?

My mind was suddenly in gear. I got out of the bath and, fetching my bag, spilled its contents on the bathroom floor. There was nothing valuable there – there never had been – but now that I had it all in front of me I knew that there was nothing missing either. I had not left the code inside the bag. Which meant that the muggers, who weren't pro enough to crack the alarm without the code, had been telling the truth: they hadn't come into this house.

So who had?

The man at Agnes's estate? Although I had never met him before, he had known who I was. And then there was the sleaziness of the break-ins – the poem and the pornographic photo both suggesting the kind of warped mind that the man in the wheelchair obviously possessed. Except ... how could I have forgotten? Someone had followed me up the stairs, switching off the lights. And I didn't know the man in the wheelchair. His crack about a detective must have been mere guesswork. I was sure I'd never met him. Our only connection was Agnes Wilson and she was dead.

And ... My frown was taking up residence in the craters of my forehead. Apart from that. Nothing.

Nothing except emotion. And even that wasn't right – they were only glimmerings of emotions, of fear and anger which had both been absent during my night's escapade. They were strange. I stood naked, no longer wet, and realized that in the five years I'd been gone I hadn't felt much of any of them. And now these glimmerings suggested that others, even more potent, might be waiting in the wings.

I shook my head. I would not let them in. I had built a wall around me; it would not be breached. I left the bag's contents scattered on the floor and went to bed.

★

We slept together, the cat and I. We didn't sleep well. I kept waking up, jerked into consciousness by dreams whose phantoms fled as soon as I opened my eyes. My movements disturbed the cat which continued to make outraged chirping noises until I stroked it into quiescence. By eight I'd had enough. I got up and, on the basis that water cures most kinds of insanity, had another bath. After that I switched off the alarm and went downstairs.

The post was lying on the doormat. One for me, I saw, and picking it up remembered the extremity of my reaction to my first letter here. Although it was a mere three days distant it seemed to have happened a very long time ago. I couldn't imagine reacting that way now. I took the envelope downstairs and slit it open.

The woman at the pensions registry had been as good as her word; there were three PR4 tracing forms enclosed. I put them to one side; I was hungry. I made coffee and toast and, realizing that I was hungrier than that, an omelette as well. That consumed, I cleared the dishes away and began form filling.

The information I was after was a list of trustees of each of the firm's pension schemes. For that I needed to prove my bona fides. In the case of Permog, Agnes's old employer, this was no problem – since her pension had never kicked in, I was pretty sure that nobody would have bothered to inform the registry that she was dead. I filled out her name and signed as her. That left me with the other two. In the end, I decided to go for pure invention. I had nothing to lose – if the registrar checked up, all that would happen was that they wouldn't return the forms. I made up a couple of unlikely sounding pseudonyms, gave a different address for each – Anna's in one case, Maria and Jurek's in the second – and having packed the lot into different envelopes went out to post them.

When I got back, I looked at my watch. It was nine-thirty. I wasn't due at John Layton's until four. I fetched my address book, searched through it and began phoning.

It took me three calls to track down Tom Parsons. He was as usual at work and, as usual, running on all four cylinders. 'Kate? Kate Baeier?' He always had been good at the crescendo, had Tom. 'I've been following your progress through the world by newsprint. What brings you back?'

I inserted flattery in place of an answer. 'Finding you was like climbing a ladder,' I said. 'You've come a long way since the *Street Times*.'

Tom groaned. 'You don't know how long,' he said. 'I'm buried in memos here. Oh for the good old days.'

I waited. I knew there would be more.

There was. 'And speaking of the good old days,' Tom continued. 'What you after?' It was said aggressively but I didn't take offence. Tom was a ferret of a journalist who, although he always complained loudly when I asked him to do something, had never refused. I think he enjoyed both the eccentricity of my requests and being part of an investigation where libel laws would not tie his hand. Even now, after all this time, he was interested. 'Go on,' he said, 'tell me.'

I told him. I told him about Agnes Wilson and the man in the wheelchair and then I told him what I wanted.

His response was dry disbelief. 'You want me to find out the name of someone who lives on an estate in Kings Cross,' he said. 'Do you think I'm magic?'

'That is the only possible explanation for the number of women who agree to jump into your bed,' I said. 'And speaking of them – remember Sarah? Great looking, great dancer, and far too clever for you. She worked at a Camden housing office, I believe?'

'But that was years ago!'

'That should make it interesting,' I said. 'And while

you're at it, check to see if there's anything on Agnes Wilson's death, will you?' I took Tom's over-acted groaning as consent. 'Thanks,' I said, 'I owe you one,' and without giving him time to itemize exactly what that one might be, I hung up.

Not for long. I had another call on my list. I had better make it before my resolution ran out on me.

I didn't need my address book. I accessed Carmen's number from memory and dialled.

She answered fast. 'Yes?' Her telephone manner had always been this graceless: teasing her about it had once been second nature. But now . . . 'Yes? Who is it?'

'It's Kate.'

Silence. Over to me then. 'Thanks for arranging the meet,' I said. 'How much do I owe you?'

Her voice was icy cool. 'I'll send you a bill.'

It was childish, I know, but I stuck my tongue out.

'You'll get it on Monday,' she said.

'I may not be here,' I said. Which was news to me – interesting news – but better kept for a more private occasion. 'So how much?'

'You going somewhere?' She actually sounded angry!

'Would it matter?' I asked. I didn't wait for an answer that I knew would not be forthcoming. Instead: 'How much?' I pressed.

To my astonishment, she produced a sum. 'Ten pounds.'

Ten pounds?

Pathetic! I nearly said, but didn't. 'Fine,' is what I said, thinking that if it were me I would have let the ten pounds go. 'I'll post it to you.'

'You do that.' Her closing gambit – there was finality in her voice.

I stopped her from hanging up by springing in a question: 'Did you know that Agnes Wilson was dead?'

'I heard.' That and nothing other.

Time for me to up the stakes. 'Why didn't you do anything about her when she was alive?'

Success – or at least a genuine response. 'What?' That one word barked out in a voice so hard it might have been spun with steel.

I didn't let it bother me. 'You were meant to start off the Wilson investigation,' I said. 'But you didn't. Or at least there's nothing in the file to show you did. I want to know why.'

'Why do you think?' snapped in instantaneously.

'Look.' I sighed. 'If I knew that I wouldn't be asking you, would I?'

There was a long, long silence. I sat there, holding the phone to my ear, waiting for her reply.

Not that it was worth waiting for. 'Forget it,' is what she said. 'I'm not interested in playing games with your conscience.' Click. She had hung up.

When I eventually put my own receiver down, my hand was trembling. I let it lie against the phone. I sat there, working on my fury. *My conscience* – what the hell did she mean by that?

But no: I would not dwell on it, would not hand her even the partial victory of making me worry about what she said. I had other, more important things to think about. I sat some more until the force of my initial anger was dissolved. Then I wrote a cheque to Carmen, shoved it, unaccompanied, into an addressed envelope and left the house with it. As I got rid of it, pushing it briskly into the post box, I also rid myself of thoughts of Carmen.

I had more than five hours before my next engagement. I decided to spend it out of the house.

Chapter
nineteen

I went to a library, got hold of an ancient *Who's Who* of company directors and used it to check out each of the names from my Companies House microfiches. It was tedious work and by the time I'd finished all I had was an expanded list of company names and the prospect of a return to Companies House to track them all down. Since this was unlikely to do anything other than lead me into a sub-section of the old boy's network which is perpetually England, I decided to put off that dubious pleasure.

I closed the *Who's Who*. All the time I'd been referencing and cross referencing, I had also been thinking of what I had said to Carmen – that I might soon be gone. The more I thought about it, the more sense it made. Whatever delusions had kept me in London had been punctured. I had faced my past and the way I had fled from it; Matthew was the last remaining fragment and I would soon dispose of him.

Which meant that there was no reason to stay. I gathered my papers together, and stood up. Unless Tom came up with something really dramatic about Agnes Wilson or my biting foe I would leave – and within the next few days. I began to walk towards the door, feeling my muscles unwind. I remembered the man in the wheelchair telling me to go. The old Kate would have taken this as a challenge, a reason, even, to stay. But that Kate was gone.

The new me had seen how often giant slayers turn into their own dragons: I wasn't into fighting giants, not any more.

The day had brightened. I stood in the library's uninhabited forecourt and looked up at clear blue skies, winter on its way. I found myself yearning for hot hazes and long, low horizons. Whatever Tom comes up with, I thought, I'll still go.

I took a walk. I strolled into the heart of the city, which on Saturday was so abandoned it looked as if a neutron bomb had struck. That's the way I liked it – the buildings and I, alone. I weaved down the narrow streets, my head craned to view the fluctuating skyline – the narrow, old structures edged in by new plate and glass, all of which spoke of a now vanishing prosperity. When I'd had enough of that I got my car, drove it to the South Bank and bought myself a late lunch. I sat there, eating slowly, looking out on the Thames, until finally it was time to go.

On my first visit to Kingston Hill I had driven through the open gateway and up the drive. This time the gates were firmly closed. No problem. There was a bell embedded in the wall. I got out of the car and walked towards it.

I needn't have bothered: before my finger made contact, the gates opened, nudging me aside. Wrong footed, I went back to my car and drove on through.

Parking the Renault, I crunched through the forecourt. I steered clear of the stone lions, going straight to the front door. It was opened by Lilia decked out in full regalia – white frilled apron pinned to neat black dress, white cap on sleek black hair, and solemn respect on whitened face. She was a model of a dependable domestic, not at all the type who would willingly stick her head under a van.

Nor would she chat. She took my coat and, uttering a

polite, 'This way,' blanked her face against my smiled attempt at contact. I followed her rubber soles across thick pile.

She guided me to the far end of the hallway and then, opening a door, stood aside. I walked over the threshold. The room I entered was on a majestic scale, stretching from one end of the wide house to its other. Different blocks of furniture – the grand piano with accompanying chairs, the two sitting enclosures, the place for a desk tucked into an alcove by one of the many windows – served to demarcate each separate zone. The interior designers had done their job well. It was too puffed up for my tastes – soft pinks, hushed blues, plush fawns hustling each other – but it was certainly very effective.

I heard the door close. I took another step inside.

'Kate.' John Layton was on his feet, welcoming me. And what a welcome. His voice was robustly hearty, his eyes moist and open, and his beaming mouth added a loud: 'So pleased you could make it.' He shook my hand more vigorously than was necessary. I got the message: we were playing charades, our roles pre-assigned. John was to be the genial host, I the charming guest. Which left – I looked around – yes, there he was in the furthest corner of the room, slouching in a straight back chair – our audience. Matthew.

The sight of him drove out my smugness. Only a few hours ago I had thought that this visit would dispose of Matthew; now that inappropriateness fled. I couldn't tear my eyes away. The absurdity of what I had imagined by the Dulwich playing fields, that I might not recognize him, was exposed. I knew him. I would have known him anywhere. Not that he hadn't changed – on the contrary, his boyishness had been sloughed off. His face was much more angular, what had once been a chubby body was now thin and wiry. But none of this counted, for what made him so easily identifiable was how much he looked like Sam.

It wasn't his colouring – where Sam's eyes had been blue, Matthew's were hazel, where Sam's hair had been almost fair, Matthew's mouse was edging close to chestnut – nor even his shape – Matthew was much more angular than Sam had ever been – but rather the whole effect. Movement made it more pronounced. As he shifted uneasily, I saw my Sam.

And I saw what I had forfeited. During the past five years when I'd agonized about the severing of our links, it was the child I could have comforted and who could have comforted me that I was thinking of. But now, seeing him, I knew what I had really lost – not his past but his present and his future as well.

I tried to speak: 'Matthew,' my voice no louder than a whisper.

A crashing echo drowned it out. 'Matthew,' John boomed. 'Come and greet our guest.'

He responded immediately, jumping up, approaching me, his hand outstretched. I had wanted him closer but was sorry to see him so compliant.

He was upon me. 'Pleased to see you,' he said in a cultured Dulwich voice that Sam had once disowned.

My gestures were all out of proportion. When he broke the intensity of my gaze by looking down, I followed suit. I saw our two hands locked – I was holding his too hard. I loosened up and said the first thing that occurred. 'Do you remember me?'

The uncompromising part of the ten-year-old Matthew – that which I had once admired and detested in equal measure – had gone. In its place was bland politeness. 'Yes,' he said, although the expression on his face seemed to say he wished he didn't.

'Why don't we have tea?' John's uncharacteristic

jocularity bounced out. With Matthew in tow, he lead me to a section of the room which had been designed for intimacy – three small sofas arranged around a low, central table and looking out on to the garden. He must have been wired to the kitchen. Within moments of us sitting down, Lilia appeared. She was quick and efficient. She laid the tray down, served us each in turn with tea and Matthew with cake, and left.

I came up with conversational gambit number two: 'How's school?'

Very original, I thought, but Matthew seemed relieved. 'I like it,' he said and, without the need for further prompting, proceeded to fill me in on Dulwich College's major points of interest.

When, two cups of tea later, Matthew ran out of steam, John took up the baton. He veered on to something other – cars, perhaps, or university choice, – and between the two of them they kept the conversational ball rolling until John repeated his secret summoning act.

Lilia removed the tea things. Since chatting in front of the help was evidently considered bad taste, the conversation faltered. Which gave me the chance to ask Matthew something that I had not, until that moment, known I wanted. I blurted it out: 'Would you like to visit Sam's grave with me?'

Matthew blinked and I, in my surprise, blinked with him. But I'd said it and I had to follow through. 'Tomorrow?'

Whatever Matthew had been about to say was blocked by John. Quite literally – he jumped to his feet and, his back exuding anger, stood between me and Matthew.

'I would be happy to go with you if you wanted,' he told Matthew, his tone saying clearly that a trip with me would be forbidden.

That's that, I thought.

But I was wrong. Contrary to my first impressions, Matthew was no pushover. He cut straight through his grandfather's bluster. 'It's OK sir,' he said, cracking the whip on that last word. 'I would like to go with Kate.'

I held my breath. Knowing John Layton, I expected charm, toughness, or outright prohibition (and perhaps all three in that order) to be thrown at Matthew. But no: shrugging his shoulders in weary consent, John reseated himself. Instead of recrimination, he chose small talk. 'Has your stay in London been productive?' he asked.

I answered with platitudes issuing from only half a brain. The other half was trying to understand John's docility. One explanation kept presenting itself – love. Love? Surely not. Sam's voice reverberated: *John doesn't know how to love.*

I looked at Matthew. He looked away. John's eyes followed him. I watched him watching his grandson and I knew that Sam had been wrong. The fierce light of love burned in John's eyes. I felt something hit at my chest: I wished that Sam had lived long enough to see this.

Matthew was on his feet. 'I'm afraid I have some homework to finish.'

'Of course.' I got up. 'I'll pick you up tomorrow at eleven.'

'No.' Sharply. The spirit of his resistance burned deep. 'I have some errands to run,' he said. 'I'd rather meet at Highgate tube.'

'Sure,' I said, seeing, out of the corner of my eye, John's faint protesting movement.

'I'll see you then,' Matthew said and, smiling briefly at his grandfather, left the room.

Leaving John and me. 'Well,' I said, frowning, trying to remember where I'd put my keys.

'Can I get you a drink?'

A drink? I looked outside and saw how dark it was. I

shook my head. 'No thanks.' Of course, my keys must be in my coat pocket. I smiled. 'I'll be on my way.'

'Stay a moment.' It was an order.

My smile froze. John might have found the capacity to love but he was still a bully.

Well, Matthew had shown me the way; I would follow. 'I have to go,' I said.

'Stay. Please.' His voice was soft.

Another first: John pleading. Astonishing.

He pressed home his advantage. 'A drink?' he asked again. Why not? I nodded. 'Whisky.'

The malt he poured into a heavy-bottomed glass was the colour of saffron silk. It slipped down my throat as easily as a wet child on a water slide. I'm glad I stayed, I thought, taking another sip. If I have to be berated, then this is the only way to go. I rested my head back, closing my eyes as my taste buds indulged themselves.

'Sam was a very rich young man,' I heard.

My relaxation fled.

'If Sam had made a will . . .' John continued.

Here it came. My guess had only been slightly out. I was going to be accused not of speaking out of turn but of gold-digging. Oh well, I'd heard it all before – on at least three separate occasions when Sam was still alive. Wearily I put my glass down. 'Look . . .'

'No. You look.' He modulated his tone. 'I know we have not always been friends . . .'

I raised an eyebrow: now that's what I call understatement.

'But I'm sure you also know that I have a reputation for fairness,' I heard John saying.

A second eyebrow joined the first. *Fairness?* Who the hell was he kidding?

'And I know,' John continued, 'that if Sam had had the foresight to make a will . . .'

I sighed. Back to the will.

'He would have left you with a substantial sum.'

What?

'I have control of the trust,' John said. 'And I think it only fair that you be given a share.'

I shook my head. Violently. Both to prove that I wasn't dreaming and to rebuff this madness. 'I don't want Matthew's money,' I said.

'It's not Matthew's. It is money I set aside for Sam. It is your money.'

I was so agitated, I was on my feet.

'I don't expect you to decide immediately,' he said. 'Sleep on it. Let me know. But remember, it was Sam's money and he would have wanted you to have it. Of that I'm sure.'

He sounded so definite. As for me – I wasn't sure of anything. Except, that is, that I wanted out.

'You'll think about it?'

I was already walking off. 'Thanks for the tea.'

'Lilia will show you to the door.' He had settled back, whisky glass in contented hand.

His smugness provoked me. I stopped. 'Tell me one thing.'

'Hmm?'

'How much?'

'I beg your pardon?'

I spat the words out. 'How much money are you planning to give me?'

The way he looked at me confirmed what I'd suspected. I was livestock and he was assessing me, weighing up how much he'd have to pay.

A lot apparently. 'I would have to look at the accounts,' he said. 'But rest assured, we're in the region of six figures.'

'Oh.' Six figures. Quite a bribe.

'Think about it.'

I kept on walking. I sure would think about it. In fact, I already was thinking about it, thinking that behind such a hefty bribe must lie a cost. But what? All that money, just so that I would leave Matthew alone?

Lilia held out my coat. I slipped into it. Six figures – at least a hundred thousand pounds. If this was the way John Layton reacted to a threat to his love object then the price of his love was too damn high.

Chapter
twenty

Sunday morning. I arrived at Highgate tube to find Matthew waiting. I opened the car door. He got in. He smiled briefly and returned my greeting but the way he settled into the Renault's narrow passenger seat told me he'd taken a rain check on further conversation. I pulled out and drove up the hill into Highgate village. There I turned into its calm back streets, heading west towards the cemetery. As I manoeuvred the car, I stole the occasional glance at Matthew.

He sat coiled, his shoulders hunched, his eyes fixed firmly on the outside. In profile his face was pinched and sullen. Remembering how he had stood up to his grandfather, I wondered whether he had agreed to come only so as to annoy John. Another glance: he was frowning. I wondered whether he was regretting his decision.

When he turned his head suddenly, he caught me looking at him. 'We're almost there,' he said, his man's voice cracking to reveal the boy. He cleared his throat. His stiffness, I realized, was not resentment but nervousness.

I tucked the car into the side of the steep hill and, to be extra safe, put it in first. I looked at Matthew. 'Do you come here often?'

His reply was deadly serious. 'Once every two months or so.' He nodded. 'John brings me.'

So it was me, then, who was making Matthew nervous.

I didn't blame him. I was nervous too.

'Shall we get out?' He had opened his door but my hesitation had thrown him off stride.

'Sorry.' My smile was strained. 'Yes, let's go.'

We walked across the road and through the cemetery's gates. Things had changed. Beside the small gatehouse was a new addition: a manned table at which a line of people was patiently queuing. I heard pound coins chinking. I turned to Matthew: 'You mean they actually charge entrance fees?'

My indignation annoyed him. 'I've got a grave pass,' he said tersely, and pulling out a grubby white card flashed it at the woman behind the table. She nodded us through.

It had rained heavily overnight. The ground was sodden and nobody had yet bothered to dispose of the last of autumn's rotting leaves. We squelched our way down a narrow path that ran between two grave-filled sections of undergrowth. Without my trainers on it was hard going: as we rounded a corner, I slipped. I cried out.

Matthew's reflexes were good. One arm grabbed mine, the other steadied my left shoulder.

I smiled. 'Thanks.' It was the closest that we had come. He was taller than I had thought – he was taller than me. I looked up.

His face flushed. His fingers fled my shoulder as if they had been burned. He covered the abruptness of his movements with a gruff: 'Over there.'

Over there was our own white elephant, the Layton mausoleum. I had seen it only once before – when we'd buried Sam – but its image had been burned upon my retina. Over the years the picture I'd built up had seemed increasingly ludicrous but now that I stood and compared it with reality, I saw that I hadn't been far wrong. It was a mess, this monument to the Layton clan, a clash of styles, a miniature temple with a domed top and thick, white alabaster colonnades guarding its entrance. I bit down an impulse to laugh.

'Are you coming?' Matthew had undone the padlock that held the small iron gate closed. He was standing at the entrance. I followed him down two steps and into the vault.

Even though Matthew turned the light on as we entered, it took a while to accustom my eyes to the gloom. What I saw first were the place's walls, not damp but somehow dank, a murky grey, the colour, I thought, of despair. I stood in the centre of the space and forced my eyes lower. There were four coffins in all: Sam's grandparents', his mother's and his. His was the new one; its wood still holding off the encroachment of the inner blanketing of lead. I tried to take a step towards it. But couldn't: I couldn't move. I felt my eyes fixated on Sam's coffin. I spoke involuntarily: 'What are you doing here?'

Matthew knew I wasn't talking to him. 'I think my father might have preferred to have been out in the open,' he softly said.

I nodded. 'I loved him,' I whispered. I don't why.

A moment's silence and then: 'Sometimes I think I remember you better than him,' I heard Matthew saying.

That shook me. I turned.

Matthew was by the door, his face partly illuminated by light from the slit window which had been dug out of the vault's dome. He no longer looked grown; he looked young and embarrassed and he wiped roughly at his eyes. But that didn't stop him continuing: 'But maybe,' he said, 'that's only because I remember you at his funeral.'

I took one step towards him.

'Funny how some things stick in the memory,' Matthew said, his voice cracking.

Ever since we'd arranged to meet, I had told myself that there was one thing, one vain, meaningless thing that I must not say. Now, going even closer, I found myself saying it anyway. 'I'm sorry.'

'Sorry? For what?' Like that – sharply.

I dropped my head. 'For going.'

His voice, pitched higher than it had been before, pursued me into isolation. 'You aren't my mother.'

My eyes twitched. 'No.'

'There was no reason why you should have stayed.'

I stood biting my tongue both against his denial and his hostility. There was nothing I could fairly say. The damage I had done was in the past: no apology, no matter how well phrased, could change that.

'I'm all right,' he said, sounding far from all right. But when I eventually lifted my eyes and looked at him, I changed my mind. Despite the welling tears, despite the trembling lower lip, despite the coiled quality of his shoulder muscles, Matthew was probably all right. He had accepted reality and he was dealing with it. It was me, with my hope that this would ever be easy, who was at fault.

'Shall we go?' He turned and walked away.

I didn't follow, not immediately. I stood, quite still, looking at Sam's coffin. Matthew was right; Sam should not be here. He should have lain outdoors, in the open, free, not caught up in this lurid Layton fantasy.

I shook my head. Even that was wrong. Sam should not be dead. He should be living with me and with his son. Stupid. Stupid of him to have gone outside, straight into the path of some maniac's car. I'd never understood it – why he'd gone out on that dark night, wrapped so tightly against the cold. 'You shouldn't have done it,' I told his coffin, softly, so that the cold stone walls absorbed the sound.

I went outside, walked through the gate and waited as Matthew closed it. While we'd been in the vault, the skies had darkened: I shivered and pulled my coat more tightly round me. Matthew was taking a long time fumbling with the lock – I was sure he should by now have finished. I stood there wondering why he didn't turn.

When he spoke, he kept his back to me. 'He hates you,' he said.

'He?'

He turned. 'My grandfather.'

I shrugged. The antipathy between John and myself was no secret, but I saw no reason why Matthew should be involved. 'We're from different worlds,' I said. 'With different standards.'

But Matthew was ahead of me. 'It's not about who you are,' he said. 'It's about what you did. He blames you for my father's death.'

Me? My jaw dropped.

'I heard him talking about you,' Matthew continued. 'He thinks you've come back to make trouble for him.'

'Trouble?' It was news to me. 'What kind?'

His mouth was shut. Tight. He had said as much as he was prepared to say, or perhaps as much as he knew.

But I was not yet finished. 'John offered me money,' I said.

'A lot?'

I nodded.

Matthew's lips seemed to quiver. 'Are you going to take it?'

I shook my head.

The quivering must have been illusion. He was quite still now, and quite inscrutable. His face was no longer like Sam's – it was too closed for that. He stared at me, his brown eyes unwavering, looking until they were sated. And then: 'Let's go,' he said.

He had started the conversation and now he ended it. I opened my mouth. 'Let's go,' he said again.

There was nothing else I could do. I fell into step beside him. It had begun to drizzle. We walked on, heads held down against the damp. Until, that is, Matthew chose to speak again. 'Don't hurt my grandfather.'

I stopped. I was confused. Why should I hurt John Layton?

'I know he's difficult,' Matthew said, 'but he loves me. And he's all I have left.'

That hurt. I wanted to shout out a denial, to tell Matthew he still had me. I wanted to hug him, to address the hurt of this abandoned child. I wanted to try and make him better.

I didn't do any of that. I knew I shouldn't. I only looked at him.

He looked more like Sam than he ever had. It was the way his jaw was set, and the determination in his eyes, and the slight stoop so that the determination should not be misinterpreted. I couldn't help myself. I reached up and touched him lightly on the cheek.

This time he didn't avoid the contact.

'John's lucky to have you,' I said.

He smiled, and in that straight array of gleaming white teeth, I saw my Sam some more. 'We'd better hurry,' he said. 'It's going to start pelting down.'

At the cemetery's gate, we paused.

'Should I take you home?' I said.

He shook his head.

'A tube then?'

'No,' in a determined voice. 'If you don't mind,' he said, 'I'll make my own way back. I have some friends nearby. I think I might visit them.'

'I'll give you a lift.'

But he was adamant. 'Thanks,' he said. 'It's not far, and I like walking in the rain.'

I didn't press him. 'Fine,' I said. 'I'm going to Waterlow Park for a coffee. You want to join me?'

He did what I had predicted: shook his head. ''Bye then,' I said and, raising up on to tiptoes, kissed him lightly on each cheek and left.

I walked out of the gate and through the park until I was out of sight. I stopped and counted to ten. When that was over I went quietly back towards the park's entrance. I didn't need to go further than that to confirm my guess – that Matthew, once I was out of sight, would head back towards Sam's grave. I stood there, watching his teenage body, large but not yet entirely formed, loping his way deeper into the cemetery's grounds. I let him go.

Chapter
twenty-one

The rain had graduated from discrete to continuous. I was cold and wet. I walked through the nearly deserted park and into Lauderdale House. As I pushed through the glass doors leading to the self-serve counter, an inner door was opened. Kids came flooding out. Kids of all kinds, colours, ages – the only thing they had in common was that they were all loud. Sheepish adults followed but they didn't stand a chance: the kids were king, pushing and shoving to the front of the queue where they issued forth bawdy instructions as to which brand of sweet or cake they wanted.

I was no match for them. The first jabbed elbow in the small of my back and I was out of there. I walked round the elegant building and on to the pavement. The rain had built up and started sliding down my neck. Tom had phoned me that morning and we'd arranged to meet here; I didn't feel like driving soggy to Chelsea, only to return. I saw a queue of coaches lined up outside and, gambling that they were there to scoop up the kids, I made a quick decision. I let my car alone and walked, as fast as my wet shoes would take me, to the nearest newsagent. There I bought Sunday papers, most to read, plus one for my head, and then walked back.

Arriving back at Lauderdale House, I took a short cut through the long wood-floored gallery. Its walls were in full exhibition mode – jagged space age mountainscapes jostled against still lives composed almost entirely of teddy bear families. I tried not to look too hard. At the room's end I took a deep breath and pushed the door open.

My gamble had paid off. The place was almost entirely child free, the remaining snivelling stragglers in the process of being ushered out. I ordered a cappuccino and settled myself down. When my coffee arrived, I opened the first of the newspapers.

It was sheer luxury, the hour that followed. Against the occasional blast of cold as refugees burst in from the rain, I ploughed through acres of newsprint. By the end of it I had learned considerably more about the Royal Family's emotional problems than I considered strictly necessary but I had also sloughed off most of the uneasiness left by my visit to Sam's grave.

The noises had changed. I looked out and saw that the rain had stopped. I decided I needed air. I stepped out and then, sticking to the paths, did a couple of circuits around the park. It was beautiful, even on this disheartening day, the trees, their branches almost bare against the lushness of its undulating slopes.

Back in the restaurant I ordered a vegetable lasagne. It took some time to arrive and when it did it was pretty flavour free but it was hot and accompanied by an imaginative salad. After that, I ordered an espresso and a cheesecake that wouldn't have felt embarrassed in a Miami deli. I was just finishing up when a voice spoke directly into my ear. 'Struth,' it said. 'A sleuth.'

I looked up. Tom was standing by my chair. 'We're both early,' he said. 'Must be the nineties.'

I stood and we hugged. His body felt spongy against mine – what had once been a vaguely aspiring belly had grown into a fully fledged paunch. When we parted, I looked more closely. He had aged, but not unpleasantly.

The lines etched into his forehead gave him a solidity that his young face had lacked while the now predominantly grey hair looked more at peace than the original unkempt brown ever had.

'Power suits you,' I said. 'And fatherhood?'

He grimaced. 'The kid's great,' he said. 'But divorced parenthood's the pits. Don't ever try it.' He looked at me anxiously – afraid, I suppose, that he might inadvertently have offended childless me.

I moved us quickly on. 'Coffee?'

'Sure.' He sat down and spent some time arranging himself. What I had felt in his hug – a residue of discomfort – now seemed to be increased. He, who was normally relaxed to the point of insensitivity, was now incredibly edgy. He's just too big for the space, I told myself as he pushed the third chair away from the table, or else life has served him ill.

He caught me looking at him. He swallowed. 'Black, no sugar,' he said.

Since I was heading down caffeine poisoning alley anyway, I decided to go for broke and matched my order to his. When the coffee arrived we drank it slowly, exchanging news of what we'd each been doing. The purpose of the small chat was to help us relax in each other's company. The effect on me was the opposite. As the minutes ticked by my first uneasiness thickened into bewilderment. Tom's behaviour was definitely odd. For a man who prided himself on his sophistication, he was leaning forward too far, looking at me with eyes too suspiciously moist and laughing too loud at my occasional jokes. If it hadn't been a wet Sunday afternoon and in a public place to boot, I might have assumed that this was one big come on. But no, I frowned, Tom's success with women would hardly have been won by such obvious tactics as these.

Catching my frown, his face turned serious. 'Ready for

what I found out?' He didn't wait for my assent, he was already primed. He pulled a small reporter's notebook from his pocket, flicked through it until he came to a page, dated and covered with his own special shorthand hieroglyphics, cleared his throat and spoke: 'Agnes Wilson.'

Agnes had been my afterthought. My ears pricked up. Strange that Tom chose to start with her. Perhaps he'd found something really interesting.

But no: 'Nothing much known on her,' Tom said. 'Died 1991 aged sixty-four. Natural causes.'

So I was wrong: Tom had started with Agnes because, like all good journalists, he was going for a crescendo.

'Your man in the wheelchair,' he said. His voice was dutifully unengaged. 'You were quite right, Sarah tracked him down. Name of Gary Brown. GB for short. Which is relevant.' He glanced up briefly. 'You can imagine why.'

Thinking of the racist messages scrawled on the walls opposite Agnes's old flat, I nodded.

Tom was concentrating on his shorthand. 'Gary's a darling,' he said. 'There were quite a few old cuttings on him and the rest I got from a contact. Born 1950, he moved rapidly from truancy to shoplifting, to house robbery. He was a man with a mission – searching out his métier.' As Tom got into stride, his voice became more certain. Perhaps, I thought, I'd imagined the previous discomfort. 'Gary soon found what he was really good at,' Tom said. 'Intimidation. After a short freelance career which didn't really pay he began working for loan sharks. You know the kind of thing: give us our money or we'll mince your kids. Got greedy, stepped over the mark and ended up spending five years in Her Majesty's finishing school – Pentonville Prison. He came out ready for the big time. Toted himself around – "Freelance gun for hire, kneecapping my speciality" – while becoming something of a honcho in the local fascisti group. Had some hazy drug connection: took off to India at one point and on his return started boasting he'd soon be rich. But the power had gone to his head. Rumours are that he had crossed his fellow villains once too often. Result: one dark night at the end of 1986, a nasty accident and our Gary ends up paralysed.'

A dark night, a nasty accident, I heard. So did Tom; his words suddenly reverberated on him. He looked up, embarrassed.

'Go on,' I said.

Tom's upper lip appeared to have snagged on his lower teeth. 'There's not much more. Rumours are that Gary is still partial to a bit of major violence – he has henchmen to do the lightweight work but is wheeled out for the spectacular – but he hasn't stepped far enough out of line to attract the courts' attention.'

I nodded, trying to pretend I understood. Which in a sense I did – I understood the words. What I didn't understand was the undertone in Tom's voice and the weight with which he was investing his words. I saw a movement beyond us on the grass – a couple tussling laughingly with each other. I concentrated my eyes on them.

'And that's all,' I heard Tom saying, 'except . . .'

There it was – that hint of danger. I refocused my eyes and looked across the table. Tom was sitting perfectly still, his gaze averted. He frowned: it was almost, I thought, as if he were making up his mind about something. 'Except what?' I prompted.

I saw his forehead clearing: decision taken. 'Except when I was searching through the files, they jogged my memory. I remembered something.' Hesitation was converted suddenly to staccato fire. 'I remembered. You weren't the only person to ask me about Gary Brown. Nor the first.'

He'd lost me. 'Did you do something on him for the *Street Times* crime beat, perhaps?'

'No.' Tom shook his head, harder than was necessary. 'It was at the request of a friend. A long time ago.'

A long time ago. 'A friend,' I said. 'Who?'

Tom picked up his cup.

His nervousness had spread to me – it made me snap. 'You finished that a good ten minutes ago,' I said.

He let go of the cup. It fell. It landed on its saucer, so hard that both were smashed. The sound sliced through the background's murmured conversations. As slivers of whiteness skittered everywhere there was a sudden silence – all eyes were turned to us.

I cut them out. I leaned against the table and, covering Tom's hand with mine, halted his inept fumbling with the fragments. 'Which friend?' I asked, knowing it must be Carmen.

It wasn't Carmen. Tom, who was sweating profusely, did not try and remove his hand. He looked up, around, everywhere but at me. 'Smmmmmm.' It came out like that, loud but indistinct as if his mind had ordered what his mouth refused to do.

I felt no pity, only impatience. 'Who?'

'Sam.'

Sam? I yanked my hand away. Sam. So that explained Tom's moist eyes and his insistence that he could not fill me in over the phone. Tom, fearless in print, had always been scared of personal conflict but, like soldiers of old, had always felt it his duty to deliver bad news personally. *Sam.* No wonder Tom, who at the time had chosen to deal with my grief by cutting out all mention of Sam's death, was acting now as if he was in front of a firing squad.

Except I had no gun, only sheer incomprehension. 'When?'

'Just before he died.'

'Why?'

Tom swallowed. 'He never said. Just asked me to dig up the dirt. I was surprised . . .'

Of course he was surprised. My gentle Sam's main preoccupation had been topology, not East End hoods.

'. . . I told him what I knew. The same, essentially, as I've just told you.'

'And?'

At that moment the waitress came to sweep up the broken crockery. We watched her in silence until she had finished. 'Anything else?' she said cheerfully. I saw her eyes flick from me to Tom and back again. That apparently was enough: she beat a fast retreat.

'And?' I was almost shouting.

'That's all,' Tom said. 'Sam asked me to check Gary Brown out. He didn't tell me why, only that it was urgent. When I produced the stuff he thanked me and . . . and . . .'

I couldn't stand to wait while Tom flailed around, searching out the appropriate euphemism. 'And then somebody squashed him flat,' I said.

Tom winced. 'It *was* just before Sam's death,' he said. 'But what I was going to say was that . . . that he asked me not to tell you about this.'

I registered that sentence but let it bounce. I didn't have room for it. Thoughts were flashing through my brain. I couldn't deal with any of them. I pushed them all, save one, away. 'Did Sam ask about Agnes Wilson as well?' was the thought.

'No.' Tom was relieved he wasn't further implicated. And now he had unburdened himself he wanted out. 'I better' – he was already getting to his feet – 'be off.'

I smiled. 'Nice to see you,' I said. 'And thanks.'

He nodded and, bending down, kissed me lightly on the cheek. ''Bye Kate,' he said. 'Keep in touch.'

I disengaged then. I sat quietly, knowing that he had walked away. I sat . . . blankly.

He hadn't gone. 'Be careful,' I heard him saying.

I looked up frowning. I had no idea what careful had to do with anything.

'Two accidents,' Tom said. 'Sam's and Gary's. Don't make it three.'

Chapter
twenty-two

I drove, fast, to Chelsea, trying to concentrate on the route and not the encroachment of disturbing thoughts. Without much success: questions kept lunging through my hurriedly constructed defences. Questions like, what had Sam been up to, using Tom – *my* source – and not telling me? I turned a corner, tyres squealing. The only connection between Gary Brown and me was Agnes Wilson, but what had Sam known of her?

A light turned red: I braked hard. I was trembling. I pulled the hand brake on and gripped the steering wheel, trying to calm myself down. I could not however stop the questions. I sat wondering whether I had told Sam about Agnes. I couldn't remember – I couldn't remember anything except the events directly surrounding Sam's death. If I were to make a guess, I suppose I might have told him – in that everyday, passing sort of way in which we used to unload our days. I felt tears sting my eyes.

The lights went green. I sat there, sluggish. Behind me someone hit their horn. I released the hand brake and began to drive, much more slowly now. Depression slithered in, edging urgency out. *Two accidents*, I heard Tom saying, and for the first time since it had happened, I wondered whether Sam's death had really been an accident.

By the time I reached Chelsea, something deeper than

depression had taken over. I felt it surging – the harbinger of my old despair, secreting numbness, disbelief, deadness.

Deadness: I thought of Roger Toms's photograph of Sam, of Sam's face, smiling and alive, and superimposed on this another image – that memory that I had so effectively kept hidden from myself – my last view of Sam. Not the Sam who had left the flat muttering something I didn't believe about needing to go out, the Sam who had smiled and dismissed my questions and kissed me, lightly, on the lips. Not that Sam. The other. That lifeless, inhuman thing arranged on a gleaming steel platform, that sickly waxen skin, too tough surely to be my Sam's?

I pushed the front door open. It was that time just before dusk neither light nor dark but gloomy. I began flicking switches – the alarm, off, all the lights I passed, on. I needed their brightness, it drove out memory of Sam. I was no longer listless. I went through every room, moving furiously, until the whole house was ablaze. I was in the sitting room. I sank down into one of Pam's plush sofas.

With a passing roll of its voice the cat jumped into my lap. When I did not eject it, it settled down, purring. I sat there, staring at Maria and Jurek's immaculately restored wall, stroking its silky back. I was left with one question, the worst of all: had Sam's death somehow been my fault?

It was not the first time that I had asked this question of myself. Could I have done something, I had thought in the weeks that followed his dying, to stop him from going out? I had, after all, protested, had told him that it was too wet, too windy to set off. But I had also, when he insisted, been too preoccupied by some petty TV programme to dissuade him. So he had gone and in going had got himself killed.

'It's my fault.' Those were the words I'd said when they came to tell me.

A hundred voices had drowned me out. And not only voices, the books that I read also, about mourning and its phases which spoke of the inevitability and the fantasy of guilt.

I had believed the voices and the books, had stilled my own doubt that what Sam had done that evening had been completely out of character. And now?

And now Matthew had burnished the guilt for me by telling me that John Layton blamed me for Sam's death.

John Layton. He was nothing to me. Nothing. I wouldn't have it. Pushing the cat off, I jumped to my feet. I wouldn't stand for this. I would not be pulled back into all those doubts that I had long discarded. I had mourned for Sam. He was dead. It was over. Over.

I was quite determined. What had provoked the stirring of this useless retrospection was my decision to visit London. I should never have come; I certainly should never have let Pam Willis, of all people, persuade me that it would be all right.

I sped round the room, clicking off lights. That was it – cat or no cat – I was going. I was allowed: Pam had come up with a solution to the cat problem. Who was it that she had said? Oh yes. Mona Hanson. Number in Greg's book.

I took the stairs, two at a time. In Greg's study, I grabbed his address book and, having located the right number, dialled. When a woman answered, I was brisk. 'Mona Hanson?'

'Speaking.'

'This is Kate Baeier. I'm staying at the Willises'. Pam said I could leave the cat with you?'

A moment's hesitation and then: 'Now?'

I told her no, I would deliver it to her first thing tomorrow. I took her address – she lived a block away – thanked her and said goodbye.

There, that was done. The cat disposed of. Now for me.

I climbed the next flight of stairs, pulled my suitcase from its storage space above the cupboard and began to pack. It didn't take me long – constant travelling had reduced my possessions to an essential minimum bulked out this time by a few sweaters most of which I could soon discard. Then I did a little extra food shopping. We ate by candle light, the cat and I. While I picked at gravadlax and salad, it mauled a huge dish of lightly poached white fish. I know which I preferred but the cat seemed elated with its lot. It wasn't as smart as I had thought. The exigencies of its stomach were too dominant; it didn't seem to understand that we were about to part. Unless of course that all the purring was because it not only understood but also approved. Either way, I no longer cared – the cat was a phase which had now passed on.

It wasn't so easy with Anna. I had phoned her and told her of my decision. I hadn't told her why – I didn't want her in there, messing with my psyche – but I think she must have guessed it had something to do with Sam. She insisted on locating an emergency babysitter and coming round – not to dissuade me, she said, but to see some more of me before I left.

And of course, when she arrived, she did try and dissuade me. She used the full range of her considerable powers – charm, anger, subterfuge – to try and make sense of my decision. I blocked her as best I could and we ended up speaking in metaphor, debating, as if this was no real concern to us, whether it was possible to change the past.

I held stiffly to my position – that what had happened was gone – while she danced around something much more intangible – a dialectical interaction between past and present which, as far as I was concerned, had everything to do with wishful thinking and nothing to do with reality. When I made this clear she backed off. I suppose she didn't want to give me the excuse of cutting out what had so recently been fostered between us.

'You will keep in touch,' she said firmly, as she left.

I nodded. I meant it. I would keep in touch, I thought, would even agree to meet her on neutral territory. That way this visit would not have been total disaster.

I spent a couple of hours tidying up the house. I'd made little impact on it. It was pretty clean and would be cleaned again before the Willises' return, but I wanted to be extra sure that everything was in place. As I went I made a list of consumables that needed replacing. I left it on the kitchen counter, picked up the cat, took it with me to the bedroom, and went to bed.

I had ten minutes before I went to sleep, reliving my conversation with Anna. Although intellectually I still stuck to the position I had taken, I didn't like myself either for that opinion or for the way I had pushed Anna off. In fact, I thought as sleep came closer, I didn't particularly like myself at all.

I yawned and rolled over. What difference did it make? Life was about movement and action. Liking did not come into it.

Chapter

twenty-three

Monday morning found me with a surfeit of energy. I woke early and, pushing the duvet back, sprang out of bed. Too fast – the cat, which had been lying nestled by my legs, got caught up in the covers. It hissed and, clawing its way out, fixed reproachful eyes on me.

I refused to feel guilty. 'You'll be all right,' I told it. 'Mona Hanson will feed you as well as I did and, anyway, Pam will soon be back.'

It opened its mouth but no sound emerged. I shrugged and, humming to myself, walked off. I was in an excellent mood. I was doing what I had come to love – leaving.

But first I had a loose end to tie. I reached for the phone and dialled my editor's number.

He answered fast and brisk. 'Yes?'

I copied his style. 'Kate,' I said. 'Did you get the article?'

'Kate.' A moment's lifting of the voice to signify pleasure and then back to curt. 'Came in the post. Fine. Good. Had to change the sub head of course.'

'The sub head?' He'd lost me.

'Your brief was violence,' he said.

Which is what I thought I had written: the effects of long-term violence.

Obviously not: 'But grief is fine,' he said.

Grief? Is that what I wrote?

His telegram was running on. 'It will provoke discussion,' he said. 'Want another commission?'

'Love one,' I said. 'But no can do. I'm leaving town.'

Nothing surprised him. 'Going anywhere good?'

It was an interesting question. I sat there, thinking that what I wanted was life and sun – and it being almost December that meant I wanted the southern hemisphere.

'Brazil's cooking,' I heard him saying.

Brazil. Now that sounded interesting.

'If you do get there, fax me. Could be a series in it.'

A series. Even better.

'Let me know.' He was fading on me. 'Cheque's on its way to your bank. *Bon voyage.*' Click. He was gone.

There – my business in London disposed of. I showered and dressed and, having eaten, phoned my travel agent. That was when I hit the first hitch.

'No can do,' she said. She rattled off a list of airlines she had contacted. 'Now tomorrow, well, that's different. I can get you on a flight then.'

What choice did I have? I agreed.

'Ticket will be waiting at the airport,' she sang and hung up.

I phoned Pam's friend Mona and told her the cat would be delivered a day late. She didn't sound like she cared either way. That done, I went upstairs to check that my papers were in order.

The files – the ones that Carmen had given me – distracted me. They were lying by my packed bags, the only disruption to the immaculate room. I stood there, staring at them, wondering what I was going to do with them.

It didn't take me long to work that out. I'd simply chuck them. I nodded. It was a fitting end. They were about the past and this visit had all been about burying the past. If I had the energy, I thought, I could even do that – dig a hole and bury them.

Not now though. I didn't have the energy now. I picked them up.

Half an hour later, I found myself sitting on the bed, the files strewn around me. I didn't know what had happened. No, that's wrong, I knew what – I had been rooting through the files and with them ancient memories – what I didn't know was why. I tried to tell myself that it didn't matter why. I would soon be gone. I began to bundle up the files.

And ended with Agnes Wilson's on top. I looked at it, and tried to turn away. It had me hypnotized, a job unfinished. I kept on looking until eventually I opened up. And found there the papers I'd collected on my various trips. I pulled them out.

My better judgement fled. Why not? I thought, it's something to do. I was doing it already, collating the names I'd got at Companies House with the details I'd obtained at the business library. I soon had a definitive list: six Permog directors with clues as to their whereabouts. Using the phone book, I began to work my way through them.

Of the six names I'd started with, one I completely failed to locate, one had gone to live in Spain, a third was in hospital and numbers four and five, although both well and in the country, were unavailable to speak to me. Which left number six, Harold Grayson, a soft-talking courteous gent who, although his voice stiffened considerably when I mentioned the name of Permog, ended up saying I could pop along and interview him in person.

He lived in Kensington in a mansion flat guarded by a suspicious doorman who grudgingly ushered me over to the lift. On the sixth floor, a stern housekeeper took over. She told me that Mr Grayson's health was delicate and that he should not be provoked, and then she admitted me reluctantly into his inner sanctum.

He didn't look delicate. He was sitting in a high-backed green leather chair, his eyes bright, his cheeks a rosy red.

'Ms Baeier,' he said. 'Come in.' He seemed very anxious to have me in, conducting me irritably with his hand when he thought that I was hesitating.

I wasn't hesitating, I was just taking in the room. It was a sight that warmed the eyes, the closest I had ever come to a human cocoon. Everything was toned to match, all dark earthy colours – the walls brick-red, the paintwork matching, the carpet a neutral beige on which a succession of dark red Turkomans had been laid.

'Sit. Sit.' He was getting tetchy.

I sat where he had indicated, in a high-backed chair that, matching his, was placed adjacent to it. He was staring at me so I, too, took a closer look. He was older than I had first assumed, his face enveloped by a myriad tiny lines that this fevered room had, from a distance, done much to conceal.

When he smiled, the lines smiled with him. 'Refreshments please, Helen,' he said.

'Tea.' It was a statement, not a question.

Which was quickly rebuffed. 'Oh no. Ms Baeier will have brandy.' His gaze was steady, his blue eyes locked on me: 'You will, won't you, Ms Baeier?'

I could take a hint. I said yes. Having vented a huff of disapproval the housekeeper left.

'I'm not supposed to drink,' he said when she was gone. 'But I do so like the sight of a grand mark Remy and, besides, I see no reason why, after my death, the vultures should be allowed to pick over my cellar.' He broke off abruptly.

The housekeeper was back, bringing with her a small side table and on it, a decanter and a single brandy glass. I looked at the arrangement, my stomach doing a double dip as I realized that I hadn't yet eaten.

'That will be all.' He could make his voice waspish if he wanted. It worked. The housekeeper disappeared.

I was beginning to understand. I looked at Harold Grayson. He looked at the decanter.

'You don't want any, do you?' His eyes did not waver.

'Not really.'

Which is what he had expected. 'Well, go on then,' he urged, his tongue darting out to lick a dry lip. 'Pass it over.'

I frowned.

'Look here, Ms Baeier,' he said. 'I'm dying. Literally. No, don't look so serious. It happens to us all. In my case I'd rather go happy than last an extra day which is all the old bat will achieve by denying me my only remaining pleasure. Come on, hand it over.'

I did as he requested. I sat watching as he poured himself a large slug into the balloon glass. He was practically salivating but still he took his time. He put the decanter gently down and held the glass between his hands, swilling the liquid round, sticking his nose close to sniff occasionally at it. And then, only after he had warmed it well, did he tip the glass back and take the merest sip.

'Ah.' A sigh of complete satisfaction. 'That's better.' He sat still, staring down into the glass.

I didn't feel like coming between a man and his love. I sat in silence watching him.

He took another sip, rolling this one along his tongue. Then, reluctantly, he put the glass down. 'I'm afraid I'm an old fraud,' he said. 'This' – he pointed at the glass – 'is the reason I agreed to see you.'

I smiled. 'I guessed as much.'

'She keeps it under lock and key,' he said. 'Only way I get it released is when I have a visitor. Only reason I tolerate visitors at all. Otherwise I can do without the encroachment of the world.' He blinked. 'Present company excepted.' This thrown out blankly, without much conviction.

I didn't care. I was there for one thing only. 'Permog.'

'Oh. Yes. You mentioned it on the phone. Something to do with me?'

I nodded and, pulling out a photostat of his name at the end of the company's most recent accounts, I handed it to him. He made a great play of placing half-moon spectacles at the end of his nose and peering through them, but what he said was just as vague. 'Ah. Yes. That's me all right.' He took the glasses off and then his hand went slack, the paper fluttering to the ground.

I picked it up and packed it away. 'Make a habit of forgetting companies which went bankrupt?' I said.

His answer was surprisingly loud. 'My dear young lady.' And snappish as well. 'I don't normally make a habit of forgetting anything deliberately. But this was a grace and favour appointment. I wasn't even on the board for long.'

I knew, from the previous years' accounts, that he was speaking the truth. I nodded.

'It does seem callous,' he said, slightly apologetic. 'But I'm afraid I don't remember much about the company. Clothing firm, you said?'

I nodded.

'Can't say I even visited it.' He reached for his brandy glass and reinstituted his elaborate swilling routine.

I waited until he had taken a few sips and put it down again. 'Remember who invited you on to the board?' I asked.

He flinched and looked, startled, in my direction: it was almost as if he had forgotten that I was there. But he hadn't forgotten what we were talking about. 'Let me see.' His nose wrinkled. 'A young man, I think. Good shoes. Not his company. He was a general factotum. Company accountant perhaps?' He shook his head. 'No – not accountant. Something else. Good eye though. Identified the Turkomans and told me something of their history I didn't know. Had travelled a lot, he said, in the Asian sub continent. Funny chap. Saw him only once or twice.' The brandy was in his hands again. He raised it up.

I spoke fast. 'So you don't know anything about Permog's pension scheme?'

'Sorry.' He only looked sorry that I was spoiling his enjoyment. He shrugged. 'That's all I know.'

And that was all I was going to get. I sat there watching him savouring his brandy until I got bored. Then I stood up.

'You're going? Stay awhile.'

I stood patiently until he had swallowed the last drop. Then I offered him my hand.

He took it and pressed it uninterestedly. 'Goodbye,' he said. 'So nice to meet you.' His eyes closed.

His housekeeper must have been listening. When I opened the door she was waiting to walk me out.

'Get what you wanted?' she asked.

I shrugged. 'I'm not sure what I wanted.'

After the musky closeness of Harold Grayson's flat, the outside felt refreshingly cold. I stood breathing it in, experiencing freedom. I've done it, I thought. I've tried my best. And found nothing. And it didn't matter. I wasn't a detective any more: I didn't have to prove myself.

I stood, pushing Agnes Wilson out of my head, making myself a plan. Now that I was leaving, there were things I had to buy and Kensington was as good a place as any. I drew up a mental list.

But didn't immediately move. I had that feeling, that sensation I'd had before, that somebody was watching me. I felt it strongly, a kind of creeping up my neck, a feeling that whoever the somebody was, he was not benevolent. I looked about me. All I saw were strangers bustling through their busy lives. Maybe it's Harold, I thought, looking up. But the mansion block was still and quiet, no chink in any curtain.

You're imagining it, I told myself and, walking briskly down the road, I headed for the shops and consumer oblivion.

Chapter
twenty-four

I prised my eyes open. I was lying at an odd angle. I'd slept deeply but not calmly – I was spread out across the bed, the sheets rumpled and falling off. I stretched my hand out and grabbed my watch.

It was gone eight. I had overslept. I felt sluggish. I dragged myself into the bathroom and immersed my face in a basin of cold water. I came up only marginally more awake. I needed something even more extreme. I turned the shower full on, cold.

When that was over, I was definitely conscious. I dried myself and, having packed my toothbrush, I dressed casual – jeans, a T-shirt, a jumper and an extra pair of socks for my travelling bag. I stripped the bed and bundled the sheets up with the used towels. I was efficiency personified. I knew exactly what I had left to do – the laundry, the resupplying of the house and the moving of the cat – and then I could be gone.

The cat: I hadn't seen it that morning. I glanced around the room, wondering where it could be. No luck. Oh well. It was probably hiding somewhere, sulking because it knew I was going. I walked to the door and stretched out a hand.

I froze. What I had been intending to do – demobilize the alarm – was no longer necessary. The alarm was already switched off.

I hadn't done it. I was sure of that. Panic engulfed me. I stood rooted to the spot, as a memory of the man who'd stalked me through the house returned. What if he was here again? What if he'd never gone?

The thought was so ridiculous it brought me to my senses. It was daylight, after all, and I was fine. There was no one in the house. No one but me.

I knew what must have happened. I'd had too much to drink the night before and had forgotten to switch on the alarm. Yes – I felt myself relax – that was it. Opening the bedroom door, I called out for the cat.

It didn't answer. Definitely sulking, I decided, and leaving the door open I went downstairs. I shoved the washing into the machine, put the kettle on, tucked two pieces of bread into the toaster, and got out some marmalade.

Marmalade, I thought. Must add it to my shopping list. I looked around for the one I'd made the night before. But it was missing. The kitchen counters were as clean as I had left them – except no list. I frowned. I must have left it somewhere.

My brain was still fuzzy, despite the cold shower. I made myself a cup of strong coffee and drank it down, using the toast to take the edge off the caffeine rush. There, that was better. I could mobilize.

The list, I thought. Upstairs. I made my way upstairs. The sitting-room door was closed. I had done my drinking there the night before, I must have left the list inside. I opened the door.

The room was quiet, and as neat as I had left it. The list was nowhere in sight.

Perhaps I dropped it, I thought, beside the sofa. I walked across the pale pink carpeting which absorbed the sound of my approach. Not that it mattered. What lay behind the sofa was oblivious to sound.

At first all I saw was fur. The cat's fur. Lying by the sofa's edge. I was frowning. How did it get in here? I thought. The door was closed. My mind was one step behind my body. I was upon the cat before I realized that the way it was lying, its limbs sprawled out, wasn't right. I bent down.

The cat was still. Like a Noh mask its life's end grinned up at me. The cat was dead.

Long dead. It was cold, its blood congealed. Its blood that had spread out from the gash around its neck, staining the carpet. The knife that had done the job had not been removed. It was there, piercing the cat, a skewer through a torn-off piece of paper. I yanked at the knife. There was a slow sucking sound and then I had the paper, stained blood-red, in my hands.

One side was familiar: the list that I had left in the kitchen the night before, its domestic vocabulary now smeared by red slime. I turned it over. On the other side just two words: *You're next.*

What happened next was out of my control. The contents of my stomach went spewing out. In an almost elegant arch it fell, although when it landed on the cat it was far from elegant. The sight set me off again. I stood there retching.

When it was finally over and I had stopped gagging, I went downstairs. I fetched kitchen towel, cloth and hot water and took them to the living room. I knelt beside the cat, gently wiping it down. The stench – my vomit mixed with its excrement – was almost unbearable but the cat was dead and I had to bear it. I wiped it, stroking its stiff cold body until it was clean.

'It's all my fault,' I said.

Its eyes, glassy and open, stared unseeing. It had no eyelids – I could not close them. I found a cardboard shoe box, lined it with a tea towel, and gently, gently laid the cat inside. And then, only when the lid was closed, did I begin to take stock of what had happened.

I knew exactly what had happened. Someone had got into the house and killed the cat. The same someone who had got in twice before. Who knew how to immobilize the alarm – I had left it on – and who, last night, had entered the house, come into my bedroom, removed the cat, taken it downstairs, killed it, found my note, skewered it and left.

And all that time, I had been asleep.

That was the last coherent thought I had before I found myself on a crumbling Camden Road doorstep. As I thumped at the already splintered wood the morning traffic went thundering past. Knock harder, I told myself and, pulling my arm back, prepared for a second assault.

'Katherine.' Jurek was there suddenly, on the doorstep, dressed in the faded silk of an Ivory/Merchant Polish count. 'Katherine.' I felt vaguely reassured that he'd gone back to the long form of my name. 'What are you doing here?'

My mouth was shut tight.

'You look bloody awful,' he said.

I half walked, half stumbled in.

'Coffee.' Jurek announced. 'That will help.' I was too far gone to protest. I let him lead me into the ground-floor room that, with a two ring burner and a porcelain sink, served as a kitchen and bathroom combined.

And as it turned out, Jurek was right: his coffee did help. It was the modern equivalent, I suppose, of a hefty dose of smelling salts: one whiff and language came. 'I can't possibly drink that,' I said.

I really must have looked bad. All Jurek said was: 'Tea?'

I nodded.

'And toast.'

The memory of the toast I had consumed, spraying in slow motion over the cat, came back to me. I shook my head.

That was too much for Jurek. 'But, Katherine,' he protested, 'you must eat.'

The continued shaking of my head silenced even him. He'd dealt with a lot in his lifetime but my autism was too much. When the door opened behind me, I saw his eyes light up in relief.

'Kate.' A soft voice. Maria's voice. She didn't waste time.

She came up to me and put her arms around me. She was tiny, a good few inches smaller than me, but she held my weight. And held on to me, with all the strength of her determination, just as she had done once so long before.

And just as I had then, I started weeping – although that's where the similarity ended. The time before I'd been crying out my fear, my anger, my contempt of my own powerlessness: this time my tears were quieter. And focused as well. I knew why I was crying. I was grieving not only for the cat, but also for the person who had died before it. I felt Maria holding me and I remembered the cat's unnatural rigidity and Sam's body stiff against steel and I wept the more. I had failed, I thought, to protect the cat just as I had once failed to protect Sam. I had been oblivious, too caught up in my own petty concerns to stop Sam going out. Just like now: I'd been too caught up in sleep to stop someone opening my bedroom door and taking away the cat.

I hiccupped.

'Come,' Maria said and led to me to a chair.

I sat where I was put and sipped dutifully at the glass of water that was laid gently into my cupped hand. I was no longer crying. I put the glass down. 'What am I going to tell Pam?'

Silence until: 'It wasn't your fault,' Maria said.

She was wrong. I might not understand what it was that had happened, but somewhere in the back of my mind I knew it was my fault.

I shook my head. I wasn't going to worry about that – not now. I had something else to do. 'Will you help me bury the cat?' I said.

They nodded.

Chapter
twenty-five

We were in the garden, standing under the ornamental cherry's threadlike branches. Jurek was in charge of ritual. In front of us was the hole he had dug, perfectly sized and perfectly rectangular. The box was in his hand.

As I watched he removed the top, glanced quickly inside and then just as quickly re-covered it.

He caught me looking at him. 'It is strange,' he said. He blushed.

It was strange, I thought, to see Jurek embarrassed.

'No matter that I have seen much dying,' he said, 'death of this dumb animal still has the capacity to shock.'

Dumb? I thought, ready to take offence. But then: 'It was dumb,' I admitted, half smiling, remembering the cat's many idiosyncracies. For a house pet it had been an odd creature – the way it sneaked around, the way it slunk off with its food, the way . . .

I cut the thought mid stream – what had accompanied it was just too dangerous. It wasn't the right time.

Jurek handed me the box.

I was beginning to feel faintly ridiculous. This was too solemn a ceremony for that streetwise cat. I knelt and laid it in the hole.

'Ready?'

I nodded. When I stepped out of the way, Jurek took my place. He began shovelling in dirt, covering the box.

Streetwise. The word repeated on me. I tried to push it off, to force my brain into quiescence. Without effect. My suspicions would not let go.

Since I didn't have a choice, I let them take control. And found that the more I let them in, the more sense they made.

I turned abruptly and began walking towards the house.

'Kate?'

That was rude of me. I stopped.

'Shall I mark the site so your friend would know?' Jurek said.

I didn't think it mattered. Not any longer. 'I have to go out,' I said.

They looked briefly at each other and then again at me. I knew what they thought: they thought I was in shock.

Which in a sense I was. 'I won't be long,' I said. 'Will you wait?'

Of course they would. I walked back into the house, went upstairs, washed my face, powdered it with enough blusher to give at least a hint of colour, brushed my hair and left the house.

I rang Mona Hanson's doorbell, short and sharp. In the time it took her to answer, I practised smiling. It wasn't easy. My lips were rigid; lifting them meant lifting the entire lower half of my face. Which is how she found me, grimacing terribly.

She kept a firm grip on the door. 'Yes?'

'I'm Kate Baeier,' I said, 'Pam's friend,' thinking that if what I imagined turned out to be true, then Pam was no friend of mine.

'Oh yes,' Mona said. Her hand relaxed. 'You've brought the cat.' She looked down, expecting to find its box.

'It won't be coming.'

Her eyes, confused, focused back on me.

'It's dead,' I said.

'Oh dear.' Her jaw went slack. 'I'm sorry.'

She did sound sorry. And surprised. Which meant that whatever had gone on, she was probably just an innocent bystander.

Even so, I couldn't let her off the hook. I thought of the cat's eating habits. 'Lucky it was only a stray,' I said.

She wasn't going to be that easy. Her echo, 'A stray . . .' was halfway between a question and a statement.

I went one further. 'Quite a charade Pam involved us in,' I said. 'Pretending that the cat was hers.'

It didn't work. Although uncertainty flitted across Mona Hanson's face, her mouth stayed shut. I needed another way of getting the truth out of her. Bullying was no good – if I tried that, she'd just clam up. Think, I told myself, think. What currency would Pam have used to buy this woman's complicity?

I looked away. I looked at the fenced park across the road, its railings gleaming, its lawn immaculate, picked bare of falling leaves. Life's so safe here, I thought.

And got it then – what Pam might have said. I turned to face her. I smiled. 'I know Pam only did it to make me feel at ease.'

The settling of Mona Hanson's uncertain frown made me know that I was right.

'Pam thought I needed somewhere to stay, didn't she?' I said. 'And she thought I was too proud to accept. So she went to all that trouble – finding a street cat, giving it a home.'

I was still living in a gentler world. I said the words, hoping they would be denied.

But of course they weren't. Instead: 'That's Pam all over,' Mona said. 'She's so considerate.'

*

Maria and Jurek were in the sitting room, on their hands and knees, scrubbing at the carpet.

'Don't bother,' I said.

They looked up, startled. I turned my head. I gazed around the calm pink room. It was so perfect. Like the rest of the house. It made me wonder. What if . . .

My thoughts were crystal clear. I fetched the phone directory and was in furious motion, whipping the pages back, one after the other, until I found the one I wanted. My finger sped down the list, stopping finally dead centre, middle column.

I punched in the number.

'Scots and Lacey,' a plush voice answered.

'This is Kate B. Willis,' I said. B as in Baeier, Willis as in Liar. 'Remember me?'

'Of course. The Friedrich.'

'That's it.' I was all efficiency. 'I'm checking on Pam's drawing-room maroon. Is it ready?'

Apparently not. 'Mrs Willis stated quite specifically,' he said, indignantly, 'that the paint would not be required until after her return from the Caribbean. I cannot tolerate . . .'

What I couldn't tolerate was his whining. 'It's OK,' I said. 'I'm just double-checking. How about the carpet?'

He was insulted at the very suggestion. 'We do not deal in carpeting.' His voice moved from irate to glacial. 'Mrs Willis ordered the grey twist from Kemble's.'

So I was right.

'If Mrs Willis has a problem . . .'

'Thank you,' I said. I hung up.

I looked around. And spoke out loud.

'The only room that ever came to harm,' I said. 'Was this one. The one about to be redecorated in maroon and grey fleck. Must have been part of the bargain.'

'Bargain?' Jurek looked at me as if I were mad.

I did feel slightly mad. 'You know the kind of thing,' I said. 'Scare the shit out of Kate, sacrifice the about-to-be-changed drawing room if you have to but don't muck up the rest of the bloody décor.' My voice was loud. 'I was set up. By Pam. She got the cat as a reason to persuade me that she needed me here. And then she gave somebody else her personal alarm's code – the one I couldn't change. That's how he got in and out.'

'He?'

Good question. I didn't know who. I knew it was a man – the photograph of the naked woman proved that. I scrolled through my options. Not the man in the wheelchair, I thought, he wouldn't have been able to climb the stairs. And not Greg either – he was with Pam.

I stopped trying to name the man. Something else was nagging at me. I thought of Pam. I remembered her as she had been on the Rumanian border – her tailored suit, the scent of her expensive perfume, her loving smile. And then I thought about her recent call and the tension in her voice. She'd been trying to get me out.

It made no sense. First she persuaded me to stay, then to go?

Unless . . . Unless someone else was pulling Pam's strings. Someone telling her what to do.

I bulldozed the thought. To look for blame elsewhere would let Pam, good old considerate Pam, off the hook.

I was on my feet, furious. I wanted to hit out. I leaned down, picked up the bucket of reddened water and, swinging my arm in a wide arc, flung it. 'I'll give her redecoration,' I said. The water splashed against the perfect pink paint job, staining it dark before the bucket landed on the phone.

The phone. Greg was involved as well. I remembered Pam during those nights at the border, talking urgently to England. Now I knew what she'd been doing: she'd been phoning Greg, working out a way to lure me into their house. Greg had probably invented the cat riff, I thought: Pam was too bloody genteel.

A disembodied voice sounded. 'Please replace the . . .' I killed the phone, yanking the cord, pulling it out of the wall.

All this trickery to get me here – and then these warnings to make me leave. What kind of sucker did they take me for?

I wasn't finished, not yet. I went storming out of the room and down the stairs. In the kitchen I grabbed a bottle of wine and used it as a baseball bat, my targets a conveniently close row of glasses which shattered as I swept the bottle along.

'Kate!' They'd followed me down and were standing open mouthed by the door.

I was feeling better and I wasn't even finished. I opened another cupboard and began removing plates, the specially glazed, specially commissioned dinner-party plates that Pam probably produced for minor royalty. One by one I took them, held them high above my head and then let go. One by one, one after the other. Until that is, the last of the set was gone.

There. I breathed out. That was better.

A voice, Maria's voice, stiff with disapproval, sounded behind me. 'Are you done?'

Done? Yes I was. I dusted my hands, one against the other. 'Yes I am,' I said, save only . . .

I picked my way carefully through the debris. Maria was standing in my way. I circumvented her.

The violence was gone out of me. I climbed the stairs and fetched my suitcase. On the way down, I stopped at Greg's study.

Pam had been so efficient, leaving their contact fax number visible in case anything should go wrong.

Go wrong. Funny.

I didn't laugh. I typed a message, short and sweet: 'Your drawing-room maroon is ready. The cat's buried in the garden. The alarm's off. Kate.' I made a copy of what I'd typed and sent it. I waited for the bleep which told me the machine had cleared and then, with copy in hand, I got out of there.

Chapter
twenty-six

My new room was not nearly as luxurious as the one I had just vacated. It was in the attic, above Maria and Jurek's, a vast unconverted space that could have done with a little more paint and a lot more heat. There was no cupboard. To show that I meant business I unpacked my clothes and hung them over the rafters. There: room decorated.

I went down the rickety stairs and joined Jurek in eating a Polish equivalent of brunch. After that I began phoning.

I phoned Anna to tell her that I was staying in London.

She sounded pleased until I told her that I was staying with people she'd never met. After that her question: 'You didn't feel like staying with me?' was delivered on a crescendo as sharp as Tom Parsons'.

I tried to explain that I was safer where I was – that whatever was happening was connected to a past to which Maria and Jurek did not belong – but I don't think she believed me. She was quite persistent: by the time I hung up, I wasn't sure I believed myself. She was probably right: my resistance to staying with her probably did owe more to my fear of the closeness we had once had than to considerations of personal safety.

I pushed the thought away. This was no time to dwell on the convoluted workings of my psyche. This was time for action. I had no present in Britain: I had to assume that what had happened was connected to my past. I picked up the receiver and dialled again.

My call to the pensions registry was only marginally more successful. No matter what I said, the woman went on repeating that all requests were dealt with in strict rotational order. And she meant it: applying pressure only made her more resistant. I changed tactics and by going into full pleading mode defrosted her slightly. We were, however, talking deep, deep freeze: all I really wrested from her was a reluctant half-promise that she would see what she could do. Which I dare say, I thought as I hung up, was the way she usually approached the job.

I phoned Carmen but got her answerphone. It didn't feel right to leave a message – certainly not the message I felt like leaving – so I hung up.

Dead end.

But I wouldn't let it beat me. I wasn't going to wait around for the pension forms to pitch up – only to find that they told me nothing. I thought about what I should do next.

If I had no leads, I thought, I'd better make my own.

I got up. 'I'm off,' I said to Jurek.

Which delayed me considerably. He insisted that I tell him precisely where I was going, what I was going to do and when I would be back. I refused: I'd had this battle before, with Sam, and I told Jurek what I had once told Sam – that his urge to protect me would only make me vulnerable. Jurek, just like Sam had done, felt it his duty to remonstrate with me but, unlike Sam, he didn't know when to stop. It got quite heated and only Maria's considerable negotiating skills left Jurek and I at least as partial friends. To achieve this, I had, of course, to give some ground. I had to give them the general drift of my proposed activities and agree to ring if I was going to be longer than three hours. When I grudgingly consented, I was released.

*

It was my third visit to the Kings Cross estate. Each time I had come, I liked it less. This time I stood, hesitating, outside its gate. There were two possibilities – a second visit either to the wheelchair king, Gary Brown, or to the woman who lived in Agnes's flat.

The woman, I knew, didn't want me there and, having met Gary Brown, I thought I knew why. I didn't want to put her at risk, but, on the other hand, having met Gary Brown, I was hesitant about going back. So I was selfish. I chose the woman.

I went through the gates. It was like stepping into a paranoid bubble. As I walked under the arch, that feeling of being watched returned. I told myself that this was impossible – that they had no lookout posted there. I kept on walking, across the courtyard, up the stairs.

The balcony that lead to her flat was empty. I hurried along to its end and banged hard against the door. I heard her fumbling with the spy-hole cover. I waited patiently. And waited after that as well.

She was there, I was sure of it, standing by the door, but she wasn't going to answer.

'It's Kate Baeier,' I called. 'I came before.'

Silence.

'Please open up,' I said. 'All I want –'

Two words, an order: 'Go away!' cut across what I was going to say. The fear that underlined them was unmistakable. And infectious – it hooked my paranoia. I found myself looking furtively around.

I was alone. I was sure of that. I moved closer to the door. 'There's nobody here,' I said. 'Not as far as I can tell.'

'Go away.' Louder now.

'All I want is a lead to Agnes Wilson. Anything – a friend, a different relative, somebody she worked with . . . anything like that.'

A bang. She was hitting the door with something metallic. She followed through with a repetition: 'Go away.'

I gave it one last try. I leant down as if to tie my sneakers and as I did so I started whispering. 'I know you're scared,' I whispered. 'But don't let those bastards terrorize you. What I'm doing is important. If you want to help me I'll be waiting outside.' I named a street nearby. 'In a red Renault.' I whispered its number plate. 'Please. Help me if you can. I'll be waiting,' and having untied and tied my sneakers again I got up.

'Go away,' I heard. I went.

I was on the last flight of stairs, heading round the corner, when two men materialized. They came from nowhere. One minute I was alone and the next I was facing them. They stood, about five steps down, blocking my way. They were almost identical: in their mid twenties, with hair shorn close against white scalps, wearing jeans, open-necked white shirts and ugly scowls on ugly, scarred faces.

I stopped moving.

'What's the matter?' one sneered. 'The Paki too scared to talk to you?'

'She can't speak English, can she?' jeered the other.

I stood my ground.

They directed their poison at me. 'Piss off, cunt.' This from the first. 'We don't like your sort here.'

I didn't think it was the time to tell him that I didn't like his sort anywhere. But neither was it time to show fear. I moved one step closer.

They stayed side by side, flexing muscle.

I was sure that if I kept on going they would have to move. I kept on going. They smiled and one beckoned with his index finger. 'Come on,' he urged. 'Try me.'

Keeping my expression as bland as possible, I did a rapid calculation. They'd planned this confrontation well –

they might easily have planted somebody above me. I couldn't go back. There was nowhere to go back to. If I went back I would be trapped.

I went forward, one more step. We were separated now only by two.

'Fucking lesbian,' the first said. The other just bared his teeth.

It's broad daylight, I told myself. What can they do? I told myself. Throw me down the stairs?

It was a distinct possibility. I went down one more step. Beer – that's what I smelt; the sourness of digested beer. I took a deep breath in. 'If Gary told you to scare me,' I said, 'then you can consider me scared.'

They did a double act on that one. 'Consider me scared,' they mocked. 'Listen to her.' They made faces at each other and at me: big children whose aggression was a weapon too blunt for me to handle. But I had to. I'd been witness to enough violence in my recent past to know that hesitation could be more dangerous than making the wrong move. I stepped down.

I had, thank God, guessed right. They moved, only a fraction, but they did move. I walked between them. I felt them, one on either side. I tried not to flinch when I felt them touching me. One got a breast, the other a buttock. I kept on walking. They let go.

Down I went, willing myself to keep even pace. They followed close behind, speaking in my ear.

I heard what they were saying, one single word repeated, a word ending in a double s. I couldn't make it out.

It sounded like a football chant. '. . . ass, . . . ass, . . . ass.' Crass? I thought. No, far too literate.

'. . . ass, . . . ass, . . . ass.'

Lass, then? No, too kind.

'. . . ass, . . . ass, . . . ass.'

They were hissing the end like a . . . Like a . . . Of

course. The penny dropped. I knew what they were saying: 'Gas, gas, gas.' As in gas chambers, I assumed.

A chorus. 'Gas, gas, gas.' Unbelievable. But true.

They followed me all the way across the courtyard and to the main gate. I kept on going. I knew that I must not look back. I kept on. I thought they had left me but I could not risk looking back. I kept up an even pace, counting to myself to keep my cool. As I reached two hundred, I also reached my car.

I got in, as quickly as I could, and locked the door. I felt less safe than ever – I had visions suddenly of what might happen if they started rocking the car. I looked in the rear-view mirror – the street behind was deserted. My eyes flicked to the side mirror – nothing again. I was safe.

I felt anything but safe. I felt unstable. My teeth were chattering and I could not stop them. I fumbled with the key and managed to fit it into place but when I turned it, I turned it too far. There was a loud, grating noise and the engine died.

I left the key and withdrew my hand. Holding it up in the air, I concentrated my gaze on it until eventually by sheer will power I stilled its shaking. That was better. I started the car and drove it round the corner to the street where I had said that I would be waiting.

I had no idea whether she would come. I parked but left the engine running. I settled myself down to wait. If she did come, she would not do so immediately. I tried to make myself more comfortable. Some hope: the car was too small and I was out of practice – without even the bare minimum of a thermos flask of coffee. I turned the radio on low and, pushing the seat back, put everything on hold.

Almost three hours later I was cursing Jurek. If I didn't go and phone him soon, I thought, he'd call the riot squad out. I should never have given him that promise, I should have known better. It had never worked with Sam.

A sharp rap on the window made me jump. Wrong car for that – I hit my head. Rubbing it, I looked to the left. There was a young man there. He was thin and handsome with delicate features and chestnut-brown skin. As I looked at him, he kept his face deliberately blank, his brown eyes unblinking.

He was the wrong colour to be one of Gary's henchmen. I leaned across and rolled the window down.

He was holding a piece of paper. 'She sends you this.' He pushed the paper through the window. 'Addresses of friends of Agnes Wilson.'

'Thanks.'

He didn't want my thanks. 'She has done what you requested,' he said. 'Now she asks you to keep away from her.'

I took the paper.

Or at least I tried to take it. He held on. 'Your blundering is dangerous to her,' he said. 'I am not asking, I am telling: keep away.' He let go suddenly. My arm jerked inwards.

I glanced down, saw two addresses written there.

'Did they hurt you?' I heard him asking.

I shook my head.

'That's good.' He was about to go.

'Wait.' I tore the paper he'd given me in two and on the blank half wrote down my address. 'This is in case she, or you, want to tell me anything more,' I said, holding it towards him.

'We won't,' he said, but took the paper anyway. He turned.

'Why don't you do something?' I asked.

He turned back. 'Something?' His smile was bitter. 'And what do you suggest?'

'The police?'

His smile was gone. 'The police classify what happens

here as a domestic dispute. And even if they did take action, they wouldn't stay for ever, would they?'

'Self-defence then?'

The smile was back. 'Fascism they call domestic,' he said. 'But for self-defence they use a different term. Attempted murder. So we have to be careful. We're not strong enough to risk it yet.'

Yet. I heard the word deliberately stressed. I smiled and, through my side mirror, watched him walk away.

Chapter

twenty-seven

I rang Jurek and told him I was all in one piece. I kept the conversation short, hanging up on the disapproval that came flooding over the line when I told him I wasn't coming right back. It was childish of me: I should have told him why. Not even Jurek would have found anything to complain about in visiting two elderly friends of Agnes Wilson.

The first, Dorothy Sharp, lived in Kings Cross, not far from where I was. I walked there, down a narrow alley whose walls on either side were topped by jagged glass. The house wasn't much more inspiring: a small terraced number whose outside paint was peeling, a large damp stain running down one side where a drain pipe was hanging loose. I rang the bell.

'Yes?' The middle-aged woman barked the word out as if she hated it.

I opened my mouth. From above came the sound of thumping, somebody playing the bongos on the floorboards.

The woman grimaced. 'Look, if you're selling something . . .' She was already turning away, pushing the door closed.

I stuck my foot out.

She wheeled round. 'For Christ's sake.' Her face was blotchy with frustration. 'Haven't I got enough on my plate?'

The thumping started up again, a rhythmic tattoo that, as it gained momentum, dislodged a dusting of plaster from the ceiling.

'I'm coming,' the woman yelled and then under her breath muttered: 'Bloody cow.' She had forgotten me. She began to walk down the dingy hallway, heading for the stairs.

I went in and closed the door.

She turned. 'You still here?'

I nodded. 'Dorothy Sharp?'

She pointed one finger at the ceiling.

'Can I see her?'

The light from a bare bulb was so dim that all it did was reflect the hall's dull brown theme. The woman stood with her hands on her grubby apron. 'What do you want with her?'

'I want to ask her some questions.'

I saw the lines around her mouth turn down, a prelude to her no. At that moment the hammering started up again, accompanied this time by what sounded like a goat's bleat. The woman's body deflated, her shoulders rounding as if to ward off a blow. 'Come on,' she said grimly and, without waiting to see if I was following, walked up the stairs.

She led me into a first floor room whose blue flock wallpaper was grimy with age and damp. In the top left hand corner, along the same fault line that I had seen outside, green mould was growing. The room was barely furnished – a bed and a chair only. It was cold. The gas fire at the centre of the chimney was off.

The bed was empty. In the chair sat a woman tiny with age, her gnarled hands gripping a stout cane. As we entered she had it raised. Seeing us she dropped it down – a token blow to show that she was angry. The bleat was also hers. She used it now. 'What took you so long?' Her eyes, hidden amongst great folds of skin, looking accusingly at my companion.

'But, Dot.' The woman's voice was poised halfway between the twin polarities of reason and rage. 'I wasn't long.'

Dorothy Sharp's eyes darted in my direction. 'You see how she treats me? That's why I've reported her to the welfare.' Her voice was surprisingly fierce. She revved up. 'She shouldn't be allowed in here. She steals my money. Can't even afford to have the fire on because she eats my meter money. She takes advantage, that's what she does. She's an evil woman. You have to –' She stopped suddenly. Her heavy-lidded eyes closed and when she opened them again, tendrils of suspicion enfolded me. 'Why aren't you writing this down?'

'I'm not from the welfare.'

Her mouth quivered. 'Why didn't you say so? What you doing here?'

'I've come to ask you some questions.'

'Questions.' She banged down. 'I'm too old for questions.'

She did look too old but I tried anyway. 'About Agnes Wilson.'

'Agnes? Don't know an Agnes. Go away.' The stick hit the floor again, just missing the ugly brown shoes specially fashioned to fit her twisted feet.

I turned to the woman beside me, looking for help.

She sighed heavily. 'Wasn't Agnes the one you worked with?'

When Dorothy Sharp frowned her whole face crinkled. It made her look a million years old. This is a waste of time, I thought, thinking how best I could extract myself. I turned.

'Agnes,' I heard.

I turned back.

'You're not Agnes.'

'No, Dot,' the other woman intervened. 'This lady has come to ask you about Agnes Wilson.'

'She's dead.' The words were spat out. Then Dot smiled, her face creasing up. 'I'm fifteen years older than her and she's dead.' The creases were too deep for mirth. I saw tears forming in the pouches below her eyes. She blinked them away. 'What's Agnes to you?' She was staring at me through those lizard eyes. I took a few steps closer.

'I'll leave you to it,' I heard. The door closed.

Standing in the chill, on the bare boards, the meagreness of the room's furniture laid out before me, I felt as if somebody had just passed sentence on me. I guessed that Dorothy Sharp must feel the same.

She was watching me carefully. 'What you want?'

'I want to know about Agnes.'

'Agnes? Who's she?'

'Agnes Wilson. You worked with her.'

'Work?' She was bleating again. 'Are you mad? I'm too old to work.'

'Now you are,' I said. 'But before . . .'

Her voice cut through mine. 'Agnes never liked her biscuit,' she said. 'He gave her trouble.'

Biscuit? He?

I never got the chance to ask. Her hand went up in the air, high and down, again and again, hitting the floor so hard that the floorboards jumped.

The door opened. Her companion entered. 'What is it?'

'I've been calling and calling you,' Dorothy Sharp said. 'Why didn't you come?' And down went her hand again, banging out her rhythm of confused desperation.

The younger woman smiled apologetically. 'Some days she's lucid.'

'Don't talk behind my back,' Dorothy Sharp yelled. 'You think I can't hear?' The banging escalated.

There was no point in staying. I went to the door. The woman followed. 'I'll show you out.'

We walked in silence to the front door.

'Your mother?' I asked as I was about to leave.

'Mother-in-law.'

'Tough on you.'

She nodded but added, quickly, in case I got the wrong impression: 'She's not so bad, really.'

I thought of the cane's incessant hammering.

The woman saw my disbelief. 'This is one of her difficult days,' she said. 'She's cold and she's lonely. But she was good to me when I was young. I don't begrudge it her.' I looked at her, seeing how kind was that face beyond its surface of weariness. She must have seen sympathy in my face: it gave her the courage to continue. 'It's the same all the time, isn't it?' she said. 'It's money, that's the problem.' Suddenly it came pouring out: 'We never get a moment's rest, me and my husband. When he works, I'm here. When I go out, he pops in to see she's all right. If only her pension hadn't turned out to be worthless – we could hire a nurse occasionally. She won't go into a geriatric ward, you see. Not that I blame her. She'd go downhill that way. You see, you got her on a bad day. She's not always like that: she has her flashes, you know, her moments of lucidity. You should see her . . .' The woman stopped abruptly in mid sentence as if she had just noticed the speed at which her words had come tumbling out. She smiled, wanly. 'I don't often get a lot of chance to talk to a sane adult in the day,' she said. 'You know how it is?'

I nodded although I didn't know. I didn't know anything – I didn't know how she could stand to be tied this way and I didn't know how it happened that the woman upstairs must do without a gas fire in winter because of men in suits who had played Monopoly with her money. I opened my mouth to say something – anything that might give comfort.

I didn't need the words. From upstairs came the sound again, Dorothy Sharp hammering for attention.

My companion looked relieved. 'I'd better go,' she muttered.

'Sure,' I said. I walked over the threshold.

Her voice pursued me. 'Thanks for listening,' but when I turned she had already shut the door.

Chapter
twenty-eight

I wasn't sure that I wanted to go on but I knew that if I didn't I would only regret it. I glanced quickly at the piece of paper I'd been given. My next venue sounded more in control: an old-age home tucked away in some Islington recess. I walked back slowly to my car, pursued by the sound of monstrous drumming. I got in, all my concentration focused on mapping out a route so that none was spent on thinking about Dorothy Sharp in her empty room.

I found the place easily enough, standing slightly set back from its leafy avenue. It was a relatively new building, one L-shaped storey with lots of square glass and not much else to distinguish it from a sixth form science laboratory. I left the car in its forecourt and walked to the door. It was open. I went in.

Inside was as uninspired as out – mostly anonymous corridors lined by numbered doors. Opposite was an unoccupied nurses' station backed by hanging brown files. From the right a hum of conversation which did nothing to warm the dull grey walls. There was nobody in sight. I turned, heading towards the sound of life.

A woman, whose dowager's hump had almost folded her in half, came shuffling towards me. She stopped in front of me, her hair wispy and white, her face blotchy, her eyelids hanging heavy over rheumy eyes. 'Do you know what I'm doing here?' she asked.

Wondering how much more of this I could take, I shook my head.

'I need help.' There was no expression in her voice. 'Look at me.' Her hands played helplessly with a dressing-gown collar stained yellow. 'What's happened to me? What am I going to do?'

It was too existential a question for me. I stood there helplessly.

'There, there, Daisy,' a cheerful voice announced. Its owner, a stout woman in nurse's uniform, bore down on us.

'What am I doing here?' the woman muttered.

The nurse had no trouble answering. 'You're going to take part in the sing song and then you're going to have lunch,' she said. She nudged Daisy gently into motion before turning briskly to me. 'Can I help you?'

I told her that I wanted to see Trevor Carter.

The expression on her large cheerful face was quite relaxed. 'You a relative?'

I toyed momentarily with the notion of a grand-niece or a goddaughter but settled in the end on a simple: 'No.'

It didn't bother her. 'We like to keep a track on the old dears – see who's visiting them. Mr Carter's in the day room. Go straight down the corridor and take the first left. You can't miss it.'

She was right, I couldn't miss the day room – although what it had to do with day, I couldn't tell. It looked like a cross between a waiting room and a night club – red brocade curtains hung limply beside purple walls, and an electric piano stood deserted by the window sill, with a long low table covered by torn magazines alongside it.

'Council's brilliant idea to make the place look less like an old people's home,' a voice in my ear proclaimed. 'As if anything could . . .'

I looked around the room. The hum I'd heard had come from here. Ranks and ranks of residents lined the wall. There were too many to be restricted to the sides: a double layer of chairs had also been laid along the room's centre and each of these was occupied. I looked more closely, distinguishing separate groupings amongst the mass. In one corner, some women huddled together and as I stood watching, one of their number turned to look at me. When she turned back she said something out of the side of her mouth; a cackle of derisive laughter issued from the group's centre. I looked away. My eyes got ensnared by a thirty-inch colour TV high up on the wall. The sound was turned down low but the sight was mesmerizing. A man, grinning fiendishly, was jumping around on what appeared to be a model of the British Isles. I shook my head.

'And they think some of our inmates are crazy,' the same voice said. I turned to face its owner – another nurse. She was five foot high and wide with breasts as close to a shelf as I had ever seen.

She smiled. 'Who are you looking for?'

When I told her, she lead me there. We weaved through the tiers to the far corner of the room. We had to walk slowly – she was stopped continually by people passing comments, asking for something, continuing conversations that had no apparent start or stopping points. While my escort patiently responded, I stood by, trying to unwrinkle my nose's response to the stench of urine that pervaded the room.

She caught me doing it. 'Don't worry,' she said cheerfully. 'You'll get used to it. Now. Here we are. Mr Carter.'

She was leaning over a frail old man whose cheeks were sunk hollow in his emaciated face. His eyes were closed and he appeared to be asleep, his chest visibly rising and falling to the accompaniment of a bronchitic wheeze. 'Mr Carter.' As she yelled his name, she shook his shoulder. 'Mr Carter.'

He opened his eyes. 'I'm not deaf,' he muttered and closed them again.

'You've got a visitor.'

This time, his glazed blue eyes stayed open. They flickered at and then on past me. 'I don't know you.' His voice was surprisingly clear.

'Come on, Mr Carter,' the nurse jollied. 'Be nice.'

'No.' I stepped between them. 'He's right. He doesn't know me.' I offered him my hand. 'My name's Kate Baeier.'

He sniffed. 'I still don't know you.' He stuck his hand between his legs. 'You a social worker?'

I shook my head.

'Good. I can't stand social workers.' The hand re-emerged, but wasn't offered. 'I can't stand most people.'

'Give over.' The nurse's voice was an unrelentingly cheerful boom. 'You like me.'

He scowled ferociously. 'I can't stand you most of all,' he said. He batted a thin, veined hand in the air. 'What are you doing here anyway? This is my visitor. Go away.'

She didn't seem to mind. She pulled up a chair for me and left.

'Thank God for that,' Trevor Carter said in a voice pitched artificially loud. 'It's bad enough being in a room full of senile biddies and incontinent old men without having to listen to that woman's senseless chatter.' He turned his head abruptly and I heard a hawking sound before something globbed into a steel container. I swallowed.

He was glaring at me. 'What do you want?' A white crust had stuck to one corner of his mouth.

'My name's Kate Baeier.'

'It's not such a great name that you need to keep repeating it.' He used the back of his hand to wipe the detritus from his lips.

Someone laughed.

Pathetic as he was, Trevor Carter was making me nervous. I tried to buy some time. 'Is there anywhere more private we can talk?' I asked.

'Plenty of places,' he said. He put one hand on each of the chair's armrests. 'But it'll take me at least twenty minutes to get there.' Groaning ostentatiously, he began to push himself up.

'Let's stay here,' I said hastily.

As he fell back, he began to cough. The cough accelerated huge, hacking movements, robbing him of breath. He was gasping by the time the fit was over but he managed to deliver words. 'If you want my advice about getting old,' he said, 'all I can say is – don't.' He stared ferociously at me, willing me not to pity him. 'Now what are you after?'

'I'm a friend of Agnes Wilson,' I said.

He looked at me – his eyes cloudy with suspicion. 'What kind of friend?'

I shrugged. 'I knew her.'

'You weren't at her funeral.' He sounded angry.

I tried to smile. 'I was out of the country,' I said. 'I met Agnes five years –'

He pushed himself upright. 'I know who you are.' His clawlike hand was in the air, pointing at me. 'You're not a friend of Agnes. You're that woman. Baker. That detective she went to for help.'

I nodded.

His bloodless eyes bored into mine. 'Fat lot of use you turned out to be.'

I didn't know what to say. I tried flattery. 'You've got a good memory.'

'It's not often you get involved in a murder, is it?' He winked.

My breath caught in my throat. 'A murder?'

It wasn't a wink – it was a nervous twitch. It gathered speed, began flickering madly until he used one hand physically to restrain the offending eyelid.

'A murder,' I prompted.

'Yes, yes.' Tetchily. 'I heard you the first time.' He scowled. 'Why should I talk to you?' he said. 'You haven't given me any proof that you are the Baker woman. You could be an impostor.'

I reached into my pocket, and pulling out the passport I usually carried, handed it to him.

He fumbled at it, turning the pages. His eyes were focused at the right point in space but they weren't focused right.

He must have guessed that I had noticed. The fight went out of him. When he spoke his voice was all deflated. 'There's not a lot to tell,' he said. 'Agnes went to see you, fighting fit, and a week later she wouldn't talk about it, any of it. She said that somebody had been murdered.' He stopped talking and stared into the distance. In his lap his hands lay, pumping feebly as if searching out a reservoir of strength that was now only memory. A movement convulsed his scrawny neck – he was swallowing down tears. 'It was the death of her, you know,' he said quietly. 'She got scared and that was never my Agnes.'

My Agnes.

'The spark went out of her,' he said. 'It was as if she just gave up.'

'Was it Gary Brown?' I asked.

He frowned.

'The man in the wheelchair.'

'Who? Crackers Brown?'

Crackers, I heard, and alongside it, Dorothy Sharp's voice: *Agnes never liked her biscuit.* 'Did he do it?'

Trevor Carter's face was vague. 'Some said Crackers was being paid to keep an eye on Agnes,' he muttered. He frowned as if memory evaded him. 'But Crackers was more interested in the blacks on the estate. Nah.' He shook his head, shaking the frown off. 'What did Agnes in,' he said, 'was the thought that she was to blame for what happened.'

'Why? What happened?'

He didn't answer. His shrug said he couldn't. He slumped back in his chair, his eyes closed, all his energy concentrated on the clumsy rise and fall of his chest. I pursued him into his silence, asking him something that had always bothered me. 'Do you know why she came to see me?'

His lips moved reluctantly. 'She wanted a detective.'

'I know,' I said. 'But why me?'

He opened his eyes. 'It's obvious, innit?'

'Not to me.'

A sneer of contempt. 'Because of your connections.'

'My connections?'

He managed to curl his lips without producing even a semblance of a smile. 'No wonder you did Agnes no good,' he said. 'You set yourself up as a detective and you don't even know your own bleeding connections. Pathetic.' His eyes closed again. His lips moved. 'Pathetic,' he said again.

That was the last I got out of him. I sat and prodded, with fingers and with questions, but no joy. So then I just sat, thinking that if I waited long enough, he would return to the land of the living.

Something caught in his throat – he coughed it out, great racking coughs to clear it. The nurse was right – I could no longer smell the room, I had merged with it. He opened his eyes once, looking at me from behind half-closed eyelids. No recognition there. I waited some more but realized, in the end, that there was no point in waiting – he had far greater staying power then I. I stood up.

Trevor Carter's nearest neighbour, a tiny wrinkled woman, was beckoning me closer. I went closer. She beckoned again. I put my face almost against hers. 'Don't listen to him, darling,' is what she whispered. 'He's as blind as a bat and as nutty as a Magritte.'

I walked away fast down the corridor.

'Get what you came for?' The second nurse, she of the magnificent breasts and high cheer, passed me on the trot.

I didn't answer – not that she had stayed long enough to hear if I did. Opening the door I stepped out into the cold, fresh air.

Chapter
twenty-nine

I got into the car, but didn't start it up. I sat there, straight backed, staring unseeing at a brick wall. Trevor Carter's vexed old man's voice repeated on me. *A murder*, I heard him saying and merging with what Tom Parsons had said: *Two accidents. Don't make it three.*

I shook my head. I was angry. 'It was an accident,' I told the wall. Of course it was. Sam's death had been accidental, I knew it had. He went out, that's all, one wintry night, and he didn't even get very far. He was killed within walking distance of the house. If I hadn't had the television on so loud I would probably have heard it happening.

I sat there, thinking of my last sight of him. What I had relived so recently came back again, this time in slow motion. Sam's lips wafted over mine, a sketchy contact made to stop me asking him where he was going. I saw their redness hovering, about to touch, the last warmth of him, the last . . .

'Are you all right, dear?'

I jumped and, turning, saw a nurse whose expression of professional concern was focused on me. I lifted my hand up to my cheek. It was wet.

'Are you all right?'

I nodded and swiped my tears.

'Can be upsetting visiting the elderly,' she said and walked off.

I turned the key to reassure her. I sat there revving at the engine until she was gone from sight. I put my foot down on the clutch and moved the gear stick.

And saw suddenly, in my mind's eye, another sight. A flash of red cashmere: not Sam's lips but Sam leaving with the scarf I'd given him around his neck. My foot went up. The car jumped forward and hit the wall. I heard a crunch and then the car stalled. I turned it off.

His red scarf. Which had not been amongst his belongings when I had picked them up. His belongings: John had taken Sam's son but had left his bloody clothes to me. I remembered how I had unpacked them and laid them out, all of them, his coat still damp, his shirt which they must have torn off him to get to his chest, included. All of them – but no red scarf. I remember asking if this was all – meaning was this all that was left of my Sam – but the man in the hospital had misunderstood, had told me that the police had searched the area carefully. 'In case of foul play,' the man had said.

Foul play. It had happened. Sam had been killed. After he had gone somewhere first. Somewhere where he had left his scarf.

Somewhere . . . but where? It had to be near – Sam had died close by within half an hour of his leaving me. It was late at night, too late for him to have taken refuge in any of the nearest coffee places.

Somebody's flat, perhaps. Somebody nearby. Except if it was that why had he bothered to take the scarf? Although it had been raining heavily that night, it hadn't been cold. It wasn't like Sam to wrap up so well – not if he was merely walking a few hundred yards to somebody's warm flat. And he was going somewhere. I remembered him striding purposefully to the door – a man with a destination.

Which left a car. As the thought occurred, I knew it was

right. Sam had been going to meet somebody, and had wrapped up warm because he had thought he might be kept waiting out in the dark and rain. And was – that's why his coat had been damp.

So now I knew. Sam had waited at a street corner for the someone to drive up, had got into their car and stayed there long enough at least to leave his scarf, had stepped out, had tried to cross the road and had been deliberately killed.

I knew that now. What I didn't know was who had killed him . . . Gary Brown was the obvious answer. But why?

I pushed those questions aside. Something else was occupying my mind: my own culpability in Sam's death. *Your connections*, Trevor Carter had said, had led Agnes to me. Mine. My connections. Which had ended up killing Sam.

I couldn't think of it – not now. I turned the key, backed and, turning rapidly, drove, wheels spinning, out of there.

It was only when I got back to Maria and Jurek's that I remembered the sound of metal tearing as I had hit the wall. I parked and, getting out, walked slowly round the car. It was dark already – I had stayed longer in the forecourt than I'd thought – but a nearby streetlight illuminated the damage. It wasn't quite as bad as I'd feared, but it wasn't nothing either. That one jolt had been enough not only to bend the bumper back but also crumple part of the car's metallic front. I stood there, gazing at it, wondering whether Sam had made the same kind of impression on the car that had been the instrument of his death. I frowned. Probably not – Sam was much softer than the wall. And yet – the frown deepened – whoever it was that had killed him must have been accelerating wildly. That's right – I remembered that the only person who admitted to hearing the accident had spoken of the gunning of an engine. We – the police and I – had assumed that this was the hit-and-run driver taking off; now I wasn't so sure.

I bent down and placed my hand gently on the ripped metal. Whoever had run Sam over would have had plenty of time to repair their car. Five years to make it new; five years while Sam's body rotted.

'Where have you been?'

Where have you been? I saw Sam sprung to life. Sam in darkness. I remembered what had happened then, I'd pressed the light and had seen him standing on the top step, his arms folded, glaring down at me.

'Where have you been?'

He'd repeated it as well, shouting out the question as I'd slowly begun to climb the stairs. I don't remember what I answered and I don't remember what else he'd added. All I know is how quickly our argument had escalated. I could hear it now – the sound of our voices, distant like my parents arguing behind dense wood which, although it filtered out the words, could not prevent the intensity of their mutual ferocity from getting through.

'Where have you been?' I felt an arm as well. I looked up. It was Jurek, not Sam. I shook his arm away. 'We have been worried,' Jurek said, his eyes flashing not in concern but in anger.

I got up. 'I'm sorry,' I said, and, turning heel, walked quickly away.

I went to bed. I went and lay there on top of the covers, staring blankly at my clothes hanging above me. There was a knock on the door. I didn't move. Maria came in anyway. As she opened the door a gust of wind blew the clothes about, twisting them.

Maria was standing by my bed. 'You must eat,' she said.

I nodded.

'Jurek gets angry when he is concerned,' she said.

So it seems do all men, I thought. I kept my mouth shut.

'Anna rang,' she continued. 'She would like you to phone her.'

'Thanks.' I looked at Maria, smiling, wishing her gone. She got the message. She laid the tray she was holding down on the floor and then padded softly away. I waited until she shut the door. When, finally, it was closed, I turned and faced the wall.

Chapter
thirty

The next thing I knew I was being shaken from sleep. 'Katherine.' It was Jurek. 'It is time.'

Time? I raised one eyelid and squinted at my watch. Eight o'clock.

Eight o'clock. Surely not in the evening? I lifted my head. No, not in the evening – grey light was filtering through the makeshift curtain. I shut my eyes.

'You must get up.'

I groaned: 'Leave me alone.' And turned over.

But Jurek would not let go. 'All this sleep,' I heard him saying, 'is bad for the constitution.' I burrowed deeper into the blankets. 'I have seen this happen before,' Jurek said. 'You are turning anger into hopelessness. Do not let this happen to you.'

I lay there quietly. I didn't feel quiet. Jurek was right – I was furious. With him. What right had he, I thought, as I lay there, to psychoanalyse me?

'You have a letter,' he said.

My eyes snapped open.

'It is not addressed to you.'

I turned and saw it in his hand.

'But since it is not addressed to anybody I know it must be . . .'

I snatched it from him. The postmark showed me that it was from the pensions registry. I tore it open.

What I saw was the details of a defunct pension scheme. The company was Permole – not Agnes's but its sister. My eyes scanned rapidly down the page, skipping over the figures until I got to the list of trustees. It took a moment for me to focus on the print.

There were six names in all. Five I did not know. The other was at the bottom of the list and was extremely familiar. Greg Willis, Chelsea address supplied. I can't say I was surprised.

I was out of bed and ignoring Jurek's flow of questions, rooting through my suitcase until I found Agnes Wilson's file. At its back I had shoved the copies of the three companies' accounts I'd obtained from Companies House. I took them out and laid them on the bed, side by side with the ones I had just received.

It didn't take long to confirm what I had suspected. Large sums had been taken out of the Permole pension fund and used as unsecured loans to one or other of the three companies which had then gone bankrupt. It was only a partial picture I had here – after all there were at least two other and possibly more pension funds involved – but it was enough to show that someone had been either deliberately negligent or criminally stupid with other people's money.

And Greg and Pam Willis, who'd so kindly lent me their London house, had been involved. Sleep and its aftermath both had fled. I had to get moving. Jumping out of bed, I grabbed my jeans.

'Katherine!' Jurek's protests were aimed not so much at my changing in front of him but at the abruptness of my movements.

I stopped momentarily. 'I thought you wanted me up,' I said and, turning away from him, carried on.

He skipped round to face me. 'This haste is another side of the same currency,' he said.

'Coin,' I muttered. I pulled a sweater over my head. My teeth were grinding. What a few days ago I'd thought endearing was now extremely irritating.

Not that my irritation could stop Jurek. 'Coin – currency,' he said. 'The word itself is irrelevant. What matters is that you are unbalanced.'

Takes one to know one, I nearly said. But didn't. I put on my socks.

'Katherine!' A curt command.

I looked up.

'You cannot go on like this.'

You cannot, I heard. I nodded, confirming to myself that this is what he'd said. 'No,' I replied straightening up. Something was pulsing in my forehead. 'I can't.' My voice was clear.

Jurek knew what I meant. He backed off, just a fraction. 'Katherine,' he said, softer now. 'I am acting only as a friend. I'm trying to help you.'

'No, you're not. You're –' I paused, censoring the first words that occurred. 'What you're doing,' I said eventually, 'is suffocating me.'

I had known that Jurek, whose watchword was autonomy for all, wouldn't like that. He opened his mouth but, for once in his life, no words came out. When he shut it again, I saw how two dark red spots had appeared on each of his pale cheeks. He turned.

I'd gone too far. 'Jurek . . .' I began.

It was too late, Jurek had left.

When I reached the kitchen he was there, sitting sullenly by the table. Once angered Jurek was almost impossible to placate. I didn't even try. I washed my face and brushed my teeth and then, taking a cup and pouring coffee from the pot, went over to the phone.

'Kate.' Anna sounded pleased to hear from me. When

however I skipped over the small talk and asked her if there was any post for my pseudonym, she went into abrupt reverse. 'Hold on,' she said curtly.

I took a sip of Jurek's coffee. It was bloody awful and only lukewarm. But I needed something. I added sugar and gulped it down.

Anna was back. 'I've got it here,' she said. On my request she opened the letter and read out the list of names. Disapproval made her voice jagged.

I had Jurek sitting opposite, glaring at me, a glacial Anna at the other end of the receiver and another list which included Greg Willis. I put the interpersonal difficulties on hold. 'Thanks,' I said and, before Anna could chip in, added a quick, 'Goodbye.'

I hung up and dialled another number: Carmen's. It rang and rang and then I got the answerphone. I knew enough about Carmen to know she only left it on when she was in. I slammed the receiver down and walked quickly to the door.

Jurek said nothing. Pretending that I hadn't wanted him to, I left the house.

Outside was dank and cold, the air sharper than it had been before. I worried that I was underdressed for what I thought I'd have to do. I considered going back.

But didn't. The time for going back was gone. I got into the car and drove away.

I stopped off on the way to provision up. I went into a hardware store and bought a thermos. Next door was a down-at-heel delicatessen. I bought the makings of a set of sandwiches, a couple of overblown croissants, and six take-away coffees which I transferred into the thermos. I took the lot back to the car, and, thinking I would look like a fool if my hunch wasn't right, drove to Carmen's.

I parked opposite her flat. Her curtains were open – well, Carmen always had been an early riser. I got out of the car and, walking across the road, rang her bell. Long and hard I rang it; once, twice, and a third time for luck. No answer.

Oh well, I shrugged, and going back to my car settled myself in to wait.

Eight hours later I was crumbed up to the eyeballs. I'd seen a lot of what went on in Carmen's street. I had watched children dragging themselves off to school and skipping their way back. I'd followed the manoeuvring of a black-windowed limousine; seen bejewelled hands stretch out from it, exchanging white envelopes for tiny parcels. I'd even caught a bit of marital infidelity: the man from number 34 being replaced by someone who looked like his clone but whose welcoming smooch would have scorched a lesser being.

None of this was very interesting, nor could it save me from the cold. I couldn't leave the engine on in case I ran out of petrol. Every now and then when the chill got unbearable I would switch on for a moment and warm myself, before reluctantly switching off. I knew my quarry – only too well – and I was pretty sure she was inside her flat. If I risked going for petrol or a blanket, she would use the opportunity to leave.

My quarry. I sat there, my thoughts sharp against the background of a burbling radio. I thought about Carmen and how it had all begun. I'd met her during one investigation and she'd ended up working with me on others. She was everything I'd needed – smart, funny, feisty – and we'd jelled immediately. I sat there smiling, remembering how I used to boast about our partnership. It got so repetitive that Sam started teasing me about it: *You're infatuated with her*, he would say.

My smile faded. Sam had seemed to be joking when he uttered those words but now I sat there remembering an edge that accompanied them. I sat, there in the car, for a long time, wondering whether it were possible: had Sam been jealous of Carmen? No, it wasn't possible. Carmen was a friend and Sam my lover. Except . . .

No. I wouldn't think of it. It was gone – all of it.

I sat, getting colder. The only thing that saved me was that I didn't have the usual watcher's cramp. Since I didn't care if she saw me I would get out sporadically and stretch my legs. I even went on a couple of occasions to the phone booth on the corner and rang her, ringing her bell for good measure on the return trip.

I glanced at my watch. It was dark, I was getting hungry and going into overtime. Not that I was being paid – if I were, I thought, perhaps I would be doing this differently. For the first time since I had decided on my course of action, doubts crept in. Perhaps Carmen had changed: perhaps like other normal people she now left her answerphone on when she went out.

But no. The postman had gone up to her door and shoved letters in and when, on one of my occasional trips, I'd looked through the letter box, I'd seen nothing there. She hadn't gone away, I was sure of it; she was inside, hiding. Well, I'd had enough. I got out of the car and slammed the door. I shouted: 'Carmen!'

Pathetic, I only managed to turn a few heads, all of these close by. Something more drastic was required. I needed height. There was a low wall by the pavement. I climbed up on it. I centred myself and then, taking a deep breath, cupped my hands together and yelled: 'Carmen!'

This time my cry reached people further away but still it wasn't loud enough. I looked around, searching for inspiration. I found it in the form of a row of dustbins. Jumping lightly down I fetched one of the lids. Now for something with which to bang it. That wasn't so easy, I needed metal, not the anorexic twigs which were the only straight objects visible. Dustbin lid in hand, I stood, trying to think laterally. It came upon me in a flash: the car's jack. Going over to the Renault I opened up the boot and tweaked it out. There – I was ready.

The wall wasn't high enough, not for my ambitions. I climbed clumsily on to the bonnet and from there on to the roof. The metal sagged but held. I stood, feet far apart for balance, and I began. 'Carmen,' I yelled and banged my makeshift drum.

That did it; that was loud enough. Not only did every person within two hundred yards turn to stare at me but also, on the second drum roll, doors and windows began to open. Several doors and windows, but not hers. I took a deep breath and steadied myself to start again. By the sounds of the laughter and the insults coming my way I didn't reckon I had much longer. It was now a toss-up which was first: me flushing out Carmen or someone else summoning the police. Oh well, here goes. 'Carmen,' I screamed and lifted the jack high.

It never hit its target. At that moment I saw the first flickering of life from Carmen's flat – a light clicked on, a window opening. I saw a figure, blurred, in a hurry. It must be Carmen. I'd known it. She'd been there the whole time.

She'd looked out once and then was gone. I jumped down. I threw the jack into the car and locked the door, replaced the lid on its bin, bowed to acknowledge the applause of some tiny children who'd come out of their house to watch me and ran across the road. By the time I got there, the door was open.

'You better come inside,' she said.

Chapter
thirty-one

I walked behind her, up the stairs. She didn't speak. She was going for maximum body language – exuding resentment in every step. At the top I told her I had to use the toilet. When I came out she was still standing in the hall. She was in shadow; I couldn't see her face. All that waiting had dulled everything except my sense of cold: now I felt another sensation flittering past. Fear.

'Can't we go into the sitting room?' I asked, buying time.

It didn't do me much good. She entered first and by the time I arrived was standing by the window with her back to me.

'What do you want?' I heard her saying.

I took a step closer. 'Carmen.'

She whirled round then. I saw her face. 'What do you want?' I wished I hadn't. It was closed and hard, granite against any move that I might make. It was so hard that this most beautiful of faces no longer seemed even vaguely attractive. For the first time since I had decided on my course of action, I wondered whether I was about to hear something that I couldn't bear.

But it was too late.

'I'm not going to wait for ever,' she said. 'What do you want?'

I caught her glare and used my eyes to hold on tight to it. 'I want to know what happened.'

She seemed to think that this was funny. Her lips curled. 'What happened when?'

I matched my artificial smile to hers, but made mine wider. 'Let's not play games,' I said, consciously echoing the words she had used on me before. 'I want to know why you did nothing on the Agnes Wilson case.'

She clicked her tongue.

I moved closer. 'Why?'

'You know.' Her voice was loud.

I was almost upon her. 'If I knew, why would I go to all this trouble?'

'You tell me.' She'd lost some ground; her eyes reflected back the first flickering of uncertainty.

I didn't speak.

'You must know,' she said. She was trying to convince herself. She did not, it seems, succeed. She stood there, and as she continued to stare at me, I saw her pupils pulsate.

I held myself in check. I parried her look. I was quite determined – I would not speak. I stood there riveted by the vision of hostility and doubt fighting it out in those dark brown eyes. I'd never seen Carmen so unsure.

Noises from outside infiltrated the silence: children swapping insults, a car backfiring in the distance, a jostling of young men's voices disputing each other's manhood. And then, above all of that: Carmen uttering one word. 'Sam.'

Like that – *Sam* – delivered deadpan. It sparked images: I remembered Sam and Carmen, in the office, their heads bent close together, sharing an exclusive joke; and I thought of Sam's reference to my infatuation with her; and of the way, at his funeral, she made sure to keep her face averted. I teetered. Could it be, I thought? Could Carmen and Sam have been having an affair?

'Sam?' My voice.

'He told me to stop investigating.'

Relief made me bark out a laugh. Which was abruptly

stanched. Sam would never have interfered. And anyway, if for some imponderable, unlikely reason he had, she would not have obeyed. I was her boss, not Sam.

She read my thoughts. 'You put him up to it.' Her faltering tone belied the conviction in her voice.

'What?' I felt my forehead crinkling.

'You asked Sam to stop me investigating.'

My head was aching.

'That's what I hold against you most.' The rancour that had fuelled her righteousness was gone. 'You used Sam as your messenger.'

'Oh.' It was all I could think to say. 'I see.' Sluggish words started forming. 'And why,' I said – it was an effort to get them out – 'why exactly did I do all this?'

I had never seen Carmen on such shaky ground. 'I don't know.' She was mumbling.

My tongue loosened. I snapped my question out. 'Why don't you guess then?'

A long silence, until: 'There was something about the Agnes Wilson case that was dangerous,' she said, pausing between each word.

Dangerous. Well, that was true. Whatever it was, it had got Sam killed.

'That's what he told you?'

'That's what he implied.'

'Oh.' I sighed. 'Implied. Great. Just like he implied that this message came from me?'

She nodded.

'Great,' I said again. 'Anything else?'

She shook her head.

'Why didn't you talk to me about it?'

'You seemed preoccupied,' she said. 'You and Sam together. And afterwards . . . you left.'

Silence. I stood there, thinking only that I had nothing else to say. I tried to think of something. I even opened my mouth, trusting that words would eventually emerge. I saw Carmen watching me, saw hope flaring. But it was no good. I couldn't speak, not unless she did first, and I could see that she would not. I turned and began slowly to walk away. Slowly because I felt drained and for another reason as well: I was still expecting her to call me back. I shouldn't have; I should have known that sorry had never been a word in Carmen's vocabulary. She let me go.

She let me go downstairs and cross the road. As I was getting into the car, I looked up. She had left the sitting room and was standing by her bedroom window. She was gazing down on me. I stood there for a moment, looking back. I didn't move. Neither did she. I felt a terrible sadness. Whatever else happened – whatever I discovered about Sam's motive – I knew one thing for sure: Carmen and I were finished.

I stopped at the first pub I passed. My plan was simple: I was going to get drunk. Outlandishly, rip-roaringly, memory-annihilatingly drunk. But didn't. I couldn't. I sat there nursing a double whisky. I couldn't drink it down. Every time I lifted up the glass I was assailed by another memory: me, Carmen, Sam, swirling in and out of the viscous liquid, lips parted, laughing. That's what I had, until this point, chosen to remember.

Now I knew it was all illusion. We hadn't been laughing – our lips were twisted only in mutual misunderstanding. What Carmen had said had taken me back – not to the place that I remembered but to somewhere far more squalid. To a time when Sam had, without consulting me, warned my partner off – and where my partner had actually believed that I would let him do that.

I put the glass down. My eyes were stinging. I didn't believe her. I wouldn't. Sam would never have gone behind my back. Never.

I looked down at the stained beer mat. I was right: I knew I was. I picked up my glass. I threw my head back, poured the liquid down my throat, and got up.

'Cheers.' The woman who had been sharing the table with me raised her pint pot high. I nodded. And then I left.

Chapter

thirty-two

I stopped at a vegetarian Indian restaurant the like of which seems to have taken root in north London. This one had diversified from the usual variations on the theme of a potato and I ended up with an unexpectedly delicious curry of mango and green banana. Better still, two Kingfisher lagers did what the whisky hadn't managed: washed the worst of Carmen out of my system. By the time I stepped into Maria and Jurek's kitchen I was feeling almost cheerful.

Anna was at the table. Great, I thought, Maria and Jurek have made a sudden alliance with Anna – just what I need. 'Nice surprise,' I said, going closer.

She didn't return my smile.

I thought I knew why. I slowed myself down. 'Bad news travels fast,' I said, sitting down directly opposite her. 'Carmen rang you?' It was only half a question.

Which she answered with a nod.

'I think Carmen's mad,' I said. I lifted my hand and began to inspect my nails.

'Kate,' I heard.

My nails were jagged. They needed work.

She said it again. 'Kate.'

I let my hand drop. 'That's my name.' I looked up.

'I want you to stop,' she said.

I didn't ask, 'Stop what?' I didn't need to. I asked

another question instead: 'Did Carmen tell you Sam told *her* to stop investigating?'

Anna dipped her head. A yes.

'And you believe it?'

Her eyes flared.

'I don't,' I said. 'Sam would never have done that. Not without telling me first.'

'Wouldn't he?'

I raised my voice. 'No,' I said. 'He wouldn't.' Relief engulfed me. Sam wouldn't have betrayed me – not like that. I felt great. 'He wouldn't,' I repeated.

She didn't speak. She stared at me for a long, long time, her face empty of expression. I didn't know what she was trying to do and I didn't particularly care. But I played her game. I gripped her with my own eyes, gazing back.

I won. Her eyelids closed, she looked away. In triumph's place I felt disappointment. I kept on watching her.

She leaned down.

When she straightened up again, there was a carrier bag in her hand. She started dipping into it. I watched, absorbed by the deliberateness of her movements. She pulled objects out, placing each one carefully on the table. I saw books and notebooks, a vase, and disparate items of clothing. Then the bag was empty.

I tried to push off panic. 'What's this?' I said. 'A bring and buy sale?'

'They're yours.'

As if I didn't know. 'You kept them for me?'

'You asked me to,' she said. 'Don't you remember?'

Of course I remembered. What I couldn't remember was why.

I looked more closely. They were quite a medley: a couple of dogeared books, a vase, an album of some kind, some notebooks, an oversize sweatshirt and a cashmere jumper. I stretched across, picked up one of the notebooks and opened it.

What I saw there made me tremble. It was no ordinary notebook – it was the one Sam had used to write down the first drafts of his poems. I saw his familiar writing – that precise, mathematician's hand which took off into flights of fantasy in this his most private of possessions. Even now it felt like an invasion to be looking at it. I shut it.

And turned my gaze to the other objects, remembering why each had been selected. The vase – a fragile stalk of thin spun glass. It was made to carry a single rose like the one Sam had bought, giving me it and the vase together – the last present that had passed between us. As for the sweatshirt, the jumper and the books they were all his, favourites which, at the time I'd buried him, had seemed to hold his essence.

Now they seemed only pathetic. 'A remnant of another life,' I said, sweeping my hand out, shoving them away.

Anna pushed one back – the album, which she had opened.

I was looking at a set of photos – Sam and I, tussling playfully. Tears sprang into my eyes. I reached over, tried to shut it. Anna shoved her arm out, her flesh preventing closure.

'Look,' she said. She was turning pages. 'Here. Here's all of us together.' She was speaking with great intensity, as if the meaning of what she was trying to say was held within the photos.

I didn't get it. I tried to look.

But she'd already turned the page. 'Here's another,' she said. 'You and Sam kissing. I took it. Remember why?'

I could feel my heart beating.

'You'd just had a fight,' she said. 'That was you making up.' She turned the page. 'And here,' she said. And turned again. 'And here.' Her movements – flicking

221

through so fast – had possessed her. I saw images whirling by, Sam a blur. She went on going until the end and then she slammed the album shut. She looked at me.

'Why are you doing this?' I asked.

'Because it's important.' Her eyes were damp. She was pleading with me.

But still I didn't understand. 'Important?'

A shaft of what could only be pain seemed to flit over her forehead. But I must have imagined it; her face was bland, blank. 'You ran away,' she said.

Now I got it. What I'd always known must be there – her anger at my leaving – was coming out.

Except it wasn't. 'You ran from yourself,' she said. 'And from reality. You left these things of Sam's behind. What did you take with you?'

It was obvious, wasn't it? 'My memories,' I said. I could hardly hear myself.

'Oh, Kate.' The sympathy in her voice almost broke me. I bit my lip. Her voice hardened. 'Those memories weren't real,' she said. 'You built a graven image to replace the flesh and blood. Under the guise of remembering him, you've forgotten who Sam really was. You distanced him by making your relationship seem perfect. But don't you remember the tension between the two of you the week before he died?'

Tension? I didn't know what she was talking about. And I didn't want to keep on listening, not any longer. I pushed my chair away from the table, hearing its ugly grating.

Anna spoke above the noise. 'I didn't know that Sam had spoken to Carmen but I did know he was worried about you.'

I was looking down on her. 'If he'd been worried he would have told me.'

'He did,' she insisted, 'or at least he tried to. But you pushed him off. That's what caused the fights.'

222

Fights? What fights?

'It's the thing we used to joke about: anybody tries to help you, you run a mile. But it wasn't really a joke, was it?'

No, it wasn't. And I wasn't smiling.

'Why do you think you chose to be a war reporter?' Anna asked. She didn't need an answer, she supplied it herself. 'You've spent the last five years dicing with death,' she said, 'because you never faced the death that had happened. But it won't work. You can't keep running. You've got to face the past, not as an avenging angel who can change history, but so that you can finally sort it out. Maybe then you will remember Sam . . .

Sam. She'd said that name once too often. 'Stop it,' I said.

To my surprise she did. She stopped abruptly. The effort of what she'd said had made her pant. I heard her guttural whooping.

I didn't know what to say.

'You're not alone,' she said.

Oh, but I was. And I was something else. 'I'm tired,' I said.

She took a step towards me. 'Kate . . .'

'I'm tired,' I said again and then I did what I told myself I should have done before – I walked on out of there.

I was lying fully clothed on my bed, my eyes wide open. No matter how much I tried to push them off, Anna's words persisted. They raged about me, storming their way through memory. I batted them away. Without effect: . . . *anybody tries to help you*, I heard her saying, *you run a mile.*

No: it wasn't true. 'No,' I said it aloud. 'She's wrong.' About that and everything else as well.

Except she wasn't wrong about that. Only this morning, when Jurek had offered help, I had rebuffed him. I wasn't good with help. But did that mean that everything else Anna had said was right?

I shut my eyes. I saw Sam as Roger Toms had taken him: Sam smiling in a garden. I squeezed my eyelids tighter: remembering how I had sat in the Willises' kitchen and looked at Sam's photo and found a part of myself that I had buried, the part that felt his loss. Now I wondered whether there was another layer to uncover.

That's all it took – me asking that question of myself. I heard Sam's voice, raised in anger. 'Why?' Sam shouting the word out.

'Why? Why?'

I sat up. His roar continued unabated. Anna was right. Sam's last week alive had been fraught with tension. Over my job.

I remembered it now, how Sam who had treated my detective business first as something to be indulged and then as something to be tolerated had suddenly become stridently opposed. He'd started arguing with me, telling me that the work was too scarce to be taken seriously, and too dangerous when it did come.

Dangerous.

I swung my legs to the side. And realized then what I had been hiding from myself all these years. Anna had only half the picture. I hadn't been running from death. I'd been running from my own complicity in it, from the knowledge that Sam had been killed for something I had done.

My feet hit the ground. Anna had told me to stop. But I wasn't scared. I walked to the door. And I wasn't going to stop. Sam had been killed and I, on my own, was going to find out why.

Chapter
thirty-three

It was past two o'clock when I reached the Chelsea house. I had kept the Willises' key. I slotted it in and opened the familiar door. The action took me back: I half expected to see the cat come trilling towards me. What I saw instead was the alarm, blinking red.

Since I knew they would have changed it, I didn't bother punching my disabling code into the alarm. I was in motion, heading for the stairs. The copy of the fax I'd left taped to the banisters had been removed – so they were back. I took the stairs three, four at a time and on the second floor the force of my momentum propelled me into their bedroom.

'Switch off the alarm,' I said as I came crashing through.

A blurred movement, a muffled exclamation.

'Switch off the alarm.' I reached out and clicked on the overhead light.

I saw them clearly, trapped in its sudden glare. They looked so asinine, Pam and Greg, lying half raised up in bed, their mouths slack, blinking against the bright onslaught.

Greg was more awake than Pam. But not awake enough: he was floundering around, searching out appropriate outrage. 'Kate!' It sounded weak. 'What on earth?'

My voice in contrast was extremely loud. 'Switch off the –'

Too late. My ten seconds were up. That same ear-splitting siren that I had heard before rent the air. Greg, his tennis-playing reflexes paying off, leaped up and punched numbers into the console. The siren was abruptly cut off. But Greg kept going, grabbing the telephone, dialling and speaking softly to the other end. I stood and waited for him to finish.

'So sorry,' were his final words as he hung up. That done he turned to me. The urbane charm which his face had adopted as he spoke into the phone vanished. Now he merely looked dishevelled and very, very angry. 'What is the meaning of this?' He was walking, slowly, towards me. He was a big man, and fit, and his advance was meant to intimidate.

'Flamboyant pyjamas,' I said, nodding at his yellow-and-mauve striped affairs, which were less well suited to a modern temper tantrum than to a nineteenth-century salon. For a moment while he looked down he looked quite endearingly self-conscious. Then he spoiled the effect by remembering what he was supposed to be doing: his glance up was ferocious.

Greg always had been more image than effect. I could see him working his way into yet another version of indignation. I wasn't interested. I turned away from him, addressing myself instead to the figure on the bed. 'Pam.'

That's all I said but she cringed as if I had assaulted her. She looked strangely fragile lying there, her streaked hair mussed up, her eyes smaller than they were in the day, the whole untidy effect doing away with her usual suave sophistication. She was, however, overdoing it – holding a hand up as if to ward off a blow.

My irritation worsened when Greg inserted his manly body between me and the bed. 'Leave my wife alone,' he blustered. 'She has –'

'A lovely sun tan,' I said. 'And a great line in seductive patter.'

He was a pushover, was Greg. 'How dare you?' He was spluttering. 'Are you implying . . .?'

I could have played along but I wasn't in the mood for outraged cuckold patter. 'I'm not implying anything,' I said. 'I'm stating the facts. Pam conned me into staying here.'

She spoke up from behind him. 'You needed a place.' She sounded surprised.

I side-stepped Greg. 'I was going to a hotel,' I said. 'I would only have been in town two days.'

'But . . . but . . .' This from Greg. I could see confusion crossing his face and see him glancing – was it in reproach? – at Pam.

She started then: 'But . . .'

I stood and waited to see what the buts would produce. Nothing, as it turned out: by some unspoken signal their mouths were both simultaneously shut.

I took one step back, positioning myself so that I had both their faces in vision. 'Did Gary Brown organize your terror tactics?'

Their answer was a mutual exchange of looks.

'Did he?'

Greg's mouth trembled, which I took as no. I believed that – just about. But the thing that had occurred to me before, that somebody else was involved, somebody telling the Willises what to do, came strongly back.

I acted on it. 'Who told you to make me stay here?' I asked.

They had another identical reaction. Their lips tightened, their faces closed down.

I swivelled my head away, looking at this room I knew so well. It was so full of objects, collected painstakingly by Pam. My eyes were drawn to the glass shelf on which the most precious had been placed. I saw a vase, a delicate pale green. For a moment I saw it transposed, against the glass one that Sam had given me. That stirred me into action. I was by the shelf, grabbing it.

Someone was pulling both their strings at once. I heard them gasping, heard Greg shout out a warning 'Kate' and Pam a frantic: 'Be careful.'

I turned to face them. I was quite careful, I held the vase up to show them I had a grip and then I let my eyes drop to the floor to show them that I could easily let go.

'Do you know how much that is worth?' This from Greg.

I raised it higher.

'What do you want?' His face was flaming beetroot-red against the silver grey of his thick hair.

'I want to know the truth. I want to know the name of your partner.'

He was trembling with apprehension. 'We have no partner.' His voice was pleading.

I pushed the vase even higher, elaborating with a dipping motion.

'I'll prosecute,' Greg spluttered, sounding less like the lord of the manor and more a mortal man defeated.

Which is when Pam inserted herself into the picture. She had got out of bed and now, as she came walking towards me, her straight, determined posture confirmed what I had always suspected: that despite their convincing front – he the rich breadwinner, she the beautiful charitable wife – it was in fact she who had the monopoly of strength. Her voice was completely under control. 'We have no partner.'

'Your controller then.'

She met my gaze, her hazel eyes completely cool. 'We can tell you many things,' she said. 'But not everything. And nothing under threat. Put the vase down.'

She meant exactly what she said and besides, I didn't want to destroy their vase. I put it down.

'Good. Let us go down to the kitchen.'

I nodded.

In the background Greg was trying to reclaim his lost authority. 'This is an outrage,' he waffled unconvincingly. 'I'm going to call the police.'

I looked at Pam. She looked at Greg. 'Drop the phone,' she said. 'And then join us downstairs. With your dressing gown on. Kate is right: those pyjamas are absurd.'

The kitchen had been all cleared up. I sat down at her familiar counter; Pam filled the kettle.

'You destroyed my dinner set,' she said almost conversationally.

'You killed my cat.'

She opened her mouth as if to deny it, but seeing my eyes on her was sensible enough to shut it tight.

I looked down at the wooden surface, remembering how I had signed Agnes Wilson's name on it. My head went up. 'You have a letter for Agnes Wilson,' I said.

She nodded and, reaching into the kitchen drawer, withdrew a familiar-looking envelope. 'I thought it was for you,' she said. 'I would have forwarded it if you'd left a forwarding address.' Hastily, to forestall the obvious comment, she passed it over.

I opened it. I saw what I had seen before: a set of accounts and a list of trustees, Greg Willis's name included. The figures looked familiar – large amounts extracted in the form of unsecured loans.

At that moment, I heard the man himself. He was standing by the door, his gaudiness muffled by shining paisley. 'What did you do with her money?' I asked him.

He stopped – 'Whose money?' – and looked at Pam.

'Agnes Wilson's,' I said and saw total incomprehension pass over his face again. 'She had a pension with a company called Permog,' I said.

'Oh.' One word, tinged with guilt. I knew now, watching him, why Sam had always said that Greg was such a bad poker player.

But we had more at stake than poker. 'Remember it, do you?' I asked.

'Of course.' He was mumbling.

'Want to tell me more?'

The glorious construction of Greg's posture seemed to have deflated. He stood there, his carefully worked-on physique, his hairdresser's skilled reconstruction, his even tan doing nothing to conceal the fact that he was all caved in. 'Look, it was a ghastly episode in my life,' he said. 'I'm not proud of it, not by any means. But I didn't do anything wrong. You must believe me. I was careless, that was all.'

'With other people's pensions.'

He jerked his head to left and right. 'I never touched the money,' he said. 'I was asked to sit as a trustee and I should have paid more attention. But you know how these things are . . .'

'No,' I said. 'I don't.'

'I cannot excuse myself.' He was flailing around in his own drivel. 'Of course I should have taken more care, of course I acknowledge that, but . . .'

'Cut the bullshit, Greg.' Pam's voice was loud and drily contemptuous. She flicked another non-verbal order Greg's way and then focused her attention on me. 'What my husband is trying to tell you is that like all men with vast amounts of inherited cash, he is often asked to make more by agreeing to have his name, if not his charming presence, used. In this case he was a nominal trustee for a variety of pension funds. He never went to a single meeting – it was not required. He merely signed documents.'

'Which embezzled working people's money.'

'Perhaps. He is not implicated legally.' She said that

230

with confidence – they'd checked. 'He does, however, regret it. We both do.'

'And Sam's death,' I said. I felt them both tense up. 'Do you regret that too?'

Greg's reflexes were not played out. 'Nothing to do with us.' His words arrived a fraction earlier than Pam's: 'Of course we regret Sam's death. He was our friend.'

'Who was murdered.'

I couldn't look at them both at once. I saw Pam's eyes hardening. I don't know what happened to Greg. I did, however, hear his voice. 'We don't know anything about that,' he said.

'By the person, I bet, who killed the cat. And who threatened to do the same to me.' I paused, seeing Pam's unhealthy brown blanching an even unhealthier shade of white. 'Who is it?'

A visible but silent struggle was taking place before my eyes. I saw her skin tightening and then going slack, different hues of pallidness sinking into lines I had not previously noticed on her face. I didn't move. I stood there, holding my breath, waiting, waiting for her to tell me. I knew that she was trying to.

But I had reckoned without her husband. Like all couples theirs was a much more complex mix than I had first assumed. In general it might be true that Greg had the financial clout and Pam the inner strength but in this situation it was Greg who ended up calling the shots. 'We can tell you no more,' he said. He was back in one action-man piece, coming up to Pam and placing a possessive hand on her shoulder. 'We cannot,' he said, his hand digging in.

I saw Pam tensing against Greg's grasp but I had lost the battle. I saw her giving in. I was still holding my breath. She let hers out in one loud exhalation, and any apology that might have been there in her eyes was simultaneously disposed of.

I suppose I could have started on the destruction gambit again – they had enough to lose – but I didn't. I knew they wouldn't tell me. I knew it by Greg's unrelenting grip on Pam, and the contradictory relief which washed across her features.

But there was one other thing I needed to know. 'Who asked you to be a trustee?' Greg smiled. He actually smiled! That made me furious. 'Who?'

His answer was a facetious: 'But surely you know that. Sam . . .'

Of course. *Your connections*, I heard that old man's, Trevor Carter's, voice saying.

'Sam knew. He must have told you.'

No, Sam hadn't told me. But Greg was right: I did know. Only too well. 'John Layton,' I said.

Greg nodded.

'The companies were his.' A statement, not a question. 'All of them. And being John he kept his name out of the cesspool he'd created.'

Another nod.

So – I had it now. As soon as I had told Sam about Agnes Wilson and told him the name of the company that had defrauded her, he must have known his father was involved.

I had it – almost all of it. It was my turn to nod. And to go. I began to walk, past Greg, towards the door, up the stairs.

Greg's voice pursued me. 'Would you mind leaving your keys . . .'

I didn't wait for him to finish. I jabbed two fingers in his direction and left.

Chapter
thirty-four

I got in the car and started driving. I felt completely calm. John Layton, I thought, and in those darkest moments of the night I headed towards Kingston. The roads were almost deserted. I drove with the memory of Jurek's talking road map for company. I headed into Wandsworth's town centre. The pavement's litter was desolate in the yellowish light; a few people still walking wearily through the night.

John Layton: the name made sense of many things. Like what Trevor Carter had meant by my connections, and why Agnes had come to me, why Sam had recognized the name of her firm, why he'd been against me investigating, and why he'd been arguing with John on the day that he had died. John Layton: the last piece of the puzzle slotting neatly into place.

I'd emerged from Wandsworth and was heading towards Putney Heath. The houses were getting larger, the pavements cleaner. What life had shown itself on the streets was now gone.

I stopped at a red light: just me and the sound of the engine ticking over. I sat motionless in my motionless car knowing that the jigsaw was not complete. I could believe many things of John Layton but the one I couldn't believe was that he could have killed his only son.

I tried to look at it dispassionately. Putting the larger

horror aside, I dealt only with the peripherals. For a start, I thought, it wasn't credible that John, for whom style was everything, would have arranged to meet anyone, especially his son, in a car. As for running him over – it didn't fit.

I saw vague movement in front of me, the traffic lights turning green. I ignored them. I sat thinking that if John had wanted Sam killed he would never have done it himself. John was no delegator, he kept all power concentrated in his own hands, but he knew how to spread the dirty work around. Just as he would persuade (and of course, pay) someone like Greg to be his fall guy on a pension scam, he would have hired a professional to commit a murder.

But that was patently ridiculous: what hired assassin would operate by running people over? And besides, what reason could John have for killing Sam? The way the companies' pension funds had been stripped sailed close to fraud but John had kept his name well out of it. And even if there was a tenuous connection somewhere – and one that could be proved – would it be ruinous enough to John to make him kill?

I shook my head. I couldn't believe it, not of John. A gambler he might be, but when he acted, he always planned meticulously. Yet Sam's murder had about it the stink of opportunism, the seizing of an uncharacteristically empty street to do the deed.

I thought about what that person must be like. An impulse murderer, but, judging from the picture he'd sent to me and the way he'd disposed of the cat, a man also who liked to watch his victim squirm. A man who . . .

I was startled suddenly by the barking of a horn. I looked round. There was a car behind me, its driver with his window open leaning out and gesticulating wildly. I hadn't heard him drive up and had no idea how long he'd been there: by the sound of his cursing, quite a while.

I straightened myself up, put the car in gear and drove across the intersection.

I didn't go much further. As soon as the road widened, I indicated left and stopped. The car behind accelerated, and with a final angry blaring of its horn, passed me by.

I got out and began walking. I headed for the common, over a fence that seemed no obstacle, and across the marshy ground. I wasn't thinking. I was walking – preferably into darkness, alone, away from other people's curses and other people's deeds, into the embrace of silence.

It didn't help. My thoughts were too insistent. They came as images, a lifeless collage: Sam's waxen corpse, the cat's macabre grin, the bodies of those I'd seen in the five years that had separated those two acts – the nameless deaths too numerous to count. And above that one single thought – I was using death to block it out but it was too powerful even for that. One thought: that Sam had known about John Layton's involvement, had known that Agnes had come to me because of my connections with John, and yet, knowing all this, Sam had not told me.

Was I that impossible to talk to? I knew that John Layton and the things he did to make money was a subject that Sam couldn't broach without losing his temper, but this was different. This concerned me. And yet he'd done what I would never have dreamed he'd do, had gone behind my back to meddle in my work.

I felt tears welling. I stood in the centre of flattened land, the sky huge and dark above me, and the only thing in my mind was that everything that I had once believed about my relationship with Sam was gone. The knowledge came as quiet confirmation. I blinked. My eyes were dry: no tears would come.

I'd had enough of standing. I pushed myself into motion, walking quickly to my car.

*

As I drove up Kingston Hill I saw the first intimation of the dawn – tenuous silver and pale pink streaking across the distant sky. It was a promise only of things to come: above me all was dark. I was almost upon the crest of the hill – John Layton's gates to my left. I turned the wheel.

And found that I could drive straight in. As I approached them, the gates opened. John Layton was expecting me. I kept an even speed, driving towards his house.

He was waiting by the front door. It looked like he'd been waiting a long time. He was fully dressed, formal in three-piece black, and in the murkiness of the dawn light I could see his cheeks flushed red with cold. I began to walk towards him. I heard my feet crunching against the gravel, loud against the muted sounds of dawn. Of dawn and of mourning as well, I thought, remembering how I had sat up the nights following the news of Sam's death. I kept on going.

When I was almost upon him, he placed one finger on his lips. 'I'd be obliged if you'd keep the noise level down. There are people here asleep.'

People. 'Matthew?'

John winced. 'He stayed the night. Dentist appointment.' He looked at me, daring me to say something. When I didn't, all he said was: 'Come.'

He led me through the vast hallway, up the stately stairs and into a first-floor room. What I had seen of the house before had been grandiose and designed to impress; this was different, shaped for comfort. John's office, with a large, modern desk, a leather sofa and a matching couple of easy chairs. No books, just a sideboard containing a vast array of alcohol. John opened it. He took out two glasses and a cut glass decanter which he held, inquiringly, in the air.

I shook my head.

'Too early for you?' he said and poured himself a stiff

one. By the look of his trembling hand, it was not the first he'd had.

He gestured carelessly at one of the armchairs. I sat in it, and watched as he walked round the desk and stood, for a moment, by the window. The dawn had taken root, – the pink blush now flecked with encroaching grey. John stood looking at it through his leaded windows. He tipped the glass up, taking a long slug. And then, turning, he put the glass down and sat behind his desk.

'You knew I was coming,' I said.

His lips twitched. 'Greg Willis is very zealous.' He wasn't smiling. 'Not that I hadn't expected you to turn up soon. You never could leave anything alone, could you?' His voice was bitter in its softness.

'Is that what the money was for?' I asked. 'So I would leave you alone?'

This time his smile was genuine – and shot through with contempt. 'There's nothing you can do to harm me.'

'So why pay me?'

I hadn't expected an answer but I got one. 'Because of Matthew,' he said. 'These are important years for him. The last thing he needs is to have you playing with his affections before pulling another vanishing act.'

Another . . . I stiffened. 'You stopped me seeing him.'

He nodded, almost imperceptibly. 'But then,' he said, talking so softly he might almost have been talking to himself, 'you were so easy to stop, weren't you?'

I felt something tugging at my chest. I swallowed it back down. I asked a question that I had asked before, made more plain now. 'Why do you hate me?'

And got a different answer – 'Because you killed him' – spat out like venom. I sat quite still, wondering whether I was wrong: was this man so unhinged that he was capable of killing his own son?

'You and your sixties twaddle,' I heard, 'infected my

son.' John wasn't looking at me, he was talking to a spot beyond me. He got up suddenly, turning away.

'Sam was his own person,' I told his back. 'With his own ideas.'

John kept on talking. 'Of course I made mistakes.' His shoulders lifted. 'I admit that. After his mother died I was so busy ensuring our financial security, I didn't pay enough attention to his emotional development. But other people make mistakes' – he said it loudly – 'and their children come round eventually. As Sam would have done. If not' – he whirled round, his eyes blazing – 'for you.'

'For me?' It was all I could think to say.

It was enough. His jaw, its line so like my Sam's jaw, was tight with rage. 'You were responsible for his death.' His face was ugly. 'You his murderer.' He took a step closer. 'You turned him against me, you and your utopian ideas.' Another step. 'And then, as if that wasn't enough, you turned your childish detective agency on me – investigating my business. You did it deliberately, didn't you, you spent the years trying to find something to implicate me and when you did . . .'

I was on my feet, from fear as much as anything. 'I –'

That's as far as I got.

'Don't you dare interrupt me!' His voice was a low rumble of menace. 'I know exactly what you did. I have my sources. I know you were out to make trouble. And you did – you killed my son.' His blue eyes were flared, made purple by the outrage which propelled him forward. He was almost upon me. 'You got him so upset' – he was there – 'you forced him to accuse me of all sorts of crime and got him so upset he went out and walked under the nearest car.'

He was so close his spittle sprayed me. In that moment everything I'd thought before fled. He's capable of murder, I told myself: move.

I stayed there, mesmerized by the ferocity of his rage.

I smelt his whisky-soaked breath. I saw his arms come up. Move, I told myself. His hands were round my neck, the weight of him pushing me back against the wall. He was closing on me. I felt his breath mingling with mine, his hands, warm and hard, squeezing my windpipe, squeezing the life . . .

I heard a sound, a roaring, and in the distance beyond it, another . . .

'What?'

When John Layton let go, I slumped back against the wall, knocking my head as I slithered down.

'What are you doing?' Matthew's voice.

I twisted my head round. Matthew was standing in the doorway, rubbing his eyes as if he could not believe what he was seeing.

'Go back to bed.' This from John.

'But Kate.' Matthew took a step inside.

It wasn't right that Matthew should witness this. I pulled myself together and up. On my feet I said, in as firm a voice as I could muster: 'I'm fine. Go back to bed.'

He looked as if I had assaulted him but he obeyed, closing the door behind him as he left.

Silence. For a long time. Until, that is, John spoke: 'Get out of here,' issuing his instruction into the air.

Chapter
thirty-five

I don't know exactly how I got there but I was suddenly outside. I could feel a wind, icy against my throat. My fingers went up, touching my neck. I could feel where bruises would soon be forming. I didn't bother with them. I stood there, thinking that the worst thing was not the pain but the fact that as John's hands had closed around my throat my main thought was how similar they were to Sam's. And as John's fingers gripped my windpipe, I had yielded. I, who had never considered myself a victim, had deliberately given in. Instead of planning an escape route, all I could think was that I deserved this.

Again it came, the realization that I had not spent the last five years running away from the reality of my relationship with Sam. I had been fleeing a different foreboding – the feeling that I had been responsible for Sam's death.

I heard a sound, a window opening. I didn't want to be observed, not by anybody. I ran over to my car and began to drive towards the gate. I never got there. I was crying so hard that my vision was completely blurred. I had to stop.

I was suffocating. I got out of the car and stumbled, still crying, across John Layton's immaculate lawn. It was too exposed. I kept on going, heading for a clump of trees at one of the lawn's corners. When I got there, I leaned against a tree trunk, the tears washing down my face.

I stood there crying, thinking that I was responsible – not in the way that John had said but because, in that last week, I had not tried to wrench Sam out of his withdrawn state. I'd known it wasn't random, that it had something to do with me, but I'd chosen to ignore it. At the time I'd told myself that I was doing the right thing, that this was one of our occasional blips, that Sam must learn to separate himself and his disapproval from my work, that it probably had nothing to do with me. I'd known though, that it did.

And I'd done nothing.

That's why I hadn't moved out of John's way. Because I had felt I deserved it. And that's why, I suppose, I'd chosen to be a war correspondent – I was giving fate a more than even chance of paying me back.

My tears had slowed. As I waited for their end, I relived what had happened in John Layton's study. I was no longer scared. Although John Layton had tried to strangle me, he was no murderer. The force of his pent-up rage had driven him to shake me, not to kill: even before Matthew had arrived, I could, in hindsight, feel the pressure slackening off.

I was no longer crying. I was drained. I looked up. Above me splayed out the leafless branches of a birch, an anaemic grey-tinged sky filling out the space between them. I stared up.

I was no longer looking at the birch. A tree, but not the birch, I thought. I was running to the car. Another tree. I had it, the missing piece of the jigsaw. I drove as fast as I was able all the way to Maria and Jurek's house.

Arriving back, I went straight upstairs. My suitcase was where I had stashed it under the bed. I hauled it out and, fumbling clumsily in my haste, eventually managed to open it. It was there somewhere, I knew it, packed safely amongst a set of documents. I pulled the whole lot out and began rummaging through. Too fast – I couldn't find it.

Forcing myself into what felt like a painstakingly artificial dawdle, I began, methodically, to search the pile.

I found it easily enough: its cardboard-backed envelope wedged between two pages of notes. Slowly I withdrew it. And saw then that familiar face, Sam smiling into the dying light and behind him the flat foliage of a cedar.

I knew where it had been taken. At John Layton's house – the one he used to own. The one which had a special evergreen section and, in pride of place, that cedar.

It had clicked into place now – almost all of it.

I went downstairs. I found the business directory and looked up a number. I dialled it. It rang and rang. I held on to the receiver for a long, long time until it occurred to me to look at my watch: six-thirty a.m. Far too early. I put the phone down.

At eight Maria and Jurek appeared. I kept my head well down but still they must have seen by my posture that they'd get nothing sensible from me. They didn't even bother trying. They fixed themselves breakfast and passed some on to me. I may even have eaten part of it – I wasn't sure – if I did, my taste buds certainly didn't inform me. They were, I suppose, on hold, like the rest of me, waiting until the phone would be answered.

At eight-forty-five I tried again. Still nothing.

At that point, Maria, who'd gone to get dressed, came briefly back. I must have had my head raised when I turned. Her eyes, flaring in alarm, fixed on my throat. 'What happened?'

I kept my mouth tight closed. I had been awake for many hours, I had no energy, other than for the job in hand.

She knew enough about me not to waste her breath asking again. 'We are painting again today,' she said.

'Shall we leave you our number?'

I shook my head. Maria wrote a number on a slip of paper anyway and handed it to me. When I didn't take it she slipped it into my pocket, kissed me lightly on the cheek and then was gone.

I sat there by the phone. The time crawled on past.

I was pretty sure now what answer I would get, but at nine precisely I hit the redial button. This time a breezy voice answered promptly. 'Layton Securities. Can I help you?'

'Roger Toms,' I said, my voice so hoarse it came out like a croak. I cleared it and tried again. 'Roger Toms.'

'Mr Toms has not yet arrived.' She was unrelentingly cheerful. 'Can I put you through to –'

I put the phone down. So I was right. Roger still worked for John. Roger whom I thought I had met by accident but who must have been following me. Roger whom Sam had so disliked. I remembered now when I had last seen him – at Sam's funeral. He'd been standing next to John. Roger Toms was John Layton's henchman. And Gary Brown's errand boy as well?

I sat by the phone, watching the minute hand on my watch tick round. At nine-thirty I dialled again.

'Layton Securities.' Same voice. 'Can I help you?'

'Roger Toms.'

I got a different answer. 'Mr Toms is in a meeting. Hold on. I'll put you through to his secretary.' A click and then another, lower, less cheerful voice came on. 'Mr Toms's office. Janice speaking. How can I be of assistance?'

'Is Roger in?'

'I'm afraid he's in a meeting.' She didn't sound afraid, she sounded bored. 'Can I take a message?'

'When will he be available?' I had tried to make my voice mellow but it came out rough.

Which alerted her. 'Who is this?'

I gave her the first name that came into my head –
Agnes Wilson – and then asked again when Roger would
be out.

'By midday,' she said. 'Should I tell him –'

I hung up cursing myself for using that name.

I pushed the business directory away, and grabbing the
residential L–Z flicked rapidly through. I found him.
Toms, R, his phone number and his N8 address. But then
I pushed the phone book away. It wasn't Roger I wanted,
it was Gary Brown. I grabbed my car keys.

And changed my mind. I sat down again and hit the
redial. This time when the telephonist answered, I asked
for the boss: 'John Layton.'

It was a very long shot. I hadn't expected to get past the
first level of interference, never mind be put through to
his personal assistant. But in a surprisingly short time I'd
finessed the hierarchy and was on final hold.

'Kate.' John sounded subdued. 'I don't know what –'

'Never mind.' I didn't want to hear his explanation, or
even his apology. 'How long has Roger Toms been working for you?'

'Roger?' The old John Layton bravado resurged: 'What
business is it . . .' and waned. 'Seven years,' he said.

Seven years. I backtracked. 'He's been working for you
since 1986?'

'Nineteen eighty-five,' John said. 'He went away to India
in '86. Why –'

I didn't stop to answer why. I dropped my receiver down.

India. I remembered Gary Brown's arm clutching mine
and the Sikh bracelet around his wrist. It could not be a
coincidence. The fit was complete. Gary and Roger had
both been in India and Roger, who had been following
me, must have done it for Gary.

Grabbing my car keys, I left.

*

My adrenalin rush survived until I arrived outside Gary Brown's Kings Cross estate. I parked the car but did not get out. I sat there, wondering what I was planning to do. I remembered Gary Brown's yellowing teeth closing in on me and I remembered the words his followers had used. If Gary Brown was out I'd never get through his steel-covered doors. If he was in I'd never get out alive.

I turned the key. Well, if Gary Brown was too danger-ous, Roger Toms would have to do. I knew where he was – safe at work – and I betted I would be able to breach his defences easily enough. I pulled out. That's what I'd do: I'd go to Roger's and see what I could find.

I found his street in the *A–Z*. As I plotted out my route, I remembered how, when I'd asked Roger whether he lived close by, he'd answered: 'Sort of.' Well Crouch End was sort of close to Dalston just like you can sort of get a sun tan in Britain in December and like I was sort of going to respect his privacy by waiting for him to get out of his meeting.

I located his house – a three-storey number in a Crouch End back street – easily enough. I parked the car outside and walked up the stone steps. I rang the door bell long and hard, just to be sure. No one answered, neither then nor when I rang again. I looked to left and right. No one in sight. I put my hand into the letter box, checking. Nothing there. I crouched down and peered through it: again nothing.

Straightening up I did what I had not done for more than five years. I broke into a house. It wasn't difficult – he had it closed on one single Yale which was easily slipped. I pushed the door gently ajar, took one last brief look back and, seeing no one, hurried inside.

I was standing in a largish hallway, my feet on a varnished wooden floor. To the right were two doors; in front, a stairway carpeted by deep navy blue pile. I went to the right, choosing the first of the doors. They led the same way anyway, to a sitting room that ran from back to front. Someone had done a lot of careful shopping to ensure an ambience of black and white: black leather furniture, white walls with black-framed black-and-white photographs carefully arranged on them. I stood at the junction between its two halves, seeing glass side tables glistening, and modern black-chromed up-lighters pointing at the ceiling. It was like standing in a Conran showroom – everything in its place. Nothing, not even a newspaper, to give it personality.

The photographs – views of a vast land – were originals. Even they were somehow characterless. There was something dreamy about the composition, and something uninvolved. Where there were people, they were only uneasily present. The man standing by his two water buffaloes had a vague look on his face as if he wasn't exactly sure what he was supposed to be doing, and the children, taken from a distance, dots against the splendour of the Indian landscape, played without awareness of the camera's spying gaze.

Spying, I thought, and shook myself alert. I left the room and went upstairs. The next floor was just as sterile: a gleaming modern kitchen and leading off it a dining room, a formal glistening oval table and eight chairs tucked in. I guessed it was all for show. The double-fronted glassed-in fridge, containing a few desultory sauce jars, a pint of low fat milk, and nothing much else, indicated someone who ate mainly in restaurants. Nothing here for me. I climbed the next set of stairs.

Upstairs was where the action was. Not the bedroom – this continued the black-and-white theme, with black-mirrored cupboards, white carpets and a bed dressed in silky white. But the room next door was different. The house's precision was no longer evident.

Running the length of one of its walls was a long wooden surface, with wide drawers on either side. It continued round the corner, interrupted by a sink. On the windows, waiting to be pulled down, was the obligatory black – but by the look of the developer, the trays by the sink, and the red bulb in the light socket, these blinds were purely functional. Not that the room was one big darkroom. It served as a study as well – a portable computer was sitting on a purpose-built trolley and beside it stood a wooden scrolled desk.

This room, unlike the others in the house, was alive. If I was going to find anything it would be here. I went over to the photographic section and up to the rope that had been tied across one corner, on which pieces of paper had been pegged.

They weren't any old paper, they were photographs. And not any old photographs – they were all of Sam. My eyes travelled along the row, moving from one to the next. I saw Sam in various poses, Sam with John, Sam alone, Sam looking grim in all except one, a copy of the one Roger had sent me – Sam smiling in front of John Layton's cedar.

I must have stood there for a long time, but eventually I came to. I pulled myself away. What I was after was not memories but proof of Roger's connection with Gary Brown. I walked over to the roll-topped desk.

It took me a moment to find the button which released its covering. When I did, I pushed it too hard. The top went scrolling back, hitting the stop with a bang. I jumped and stood silent for a moment. When all I heard was the same background street noises that I'd heard all along I looked more closely at the desk.

It had three compartments, one open on either side and in their middle a set of drawers. I gripped the knob of the top one and pulled. Nothing happened. The drawer, and its two fellows as well, was locked. Oh well, I'd deal with that later. What I'd do first, I thought, was flick through what was easily available.

There was a wheeled typing chair by the computer station. I fetched it, rolling it over to the desk. I sat down on it and pulled a set of files closer. As I did so, I thought I heard a noise. A footstep. I froze.

I waited for what seemed like an eternity but what was probably only a few seconds. No other footsteps joined the first. Thinking that if I was going to be ambushed I'd rather be standing, I got up. And heard a voice: 'See you later then,' coming from outside. Nothing like breaking into someone's house to get the paranoia going, I thought, knowing that the footstep I had heard had also been outside. I made myself relax. I sat down again, and, turning my attention to the top file I began to riffle though it.

By the time I had emptied the left-hand compartment I knew a lot about Roger Toms's income – comfortable and mainly from Layton Securities – and very little else. Nothing at all about Gary Brown. I glanced at my watch. Eleven-fifteen – I had plenty of time. I packed the files I'd been examining together, making sure they were all straight, and gently put them back where I had found them. Then I reached out for the second lot.

I never got any closer. I heard another voice. It did not come from the street. It came from behind me. 'You won't find it there,' it said.

I whirled round. The voice belonged to Roger Toms. He was standing in the doorway.

Chapter

thirty-six

He was smiling. 'Looking for this?' From behind his back came his hand; in it a scarf. Sam's red scarf. 'Careless of him to leave it in the car.' His smile widened. 'I would normally have returned it but . . .' He paused and I saw that he wasn't really smiling. His eyes were still and cold, '. . . in the circumstances.' He dipped his head once, briefly. 'I'm sure you understand.'

At that moment I understood only two things: that this man was dangerous and that he was blocking the exit. The terror I felt was immediate. I opened my mouth to scream.

He was much too fast for me. He was upon me, one hand clapped over my mouth, the other grappling my arms behind my back. I could smell him, not full of whisky as John Layton had been, but faintly of peppermint and expensive aftershave. His flesh was in my mouth. I bit down, hard.

Not hard enough. He cursed and, shifting his weight, stuffed something into my mouth. Sam's scarf. He pushed it in so far that it pressed against the back of my tongue. I was choking. 'Too tight?' His voice, quite pleasant. I felt his hand tighten on mine and the scarf push deeper.

The cashmere was jammed against my throat. I was retching. Every time I took another gasping breath, I breathed in more of the scarf.

'Can't have the neighbours seeing this,' a voice said in my ear. I was hauled across the room. With one hand he held on to my arms, while the other pulled first one and then the second blind down.

We were in total darkness.

'Too dark,' he said and, shoving me forwards, forced me across the room. He stopped at the door. He lifted his hand. The light – deep red – clicked on. 'That's better, isn't it?' he whispered.

I shivered. There was an unmistakable timbre to his voice – seduction. I could feel him pressed up against me, could feel his swelling penis against my legs. I tried to pull away.

Which made it worse. He shoved me back, grinding himself into me. I yelped, the sound smothered by the scarf. He pushed me, so hard that I was slammed against a wall. His free hand pushed my shoulders. 'Down.'

I was on my knees. I was in a corner, facing the wall, Roger crouched beside me. I felt his breath hot in my ear. 'I don't want you to choke,' he said softly. 'I'll take the gag off if you promise you won't shout out. Think about it, why don't you.' As he withdrew I felt his tongue, licking my ear. I couldn't help myself: I shivered.

His hands tightened on mine, digging into my wrists. 'Are you going to scream?'

I shook my head.

'Good.' His tongue was back, moistening my ear. I held myself rigid. And felt his hands leaving mine and pulling the scarf out.

Air rushed into my lungs. I heard a sound – me gulping.

'Turn round.'

I turned. Roger had got a chair. He was sitting astraddle it. His pale skin reflected back the red.

'Sit,' he said.

I sat on my heels, my back jammed tight into the corner.

His face loomed closer. 'Why did you come back to London?'

I searched my sluggish mind, trying to find an answer.

But he didn't need one. 'Five years,' he said. 'I was safe.' A moment's silence and then he said it again: 'I was safe,' as if I'd contradicted him.

My weight bore down, heavy on my feet.

His voice caressed me. 'I was with Greg that night when Pam phoned to say you were coming back. I was in control, right from the beginning. I made Greg tell Pam that if she knew what was good for her, she'd get you to stay at their house. I wanted to know where you were every minute of the day. Because, you see, I knew what you were after.'

After? I thought. I saw a visual echo – my own hand signing my father's document.

Roger's voice overrode the image. 'I was ahead of you – your puppet-master. And then you decided to make your move – turning round like that in Dalston – playing smart, showing me that you knew I was following you. You thought you were clever, didn't you? Insulting me like that, pretending you'd forgotten my name.'

An inner voice cried out, silently – but I *had* forgotten – and then was stilled.

'I asked where you were staying,' Roger said, 'just to see what you would do. When you went along with me – giving me the address as if you didn't know I knew it. Well . . .' What flashed across his face could have been a smile but when he spoke again his face was grim. 'That's when I knew for sure,' he said. 'That I would have to . . .'

He didn't finish the sentence. He didn't have to.

I swallowed. Hard.

He wasn't finished. 'I've got nothing against you.' His

voice was soft and almost sad. 'It would have been all right. Why did you have to keep on prying – finding Gary Brown like that? If only you'd kept away.'

I met his gaze full on.

His melancholy was replaced by a flash of anger. 'How much do you know?'

I said what I was thinking: 'Does it matter?'

He was fast, on his feet, in front of his chair. He hit me across the face. My head banged back against the wall.

'How much?'

My hand went up.

'Put it down.'

I dropped it.

'How much?' His face looming close, his eyes bulging.

I talked, just to get him away. 'You used to do odd jobs for John Layton,' I said. 'I know you work full time for him now.'

He backed off a fraction. 'So I gather. You phoned my office. More.'

He was still too close. I couldn't think. I needed distance. 'I know you were involved in the pension scam.'

'A perfectly legal movement of funds.' His teeth looked yellow in his darkroom light. 'Unfortunate that the first company went broke: it took the whole pack of cards with it.' His smile was abruptly cut off. 'More.'

'I know,' I said and paused. Thoughts kept coming, separated by time, the first one me realizing how stupid I had been to leave Agnes's name when I'd phoned his office. I felt rather than saw his hand this time, whipping across my cheek. I gasped.

'Don't hesitate,' he said. 'Speak.'

My mind was finally in gear, the pieces slotting into place. 'Speak.'

I spoke. 'I know you had Gary Brown watching Agnes Wilson,' I said. 'In case she stepped out of line.'

His eyes static, fixed on me. 'Yes – that was convenient – me knowing Gary. More.'

I closed my lips, pressing them in on each other.

He came nearer. 'More.'

I shook my head.

He shoved his face closer: I closed my eyes. I felt his thumb and index finger, one on each side of my face, digging into bone. 'You don't get it do you?' I kept my eyes closed. 'Let me explain.' I couldn't shut his voice out. 'Whatever happens,' I heard him saying, 'you're finished. Not because I want it but because you've forced my hand.' His fingers pressed harder, I felt the power of it reverberating through my jaw. 'You can make it easier on yourself,' I heard him whispering, 'or,' another notch up of pressure, 'more painful.'

When he removed his hand the sharpness of the pain was converted into a dull thudding that had me moaning involuntarily. I bit my tongue. I wouldn't give him that satisfaction.

'More,' I heard him saying.

I opened my eyes, saw him crouching by me. He's right, I thought, I've got to keep talking.

The last piece of the puzzle clicked into place. 'You sent Agnes to me.'

He nodded.

'What were you trying to do? Discredit John Layton?'

His eyes glittered, contemptuous. 'No, of course not,' he said. 'I was trying what I almost succeeded in doing. I was damning you in John Layton's eyes, and with you Sam. John's sense failed him when it came to his son. He kept on thinking that Sam would eventually agree to work in the company. In my place. I couldn't have that. I had to show John how disloyal Sam was. And it almost worked, you know. John was furious when Sam told him you were investigating his companies. He thought you were deliberately trying to set him up.'

My jaw was radiating pain. I wondered whether he'd hit me again if I tried to rub it. I wondered whether it had been broken. I saw movement and I hastily spoke. 'But Sam knew of Agnes,' I said. 'He had worked in some of John's factories and got to know many of the employees. When I told him she had hired me, it must have rung a bell. He would have known then that it was no coincidence. So he got in touch with you.'

I could see anticipation in Roger's eyes – he was about to move.

'For that you killed him,' I said.

He shook his head. 'No, not for that. It was an impulse thing.' Said casually like someone else might say an impulse buy. That, I thought, is why he wants me to talk – so he can brag about what he's done. 'We met in the car,' he said. 'He told me what he knew. He was going to go to John. I wasn't planning to do anything but when he crossed the road in front of me I thought how easy it would be to squash him flat. The next thing I knew I'd done it. It was easy.'

Easy, he said and his eyes closed. His face seemed momentarily to crumple and when he opened them again I saw a flash of pure desolation crossing their pupils. What I had thought before was wrong: he wasn't bragging; he wanted absolution.

Well, I wouldn't give it to him.

'Kate,' he said – pleading.

I saw Sam's waxen skin filtered through the intervening years.

'Kate.'

I didn't say anything. I didn't need to. My eyes said no.

His face hardened. He leant down and, grabbing one of my hands, used it to haul me up. 'I always liked you, you know,' he said.

No, I wanted to shout, I didn't know. How could I have? I had hardly ever noticed him.

'Sam kept us apart.' His voice sliced through my voiceless denial. 'He was jealous of me, you see, because I was like a son to John.' He pulled me closer. I felt his body against mine. 'I'm sorry for what I have to do.'

We were practically embracing. I arched my neck back, away from his lips. 'You won't get away with it.'

He chuckled. 'That's my problem, don't you think?'

'I . . .'

His hand pressed into my windpipe. 'I've read the script as well,' he said. 'And I know that this is when you tell me that you left a note saying where you've gone.' He pulled my head forward, so that I was facing him.

I kept my gaze steady – as steady as I could.

'But then,' he said. 'That's not like you is it? You're an independent woman. Used to drive Sam mad.' I felt his hand stroking my neck. 'You're not the kind to ask for help. So I'll take the risk, that no one knows where you are.'

'Pam,' I said, gasping the word out.

He laughed. Quickly and without amusement. 'Pam won't help you. With the dirt I have on Greg's business disasters, neither of them even take a shit without asking my permission. No – I'm safe. I've got it all worked out. I have somewhere to put you and if they do find you' – his hand lingered on my skin – 'they'll blame John not me. He was the one who tried to strangle you. In front of a witness.'

A witness. Matthew.

He felt me stiffen. 'Oh, you didn't know?' he said. 'Matthew and I are great friends. I'm like a big brother. I get to take him to the dentist and in the waiting room he confides in me.' He shoved me suddenly. I fell back, hitting my head.

I heard myself moaning. I felt him coming closer, felt his knee edging up inside my legs. I twisted my head away.

'Don't worry,' he whispered. 'I'm not going to fuck you. I'm not into necrophilia.'

The scarf was round my neck. He yanked my head forward to get it round the back and, having done that, began pulling. It was too fast – closing in on me. His voice sounded in my ear, so near it could have been my own. 'Why did you come back?' I heard him hissing. 'It was gone. I was forgetting. Why did you come back?'

His voice faded. I felt the scarf squeezing, crushing the life out of me. I felt my vision blurring. My body sagged, going slack. He was so concentrated on me that my every movement, however slight, carried him too. He fell forward, momentarily letting go.

In that moment of relief, I knew one thing clearly. I knew that I didn't want to die. All those years that I'd spent in war zones the one thing that had not worried me had been the possibility of my own death. And when I came back as well – I tackled the muggers because I hadn't really cared what would happen. But now I cared. I didn't want to die.

I felt the scarf tighten. My time was running out. I had only a few seconds before it would be too late. My brain was working furiously. I acted. I let my breath out and collapsed. It worked – the weight of my body pulled him forward again.

I saw myself standing on a London tube. I saw two women standing by me. I saw them smiling as they talked. I heard their voices. *Kick him in the balls* one said, while the other had a different strategy: *go for their eyes.*

I went for the eyes. I wrenched my arm from behind my back and with two fingers, the index and the middle, pointing, I jabbed. Down and as hard as I could.

One went wide; the other hit target. I felt it prodding into something squishy, jellyfish soft. Instead of withdrawing it, I pushed harder.

I heard Roger Toms scream. I felt him let go. He fell on top of me. I staggered back. His weight had pinned me down. I pushed. No movement. I pushed again and with one giant effort shoved him aside. I pushed with all my might, past him, stumbling across the room, sending the chair flying, tugging the door open, down the stairs. I heard so much noise, none of it differentiated. I heard crying out, and panting, and someone moaning, and I wasn't sure which of the noises came from me and which from Roger. All I knew was that I had to keep moving.

Chapter
thirty-seven

I didn't know if he was following me. I didn't
dare look back. I heard something roaring. It could have
been Roger: it could have been my blood pumping. I kept
on going so fast that, at the top of the final flight of stairs,
I lost my footing. I toppled forward. My hands clawed air.
I felt myself rolling, sharp edges digging in. I landed at
the bottom. I was dazed. I lay still.

I heard a sound. An alien sound. It didn't come from
me. I looked up.

Roger was standing at the top of the flight of stairs, one
hand pressed tightly to his eye. 'I'll get you,' he said. He
lurched forward.

I was up and running for the door.

'I'll get you eventually,' I heard him shouting.

I wrenched the door open.

If I'd stopped to think I would have known that he
wouldn't dare follow me – not out into the daylit road. But
I didn't stop to think. I half ran, half fell down the stone
steps and, carried forward by my own momentum,
slammed into my car. I dug in my pockets, searching
out my keys. My hands fumbled; I couldn't find them.
I was crying in frustration. I jerked at my pocket, tearing
the lining. I felt metal about to fall through. I pulled at
it.

Too hard. The keys went flying up into the air. They

landed on the pavement – just near Roger's house. I ran to them, bent down.

'Are you all right?' I heard.

My head jerked up. I saw a woman peering at me. She didn't stay for long. One glance at my face and she paled, gasped and was gone.

I picked the keys up, ran to the car, got in and drove off.

A single look at the mirror was enough to tell me why the woman had gone scuttling off. I was a study in bruised pigment. There were gashes of crimson on my cheeks, vermilion indentations along the line of my jaw and around my neck deep bruises caught in the transition between red and purple. All in all I looked as if I'd been napalmed. I swivelled the mirror so that I could no longer see myself.

I drove turning right and left at random, twisting to get away not only physically but also psychologically. I didn't manage to. I was looking straight ahead but what I kept seeing was not the road but Roger Toms's face. He was coming closer, his eyes bulging. I saw his tongue, red, furred, darting out. I felt it licking my ear. I shivered violently. The steering wheel followed my motion. I swerved and almost hit a lamppost. I braked. And sat, my car diagonal across the road, my head resting on the steering wheel.

I didn't cry. The time for crying was gone. I just sat.

I sat for a long time until I heard a car's horn, blasting loud. I looked up. Someone's Ford Fiesta was trying to manoeuvre past. Seeing me look up, he hammered on his horn again. I straightened my car. 'Bloody maniac,' I heard as the Ford sped down the road.

Flesh closed in on me again. I screwed my eyes up, annihilating the memory of Roger Toms's face with darkness. But I couldn't stay there, not for ever. I needed help.

Maria. I suddenly remembered her giving me her

259

number. I felt in my jeans pocket, pulled out the slip of paper. I looked round, saw a phone box on the corner. I got out of the car and as I stumbled towards the phone, I shoved my hand down, past the ripped lining, pulling out coins. I had enough. I was at the phone box. I staggered in and dialled.

The phone rang and rang and with each successive empty ring, my energy was further drained. I stood there, leaning against the kiosk's wall; I didn't know what I was going to do if she didn't answer.

She answered. I said only one thing: 'Maria.'

There was silence, probably only for a moment, but to me it felt like an eternity. I concentrated my energy on holding on to the receiver and on keeping myself upright. Eventually Maria's voice sounded from the distance. 'Go home, Kate. I'll meet you there.'

They were waiting for me when I arrived – the three of them, Maria, Jurek and Anna. They had got to know each other fast enough to sit in companionable silence. I watched them, each in their separate ways, registering the state of my face. They didn't comment.

I sat down. The strength went out of me. I felt myself enveloped by lethargy. My eyelids drooped. I made a half-hearted attempt to push them open but my weariness was stronger than my will. I felt myself sinking into quiet unconsciousness. It was a tremendous relief. As my conscious brain gave up, I gave up trying to resist. It felt wonderful to give up, let the darkness enfold me. My mind emptied.

The slumping of my head, my chin hitting my chest, wrenched me awake. I felt someone close, moving in on me. My eyes shot open. It was only Jurek waiting with a glass in hand. 'Here,' he said in an uncharacteristically gentle voice. 'Drink this.'

I took the glass and raised it to my lips. I smelt brandy. I took a sip. It smoothed itself over my tongue, sliding to the back of my throat, but when it hit, it burned like hell. I started coughing. I couldn't stop. I was possessed by ugly hacking coming in successive waves, my whole body juddering with each bout. Something in the back of my mind told me that I could have stopped. I didn't. That something was also clued up enough to know that the coughing was there in place of tears. And I didn't want to cry. It wasn't time.

Eventually my coughs receded. When they had gone, speech returned. I told them what had happened. I weaved some detail into my account, describing the house, each room in sequence, the photographs on the wall, my searching of Roger's desk and his sudden appearance. At this point what had been a graphic sketch became a miniature, faithful to each microscopic detail. I told them what Roger had been wearing, what he said, what he did. I catalogued for them each separate blow up to the moment when my finger had squished into his eye. The only thing I left out was how I felt. When I had finished, I closed my eyes.

'You did good,' I heard.

I opened my eyes. They were all three looking at me. Anna was their spokesperson. 'What are we going to do?'

We. I shook my head. I was alone in this. Roger was going to get me, not them. And to get me not because I was a danger to him – what could I prove after all this time? – but because I was a reminder of what he'd done.

'What are we going to do?'

I was on my feet. 'There's only one thing I can do.'

Chapter
thirty-eight

I changed my clothes and wrapped a chiffon scarf around my throat. When I got down they were all waiting for me. I took no notice: I was concentrated on the task in hand, weighing up how I should do it, how I should ration the truth with the things I only half suspected. I left the house and went to my car. They followed. I got in. They were in perfect sync: they each chose a separate door and, grasping the door handles, stood there, waiting.

I rolled my window down. 'I've got to do this on my own.'

'In which case . . .' Leaving his doorside post, Jurek marched round to the front of the car. He stood, blocking my exit. He didn't say anything more. He didn't need to: his face's determination said it all.

I had only a short supply of energy left. If I didn't go now, I wouldn't be able to. The thought was tempting. I felt myself relax.

I'll get you eventually, I heard Roger's voice saying. I knew what that meant and I knew that he was serious. I had to go on and see this through to the end. I turned and pulled each of the car door catches up.

Instead of getting into the passenger seat, Anna walked round and opened my door. 'Let me drive.'

I shifted over, leaned back and with my eyes closed told her where to go.

I slept until the car's stopping wakened me. I opened my eyes. Anna had parked just outside the gate that led to the Kings Cross estate. I opened my door. They did likewise. I shook my head. 'You can't come with me.'

'You're not going alone.' This from Jurek.

I knew why he was saying it, but I also knew that he was wrong. With them in tow, it wouldn't work. 'I can't go with three of you,' I said. I closed my door.

They closed theirs.

'It won't work,' I said it loudly.

'You're not going alone,' all in unison.

I saw them looking at me and I read in all their faces the words they didn't say: that if I had told them I was going to Roger Toms's, or had taken one of them with me, my face would still be unmarked. I knew that they were right but I knew also that what I had to do was a delicate thing – four of us together would tip the balance. 'One,' I said.

They shook their heads.

'Or none.'

This time they communicated soundlessly and came up with a communal yes.

'It will be me,' said Maria, so decisively that no one argued.

Anna and Jurek stood watching as we walked through the gate and under the arch. My tread was heavy. I felt Maria beside me, light in weight, light on her feet. I wondered how she thought she was going to protect me if trouble came. I didn't bother asking. I didn't have the strength. I was concentrating only on getting there and on what I was going to say.

Makepeace House. I led us to Gary Brown's steel-fronted door. I reached my hand out.

But never rang. Before my hand made contact with the musical bell, the door was opened. I saw a young man, beefy fit, tight T-shirt over bulging pectorals, white face, short brown hair. I recognized him: he was one of the men who had threatened me on Agnes Wilson's stairs.

He recognized me as well. His eyes registered the bruises and the chiffon. He smiled. 'Got on somebody's tit once too often, did you?'

I stepped forward. 'I want to speak to Gary.'

I saw his eyes up close, little bits of brown mucus floating in their whites. He pulled a cigarette and a gold lighter from his T-shirt pocket. He clicked the lighter on. It was set high: the flame flared by my nose.

I held my ground.

He lit his cigarette, drew heavily on it and exhaled. A column of blue-grey smoke streamed from each nostril.

I refused to turn my head way. 'I want to speak to Gary.'

'Stupid slag.' He spat. His cigarette came flying out. It just missed my face.

I felt Maria, slight, five-foot Maria, shifting behind me. She was going to make a move. I didn't want that: I spoke to hinder her. 'Tell Gary I'm here.'

'What makes you think he wants to speak to you?'

My foot descended on his cigarette. I ground it out. 'Tell him I've got something to say that will interest him.'

His eyes narrowed. 'Nothing you have to say would interest the boss.' His hand went up.

I stepped back. Just in time. He slammed the door.

Five minutes passed before the door reopened. Gary's henchman was back. He didn't speak, but by the way he stood, slightly to one side, he made it plain that we were meant to enter.

We went in, me leading. The man stood deliberately close so that as I passed, I couldn't help but brush against him. He grinned lecherously down at me. I didn't say anything. I made sure that Maria was behind and then I walked down the narrow, red-painted hallway and through an open doorway.

I found myself in a small box-shaped room decorated to match the weirdness of the bell's lilting melody. Seeing how it was furnished, my plan felt more secure: I remembered the photographs in Roger Toms's living room and I looked at Gary Brown's collection. It was all memorabilia I associated with the sixties, the kind of stuff travellers brought back from the near east: tatty Persian carpets, dishevelled Afghan rugs, a splayed-out mounted caftan dotted with tiny mirrors, a tarnished brass stand on which stood lighted incense sticks. I wondered why Gary Brown had bothered to buy the stuff. He had thrown it together with what looked more like hate than love. As if to prove this a red-framed cloth swastika dominated the wall opposite.

'What you want?'

I whirled round. Gary Brown – I hadn't noticed him when I'd entered – was sitting in his wheelchair, the same dirty tartan covering his lower half, his hair hanging long and low around his shoulders, his hard face glaring at me.

'What you want?' Again. Unrelenting.

He wasn't the only person in the room. We made five – Maria and I, Gary Brown and his stormtroopers, the one who'd let us in and the other who was standing, smirking, his arms crossed as he leaned against the wall close to Gary.

Maria wasn't far away: standing by the door her tiny frame was dwarfed both by the room's suffocating decor and by Gary's companions. I bit my lip, wishing momentarily I'd brought the others as well.

Except, I thought, what I wanted to do required a delicate balance.

'Take a good look,' someone said and a light, a single bright spot, was shining in my eyes.

'Jesus.' Gary whistled. I was blinded. I shivered. 'I haven't got all day,' I heard Gary saying.

I skipped to the right, out of the light's glare, so that I could see his face. I took a deep breath in. 'Roger Toms,' I said.

No movement. Not even a flicker of those cold grey eyes.

'You know him,' I said.

I saw teeth – uneven yellow – bared not in mirth but in something much more ugly. 'What's it to you?'

'He paid you to watch Agnes Wilson.'

A shrug.

'You've known him for a long time,' I said.

'You asking me?'

'No.' I shook my head. 'I'm telling. You went to India together.'

Again no movement, which I read as assent.

'You never profited from that trip,' I said. 'You couldn't, could you?' I looked down, my gaze loitering deliberately on the tartan rug which covered his useless legs.

When I looked up, searching his face for a reaction, there was nothing there to see: only a blankness that I knew from past experience concealed a terrifying anger.

I had to go on anyway. 'Roger did all right,' I said. 'Bought himself a house in Crouch End on the proceeds of your joint endeavour.'

A word: 'So?' but spoken as if he really didn't care.

'It's the way, isn't it?' I said. 'Some profit. The others . . .' I forced myself to look at his legs again.

I had gone too far. I felt rather than saw a movement and then I heard a voice. Close up. 'Fuck it, Gar.' It was the man who'd let me in. 'She won't stop talking, this one.' I felt his breath, hot against my cheek. 'Want me to shut her mouth?' I felt him moving closer.

I stood my ground. The one thing I couldn't do was show my fear. I stared straight ahead, at Gary Brown, sitting impassive, and at his sidekick, who, smiling in anticipation, was no longer using the wall's support. Around me I felt the air shifting. Run, an interior voice started screaming, run. I stood my ground.

I felt a hand gripping my shoulder.

'Leave her.'

The hand was lifted.

I didn't have time to register relief. The sharpness in Gary Brown's voice was what I'd been waiting for.

'Go on,' he ordered me.

I'd got him. Now I must go for the kill.

'Five years ago,' I said. 'Roger drove his car over Sam Layton's body.'

I saw the tiniest narrowing of his eyes. 'So? What's that to me?'

'He killed Sam,' I said. 'He'd got better at it, you see, since he practised on you.'

Gary Brown's face remained completely impassive. His voice was level: 'You're saying he ran me over?'

I nodded.

'How do you know?' So unnaturally level it was terrifying.

But I did not have time to worry about that. This was the tricky bit. I gritted my teeth. 'Roger told me. He did this.' Gingerly I unknotted the scarf and removed it from my neck. 'He thought he was going to kill me. He told me everything.'

Gary Brown's gaze was steady. He spoke quietly, his order issuing from the side of his mouth. 'Get Roger on the phone.'

I had anticipated that. I leapt in, pitching my tone to derision. 'You think he's going to tell you the truth?'

For the first time an expression – uncertainty – crossed

Gary Brown's face. He held his hand up, stopping the man next to him from walking to the phone.

His sidekick spoke. 'We've got other ways of finding out the truth. Haven't we, boss?'

The indecision vanished. 'Yeah.' He smiled. 'Hold her.'

I didn't have time to move. I didn't have time to do anything. He was so close and he was upon me, his arm held tight against me. I didn't struggle. There was no point. I twisted my head, looking at Gary Brown. 'I have friends outside,' I said.

His smile stretched wider, a cruel grimace. 'Like her?' One hand waved casually in Maria's direction. 'I'm scared.'

I felt the arm pressing tighter. 'They'll call the police,' I said.

I heard a short bark of laughter, issuing from three mouths. The hand around me tightened.

'You're a popular woman,' Gary said. 'You make friends wherever you go. Including, by all accounts, on this estate.'

I turned my head away. It was physically wrenched back.

'You know what we can do to your friends when the filth has gone,' Gary said. He was enjoying himself, his eyes moving slowly across my face, lingering almost lovingly on each blow that Roger had landed. Beside him the man was jiggling excitedly on his feet.

'What do you think, guv?' the voice in my ear said.

'Do it.'

Do it. I closed my eyes. I felt a terrible sense of the inevitable – of my own stupidity in coming here. I wasn't sure that this time I would survive what would be dealt, but it was even worse than that. For this time I had brought Maria into danger. I stood, waiting.

'Don't move,' I heard. A woman's voice.

That made no sense. I kept my eyes firmly closed.

'Let her go.'

Maria's voice. The idiot: what did she think she was going to achieve?

'I'm warning you.'

Shut up, I thought. Shut up.

Except I felt the hand lifting. I stood there, holding my breath in my self-imposed darkness.

'Back off,' I heard, and then a movement.

I opened my eyes. And almost keeled over. For what I saw was my Maria standing by Gary Brown's wheelchair. She was looking at me and at the man beside me. My eyes focused on a different thing: on the gun which she was holding to Gary Brown's temple.

Her face was sheet white. 'Back off, I said.'

The man beside the wheelchair shifted. The gun did not.

'You wouldn't,' Gary Brown snarled. 'You wouldn't dare.'

No sooner had he spoken than Maria moved. She shifted the gun above Gary Brown's head and fired.

The shot boomed out. The bullet hit a lamp. A bulb shattered.

The gun was back at Gary's head. 'Wouldn't I?' She didn't sound pleased. She didn't sound anything except determined. She looked at me. 'Go to the door.'

I went. And watched her coming to join me, her hand steady as she aimed the gun constantly at Gary Brown's head. I backed off down the hallway, followed by Maria, until we were both safely out.

She closed the door, quietly, behind her. We walked away, slowly at first, but I kept pushing the pace. When I was almost at the point of running, she put one restraining hand on my arm. 'It is over,' she said.

I stopped and looked at her. The gun, I saw, had vanished. She was smiling.

'It's over,' she said.

I couldn't match her smile. 'Is it?' I asked. I kept on walking, through the gates, and straight to the place where Anna and Jurek were waiting. Anna's eyes were fixed on my face. I met them with mine. When I saw her tentatively smiling, I nodded. Her smile broadened and then she was upon me, her arm around my waist, guiding me to the car.

Chapter
thirty-nine

It took three days before I knew it really was over. Confirmation came in the form of a *Guardian* short. Maria brought the paper up to me. It was neatly folded so that only one side column showed. Her finger pointed at a sub head: 'Car park murder'.

The account was brief. It told of a man gunned down in the car park of a deserted shopping mall. There was only one witness, a cleaner working late, and a garbled tale of a man in a wheelchair emerging from behind a van and of a sudden burst of gunfire. That was all: no further details. No names.

I looked at Maria.

'It's him,' she said. 'I checked.'

I nodded. I climbed out of bed.

'I've already done it,' she said.

I frowned.

'I phoned the police and told them to try Gary Brown.' She dropped the paper on to my bed and went away.

I stood motionless in the centre of the room. In the corner was a cracked mirror. I could see my face, strangely distorted in it. I walked closer. I stood in front of it. I saw the span of a man's hand marking my jaw. Roger Toms's hand. Roger who was dead. I stood and stared at what he'd done to me, staring until my eyes lost focus. Then I turned and, going back to bed, lay down and did what I hadn't been able to do before: I slept.

I slept for fourteen hours, waking after dark had fallen. For the first time since it had all happened, I was thinking clearly. I had things to do. I got up, dressed myself, grabbed a sandwich and got into my car.

The journey to Chelsea passed quickly. I walked up the steps and rang the bell. Greg, looking much more in command in formal black and white than he had in his pyjamas, opened up. Seeing me, however, his face caved in. He managed a stuttered half-sentence. 'What do you . . .'

I pushed past him, walking into the hallway. I felt in my pockets. 'I came to return your keys.' I held the bunch up.

When Greg moved in on them, I moved out of range – taking the keys with me. His cheeks were flapping wildly but at least his verbal composition had improved. 'What do you want from us?'

I wasn't ready for that. Not yet. 'Roger's dead,' I said.

His eyes closed – twice: the nearest he would come to acknowledging that he knew.

'It was Roger who told you to make me stay in your house, wasn't it?'

He didn't answer. I didn't need him to.

'I don't understand why it was necessary,' I said. 'I was only coming for a few days, just to sign a paper.'

'We didn't know that.' Greg's voice was dull. 'Pam misunderstood. And Roger thought you would start investigating. He told us it was better that you stayed here. So he could keep an eye on you. To keep us all safe.'

Greg's voice faded. He looked down.

I followed suit. We were staring, both of us, at his hand-crafted Italian moccasins. I wondered idly whether he and Roger had shared the same shoemaker. 'Why . . .?' I began.

'Why what?' The question came from behind.

I turned. Pam was standing on the stairs, elegant in a long black evening dress, gems sparkling across her lily-white throat. I remembered her on the Rumanian border, efficient in a working suit, and I remembered a few nights before how hard she'd looked at me and Greg. Now she, the chameleon that she was, was smiling almost tenderly.

I tossed my question straight at her. 'Why didn't you warn me?'

Her face was still. 'Of what?'

'Come on, Pam.' My voice was toned gentle to match her ease. 'You didn't tell me about Roger the other night because you knew he was dangerous.' I got louder: 'And yet you left me in his power.'

Whatever she was thinking behind that plastic mask of hers, she didn't show it. She came walking slowly towards me. 'How considerate of you,' she said, holding out her hand. I looked down and saw she was reaching for the house keys. 'You could have posted them.' She was almost upon me. My fist closed, covering the keys. The mildest of frown's crossed Pam's face. 'We can always change the locks,' she said.

I didn't want to play. Not any more. 'Fuck the locks,' I said. I stepped back so that I was facing the two equally. I let my eyes move slowly from one to the other. 'You're not out of the woods yet, you know,' I said.

While Greg's jawline went slack, Pam continued to look only mildly interested.

'You're connected to Roger Toms,' I said. 'And Roger was into all kinds of things. Drug-smuggling, pension-stealing, murder, to name a few. He told me he had a hold on you – I bet the documents are in the house. A quick call to the police should get them to turn the spotlight on you.'

'They won't prove anything,' Greg said, the words robotic rather than convinced.

'Maybe not.' I shrugged. 'But I guess the newspapers would be interested anyway. It's all the rage these days, I hear: after the glorification of the eighties they're just dying to pull down the rich.'

Greg turned red. Pam used words. 'You'd never dare.' She was smiling to show she wasn't scared. 'You'll end up implicating yourself in Roger's death.'

'But I' – I returned her smile – 'I haven't got much to lose. Whereas you . . .' My hand swept upwards, taking in the palatial hallway and what lay beyond.

There was a moment's silence. As I withstood it, I inwardly marshalled up my arguments. I expected this to go on for much longer. I expected to have to turn the screws on them, to tell all sorts of half-lies about the things I had seen in their house and the conclusions I had come to. What I hadn't expected was a sudden collapse.

Which is what I got. 'What do you want?' This from Pam.

That was easy. 'Money.'

'I should have guessed.' She smiled victoriously. 'And may I ask how much?'

'As much as Greg earned from his position as a pensions trustee,' I said.

She was quick, was Pam: she'd worked out what I was going to do. 'Quite the Robin Hood, aren't you?' She was no longer smiling. She was no longer pretending. 'Give it to her,' she said out of the corner of her mouth. Her mask had finally slipped, shattered into fragments which, for the first time since I had known her, conveyed her age. She turned.

'But . . .' This from Greg.

Pam whirled round. Her face was ugly with fury. 'Give it to her.'

That sent Greg spinning for his cheque book. He put it on the side table. 'Who should I . . .'

'Leave it blank.'

He wrote the numbers first: '1000'. He looked up. I shook my head. He added a nought: the sum now read ten thousand. He filled the words in too.

'Thanks.' I took the cheque and, with it drying in my hand, walked out of there.

I wrote the name of Agnes Wilson's work friend – Dorothy Sharp – in the space that Greg had left blank and, putting it in the addressed envelope along with the explanatory note I'd already written to her daughter-in-law, I posted it in the nearest box. Then I got back into the car and drove along what was now an extremely familiar route.

When I rang the doorbell Lilia opened up. 'He's waiting for you,' she said, padding towards the sitting room. She opened the door, and after I had gone through started to close it.

'No. Don't.' It was John's voice sounding from an alcove. As Lilia hesitated, he walked towards us. 'Would you prefer it that Lilia stay?' he said, his voice formal, his eyes focused on the marks around my neck.

'It's all right,' I said, not knowing whether it was, but knowing also that the conversation we might have would be better had in private.

John nodded. I heard the door softly closing behind me.

I didn't wait for him. Walking over the carpet, I chose a high-backed chair by the window.

John had followed. Now he stood in front of me, looking down.

'Please sit,' I said.

He sat. His hands were bunched tight: he looked down, frowning, scrutinizing his knuckles. I sat quite still, watching him, waiting.

He looked up suddenly. 'Did I do that?' pointing at my neck.

I shrugged – a gesture that could have meant either yes or no.

His eyes, Sam's eyes, were softer than I'd seen them before. 'I'm sorry,' he said quietly.

I held my tongue.

He wasn't looking at me. He was looking at the floor. 'I don't know what came over me.' He shook his head. 'No, I suppose I do. I was wild. For five years I have kept this pain inside of me. That night . . .' He swallowed. I saw his head bobbing. I sat there wondering whether, if my Sam had lived, age would have thinned his hair like John's. 'I'm sorry,' I heard.

I nodded. I blinked and, refocusing my gaze, saw that John had raised his head and was looking straight at me.

'I was wrong,' he said. 'Sam's death wasn't your fault.'

'No.' I meant it. 'It wasn't.'

'It wasn't anybody's fault,' he said. He didn't sound sure.

I sat there, seeing him watching me, and I remembered him insisting that there was nothing I could do to harm him. I knew that he'd been wrong. There was one thing I could do – I could tell him that his son had been killed because of him. I sat there, playing with the idea of spinning him the story about Roger's jealousy of Sam and how what John Layton had started had ended in Sam's death.

I saw John's jaw working. He already half knew the story: he was expecting the rest. I opened my mouth.

And saw an image: Matthew's face in front of me. 'No,' is what I said. 'It wasn't anybody's fault.' Matthew pleading with me to leave his grandfather alone. 'Just a stupid mistake,' I said.

'A mistake.' John echoed it. He didn't sound completely

convinced and yet I saw relief, sweeping some of the pain from his eyes.

I got up.

He didn't move. 'You're leaving?'

'Not England,' I said. 'And I'd like . . .'

He was on his feet. 'I'll tell the school you can visit Matthew any time you want.'

'Thanks.' I turned.

His hand was stretched out, a gesture of peace. I almost spurned it. I almost walked straight out of there. But I didn't. I put out my hand, put it into his, and when he squeezed it, I reciprocated. I felt the warmth of our two skins together, remembering how as John's hand had closed around my neck, all I'd thought was that it felt like Sam's. Now it no longer did: it felt like the hand of a man aged by time and grief, clasping at me to reassure himself. Gently I pulled away. 'Goodbye, John,' I said and then, without another word, I left.